Praise for previous editions of Sorayya Khan's *Noor*:

"Sorayya Khan's narrative in *Noor* has a dark, poignant beauty."
—*The Telegraph*, Calcutta

"Poignant, powerful, and tender. Though unflinching in her descriptions of the horrors of the war, [Khan] doesn't give in to the temptation to take sides or offer justification. Her writing is remarkable because it is so subtle and so honest."
—*Deccan Herald*, Bangalore

"Khan's ability to sensitively portray the character of a child with special needs is exceptional. *Noor* [is] a rich but mysterious work of fiction with many layers to ponder."
—*Friday Times*, Islamabad

"*Noor* is a haunting book. . . . Wars may end, but the searing shrapnel they leave behind, embedded deep within the individual and collective psyche, continues to colour the present. *Noor* is such a remarkable novel because it conveys this in the most understated but convincing way."
—*New Indian Express*, Chennai

"[*Noor*] picks up momentum ending in an unputdownable work."
—*Hindustan Times*, New Delhi

"[*Noor*] is both courageous and remarkable because it breaks a long literary silence and is the first Pakistani English novel to focus on East Pakistan during the war of 1971 and comes to terms with its brutality."

—*Dawn*, Karachi

"In a series of chilling portraits, *Noor* brings the past back with an exactitude that is both fearful and astonishing. Sorayya Khan's *Noor* is a remarkable novel for the simple reason that it breaks the long tacit silence among Pakistanis of all hues to speak of the horrors of what they saw and did in East Pakistan, [and] there has been no attempt so far to flesh out the bare bones of that long-buried nightmare. . . . The novel moves inexorably towards its final cathartic question: 'What was it like? There?' and in the answer lances a long festering wound."

—*The Hindu*, Chennai

"Khan's prose is unrelentingly intense as she tells us of the tragedies of cyclone and war beating down on the fragile landscape."

—*India Today*, New Delhi

"*Noor* is the unbearable lightness of being explored . . . It's a history of wars won and lost and boundaries redrawn and barbed, to the point of a futile no-finality. It's about life without the 'happily ever after,' not because cynicism tears asunder fairy tale endings, but because in perspective, life isn't tidy, it has a messy unchiaroscuro in-between."

—*First City*, New Delhi

"It is hard to believe this is Sorayya Khan's first novel."

—*She Magazine*, Karachi

About the Author

Sorayya Khan was a Fulbright Creative Writing Scholar in Pakistan and Bangladesh in 1999–2000 and won the *Mahalat Review* Novella Prize in 1995. Her work has appeared in the *Kenyon Review*, the *North American Review*, the *Asian Pacific American Journal*, and several anthologies of Pakistani writing. She lives in Ithaca, New York, with her husband and two children, and is completing another novel.

Noor

Sorayya Khan

THE
PUBLISHING
LABORATORY
UNIVERSITY OF NORTH CAROLINA WILMINGTON

First North American edition published by The Publishing Laboratory, January 2006
Originally published in Pakistan by Alhamra Publishing, Islamabad, 2003
First published in India by Penguin Books India, New Delhi, 2004

Printed in the United States of America
06 07 08   5 4 3 2 1

Edited by Ashley Talley
Book design by Sumanth Prabhaker and Ashley Talley
Publishing Laboratory faculty: Barbara Brannon, Robert Siegel

LIBRARY OF CONGRESS CATALOGING-IN-PUBLICATION DATA
Khan, Sorayya.
      Noor / Sorayya Khan.—1st North American ed.
      p.   cm.
      ISBN-13: 978-0-9719308-7-2
      ISBN-10: 0-9719308-7-2
      1. Children with mental disabilities—Fiction. 2. Child artists—Fiction.
3. Memory—Fiction. 4. Pakistan—Fiction. 5. Bangladesh—History—
Revolution, 1971—Fiction. 6. Psychological fiction. 7. Domestic fiction.
I. Title.
      PS3611.H35N66 2006
      813'.6—dc22

                                                          2006001609

THE
PUBLISHING
LABORATORY
UNIVERSITY OF NORTH CAROLINA WILMINGTON

Department of Creative Writing
University of North Carolina Wilmington
601 South College Road
Wilmington, North Carolina 28403   USA
www.uncw.edu/writers

Your history gets in the way of my memory.
AGHA SHAHID ALI

On November 12, 1970, a cyclone hit East Pakistan.
One million people died.

On March 25, 1971, civil war between East Pakistan and West Pakistan began. On December 3, 1971, India entered the war on the side of East Pakistan. West Pakistan surrendered on December 16, 1971. Bangladesh, formerly East Pakistan, won its independence.

Between 300,000 and 3,000,000 people died.

Contents

Introduction

Cara Cilano

In his 16 December 1971 address to the nation of Pakistan, President Mohammad Yahya Khan attempted to explain to his fellow Pakistanis the military setbacks the country was facing in what was then East Pakistan and what would, in a few days' time, become Bangladesh. It was not at the hands of the East Pakistanis/Bangladeshis that the West Pakistanis were suffering; rather, as Yahya's comments make clear, West Pakistanis viewed this 1971 conflict as yet another eruption of their long-standing tensions with India: "We may lose a battle, but final victory in this war of survival shall Inshallah be ours. At this time, our hearts go out to our brethren in East Pakistan, who are being relentlessly subjected to terror and tribulation by the warlords of Bharat. To them we say: This is not the end." What is notable here and throughout Yahya's statement is his repeated framing of (West) Pakistanis as victims of Indian brutality: their brethren "are being relentlessly subjected to terror and tribulation." And later, "We are faced by a predatory aggressor whose designs are now clear. They have launched an all-out bid for the dismemberment and total destruction of Pakistan, on the strength of their superiority of numbers."[1] While holding that Pakistanis—both East and West—will continue to struggle against this Indian power, a claim that strikes one as specious given the events (including matters of language rights, as well as economic and political equity) that led to the emergence of Bengali resistance in the earlier months of 1971, Yahya reinforces the notion that it is India's "imperialist challenge" to the sovereignty of Pakistan that stands as the defining issue of the present conflict.

In other words, Bengali claims for independence remain outside of the "official" national commentary of the president of Pakistan, a position that is emblematic of how history recorded the events of that year. Most commonly, both (West) Pakistanis and Indians refer to this conflict as the Indian-Pakistani War of 1971. From India's perspective, this conflict was an act of liberation. If, in Yahya's eyes, Pakistan risked being overwhelmed because of its minority status on the subcontinent, then Bangladesh's risks were doubly threatening as this nation was and is wholly written out of the moment of its own birth.

Yahya's framing of the events of 1971, of a piece as they are with dominant historical recordings of this time in Pakistan, mask a fissure in the Pakistani national imaginary brought about by the deep threat posed by the violence perpetrated by West Pakistanis upon the East Pakistanis/Bangladeshis to Pakistan's vision of itself as an Islamic republic. This vision ties back to the end of British colonial occupation when Muhammad Ali Jinnah founded the Muslim League. Poised in tension with Jawarhalal Nehru and Mahatma Gandhi, Jinnah's purpose was to advocate the two-nations theory, which meant that, when the British finally quit the subcontinent, they would break it up into a nation for a Hindu majority (India) and one for a Muslim majority (East and West Pakistan). Religious identity trumped other sorts of identifying factors, such as shared

1. "Text of Yahya's Address to the Nation," *New York Times,* 17 Dec. 1971, late ed., A17.

language and/or culture, in the formation of these nations. The summer of 1947, when Partition took place, saw the literal drawing of national boundaries, one that cut through the Punjab and separated West Pakistan from India and another that cut through Bengal and separated East Pakistan from India on the opposite side. This period of time also saw a horrific outbreak of violence—murder, rape, abduction—across the national border that divided West Pakistan from India as Hindus and Muslims struggled to reach their new national homelands. Tensions continue between (West) Pakistan and India to this day. The transition from colony to nations went more quietly on the border between East Pakistan and India. Twenty-four years later, in December 1971, the subcontinent's second Partition, the civil war between East and West Pakistan, took place. This conflict, the culmination of cultural tensions, struggles over language rights, and economic and political disparities from which the West benefited, effectively gave the lie to Jinnah's two-nations theory. The actual fighting began in March of that year, but it took India's intervention on the side of the East Pakistanis in December to put a rapid halt to the violence. Bangladesh gained its independence before the year was through.

From a Bangladeshi perspective, as development sociologist Shelley Feldman points out, 1971 represents the more significant Partition of the subcontinent precisely because of the violence the West enacted upon the East: "The destruction and pain wrought on Bangladeshis during 1971 parallels the violence wrought on so many in Punjab during [the 1947] Partition."[2] This emphasis bears out in Bangladeshi "social and political histories," according to Feldman, as they make "only scant mention of the anti-colonial struggle and the Partition of the 1940s." As far as defining moments go, Bangladeshis look to their struggle for independence from West Pakistan as foundational, while both Pakistan and India center 1947 as their

2. Shelley Feldman, "Feminist Interruptions: The Silence of East Bengal in the Story of Partition," *interventions* 1:2 (1999), 167–82; p. 173.

foundational moment, one that continues to this day to shape how each nation knows itself and its subcontinental neighbor.

These historical events often figure prominently in literary production in the many languages of the subcontinent. When one restricts the field to literature written in English, however, representations of the subcontinent's two Partitions are more scarce. In this context, it is important to note that the bulk of authors writing in the English language hail from India and a smaller number come from Pakistan; Bangladeshi authors who write in English as a first language have yet to emerge in U.S. and British publishing markets. Pakistani author Bapsi Sidhwa's *Ice-Candy-Man* or *Cracking India* (Minneapolis, Minn.: Milkweed, 1991), the title by which the novel is known in the U.S., and Salman Rushdie's *Midnight's Children* (New York: Penguin, 1980) may be the two most famous examples of 1947 Partition novels. As it moves through the subcontinent's early national histories, Rushdie's book also touches upon the 1971 Partition. One need only recall how Saleem's sister, the Brass Monkey–turned–Jamila Singer, enjoys what Saleem deems an "apotheosis," a gendered idealization that renders her complicit with the muezzins in singing "Pakistani troops to their deaths" in Bangladesh (*Midnight's Children,* 388). The creation of Bangladesh functions as narrative background in another Indian novel, *The Hungry Tide* (New York: Houghton Mifflin, 2005), by Amitav Ghosh. Two recent Pakistani novels in English make similar background use of the events of 1971: Mohsin Hamid's *Moth Smoke* (New York: Picador, 2000) and, more concertedly, Kamila Shamsie's *Kartography* (New York: Harcourt, 2003).

Arguably, English-language literature in Pakistan possesses rich historical resources that its fiction has yet to mine. In Pakistani author and critic Tariq Rahman's view, more work of this sort is needed, particularly if Pakistani literature in English is to be counted among the global literatures in this language. Rahman claims that "Whereas the tradition of resistance is very strong in other Third World literatures as well as in Pakistani literature [in languages other than English], it hardly exists in English."[3] The absence of resistance literature may be due to how, in Rahman's estimation, "Pakistani literature in English is less politically aware or committed than literatures in other Pakistani languages." For Rahman this apparent lack of political awareness is borne out most explicitly in Pakistan's English language writers' "inability to respond truthfully and imaginatively to a great human tragedy [the events of 1971]." Rahman feels that "there is hardly anything sympathetic to the Bengalis" (227). On the topic of literary treatments of 1971 in Pakistan and in all of Pakistan's languages, Urdu scholar Muhammad Umar Memon expresses his chagrin over the paucity of imaginative reckoning with this seismic event: "Contrary to the general sense of gloom and loss pervading the discussion by Pakistanis of their corporate disaster, the incident appears to have touched only a few; fewer still are those for whom it has had any deep emotive significance at all, with ramifications in national morality."[4] Bringing the present discussion full circle, Memon concludes,

> The country might just as well have written off the whole incident, had it not been for the fact that the humiliation was caused not so much by the East Pakistanis as by India. What further kept the Pakistanis from lapsing into a state of national amnesia, for the short three-year period between 1971 and 1974 at least, was the issue of the repatriation of the ninety thousand Pakistani prisoners of war (POWs) in Indian prison camps. (106)

In the novel *Noor*, Pakistani-Dutch writer Sorayya Khan alters the terms of these historical and literary contexts considerably. *Noor* tells the story of this 1971 civil war, of the silences that surround

3. Tariq Rahman, *A History of Pakistani Literature in English* (Lahore: Vanguard, 1991); p. 229.
4. Muhammad Umar Memon, "Pakistani Urdu Creative Writing on National Disintegration: The Case of Bangladesh," *Journal of Asian Studies* 43:1 (1983), 105–27; p. 106.

it, of attempts to forget it, and of the possibilities of redemption through what Khan calls the "theater of the family." The family in question revolves around its patriarch, Ali, a veteran of the 1971 conflict between East and West Pakistan that resulted in the independence of Bangladesh. Ali returns to his mother, Nanijaan, in West Pakistan, with Sajida, a "fiveandsix"-year-old foundling who becomes his adopted daughter. To provide for his "ready-made family," which increases in size years later after Sajida marries Hussein and, untraditionally, remains in her father's house with her husband and three children, Ali builds a barricaded house, "Ali's sector," in the ever-expanding margins of Islamabad. Of Sajida and Hussein's three children, Noor, the title character, emerges as the center of the fiction. Portrayed as having some ambiguous developmental disability, Noor nonetheless possesses an uncanny artistic ability, evident within the first year of her life, an ability that acts as the catalyst responsible for changing this family's future.

Noor's artwork emblematizes the varied ways the novel's characters see themselves, each other, and the past and serves as cornerstones for each chapter. As chapters and the narrative progress, so too does Noor's artwork, moving from monochromatic abstraction to chilling realism in the final photograph-like drawing Noor creates of her grandfather in his military uniform. These paintings and drawings somehow encourage their examiners to "see" some hint, a fragment, of a memory whose recollection promises to bridge the emotional distances between characters even as it threatens to sever their emotional connections completely. Hussein, for instance, discerns the image of his long-lost Italian shoe in one of Noor's paintings. A metonym for the youthful love and joy he found in Sajida, the shoe Hussein sees calls him back to himself, pushing him to undo the estrangement that has separated him and Sajida since Noor's birth. The novel reminds its readers of the painting's abstract nature despite Hussein's conviction that the image is of his shoe, thereby suggesting how the interaction between representation and interpretation bears the potential to shore up the forgotten or the repressed. Noor's art-work affects all of the adult characters in such ways and thus become the central means through which the novel excavates individual and collective memories.

For Khan, such an excavation will help uncover the "tragedies in the drawers of [Pakistanis'] own histories" that were the impetus behind the creation of her novel. While silence and forgetting may be necessary for war, the eventual acknowledgement of such silences and attempts to remember are, as Khan further holds, integral to society's healing as a whole. Thus, to return once again to Khan's professed wish to study war "in the theater of the family," the novel enacts one possible way that a West Pakistani soldier may be recon-ciled with society, his victims, and their shared past. What remains open—both in Khan's novel and in Pakistan's national imaginary (President Musharraf's 2002 apology to the Bangladeshis notwith-standing)—is the completion of this act of reconciliation.

Though Ali is the soldier in need of reconciliation with him-self, his society, and a collective past, Sajida functions as the novel's emotional and historical core. What Ali first presents as his "adop-tion" of the young Sajida later comes to resemble an abduction, and Sajida's gradual recognition of this shift in perception finally makes of her a woman capable of self-determination. This capability holds significance due to the morally ambiguous circumstances surround-ing Sajida's becoming Ali's daughter, which irrevocably connect to Sajida's always-present identity as a Bengali. From the moment of her arrival in Islamabad, Sajida, then just a young girl, is described as "black or, it seemed to her then, almost black. Her hair, her eyes, and her skin color blended into a blue black hue absent in the girls around her." Sajida's skin color, as it marks her as Bengali, also earns her the nickname, bestowed upon her by her classmates, of "kohl-ki-larki," which makes Sajida want to "bury herself in a mountain of coal and become their insult." Sajida's (West) Pakistani schoolmates merely play out the prejudices against Bengalis, based on both skin color and language, evident throughout the west wing of the country. When Sajida can finally say, even in a "small, hushed voice," that Ali is "not really" her father, she indicates her need, her right to know what Ali did in East Pakistan and to hold him accountable for it.

Putatively, Ali brings Sajida from Dhaka in present-day Bangladesh to Islamabad in (West) Pakistan to rescue her from the cyclone- and war-torn landscape of East Pakistan. Yet, certainly, Ali's "adoption" of Sajida also represents a gesture of atonement. Although a man given to self-lacerating penitence, including the immersion of his body in scorching hot baths, Ali requires the urgings made manifest in Noor's artwork to reach beyond himself, to connect, through the tellings and recollections of brutal truths, with Sajida. Noor's strange paintings and drawings somehow represent memories to which the child has no claim and of which she has no understanding. And they foment within Ali the realization that "he remained what he wanted, so badly, no longer to be": namely, a man who not only witnessed but partook in the willful devastation of a people, the Bengalis, for reasons of national consolidation that he no longer—if ever—believed in. Not connected through biological ties, this family's relations derive from repressed memories of mass graves, making Ali "forever joined by a pit of mud" to Sajida and her children.

Khan was able to undertake the research necessary for the writing of the novel *Noor* through a Fulbright Creative Writing Research Award she received in 1999–2000. This award allowed Khan to return to Pakistan and to travel to Bangladesh for the first time. During these trips, Khan interviewed a number of Pakistani veterans of the 1971 civil war, and, remarkably, these men disclosed many details about their experiences in what was then East Pakistan. The stories Khan heard in these interviews provided her with an opportunity to consider how soldiers act as collaborators and to come to some explanation of their loyalties, their betrayals, and the possible ways they might define who they are and why. Khan's conviction that Bangladeshis must also tell their own stories drew her eastward as well. One Bangladeshi woman whom Khan met described how the horrors of the 1971 war far outstripped her childhood fear of cyclones, such as the one that struck Bangladesh at the end of 1970. One sees in this woman's disclosure some traces of Sajida. In shattering the pervasive silences around the subcontinent's second Partition, Khan's novel attempts to reconcile history and memory, while holding fast to the belief that silence's end allows us to see what we might have been.

First published in 2003 by Alhamra Press in Islamabad, Pakistan, and then in 2004 by Penguin India, New Delhi, this 2005 publication of Khan's novel *Noor* by the Publishing Laboratory in the Creative Writing Department at the University of North Carolina Wilmington represents the first North American edition of the book.

CARA CILANO
University of North Carolina Wilmington

one

Noor was Sajida's secret.

She knew the exact moment her child was conceived. Purple passed slowly, the lowest of clouds, over her eyes. Bathed in such magnificent color, Sajida lay perfectly still. Much later, she would try to relive the exact moment, as if she needed to understand how the fact of her child could have entered her body and mind at the same time. But Sajida would not summon the gentle shade ever again. Instead, the vaguest hint of it would swim in her memory like the brief feel of a distant place she might have visited when she was a child.

Except for sounds of breathing, the room was silent. Loadshedding had stopped the ceiling fan and silenced the drone of the old, straining air conditioner. The stifling heat hung thick in air made almost sweet by the faint smells of lovemaking and freshly bathed and powdered children asleep on the floor. Without opening her eyes, Sajida rolled away from Hussein. She pulled at the sheer cotton of her nightgown and blew on her chest until she felt the film of perspiration tighten and dry.

Slowly, a hum rose from across the room. Sajida, accustomed to the amplified bellow of the azaan in the early hours of an Islamabad summer morning, thought little of the interruption. But when the hum broke into an entire round of a young girl's giggles, she was startled enough to open her eyes.

In the farthest corner of the room, a soft glow lit up a scene. An adolescent girl—twelve or thirteen by the likes of her curves—hovered above a wooden chair. The girl seemed to float in her movements, her hand rising ever so slowly in the air until the arc stopped on her painted lips. Her long hair, an electric combination of oranges and pinks, was thick like a rope and waved gently over one shoulder and then the other.

Sajida stared at the strange girl. Her color was richly dark, her flat nose was bridged by oddly slanted eyes, and her perfectly sculpted miniature ears appeared as if they were meant for a far younger child. The girl's white teeth seemed too big for her mouth, yet the crowded rectangles fit one after another in an impeccable row of white. Her wrists ended in pudgy bracelets, like those of a healthy baby. Although the girl's characteristics were otherworldly, they were familiar to Sajida, as if she might have located the striking combination of grace and innocence in someone close to her or, perhaps, somewhere in her own self.

Suddenly, the giggles stopped and the suspended girl focused her attention on Sajida. The velvet texture of her big black eyes poured into her plea.

"Ammi," she called in the high-pitched voice of a young child registering an all-consuming need for her mother.

The sound of the word, the fact of it, made Sajida's vision blur. It appeared, then, to be the utterance itself that caused the young girl and her small wooden chair to dissolve like pieces of a scattered puzzle into sheer darkness.

The force of what was said stunned Sajida. The "Ammi" that grew from the strange girl was different. It had an urgency all its own, absent in the wails of her young sons who took the word for granted, blending the two syllables into expectation, repeating it again and again until it was merely a sound. The cry evoked a private set of memories Sajida had grown to forget. Among them, she now recalled how she'd begged for her own mother, calling for her again and again in the maternity ward of the government hospital when she was giving birth to her first child before an irritated nurse covered her mouth and told her that God did not intend for children, especially sons, to be born to weak women. Staring at the corner of the room, where the vision of a strange young girl bearing resemblance to herself had just dissolved, Sajida trembled. Because her past, unclear and unspoken, forever lingered just beyond her touch, Sajida immediately recognized the visit from her future.

Afterwards, Sajida got out of her bed, walked to where the girl had been and pulled back the heavy curtains from the window. She pushed her face against the screen, searching the night for an explanation for what she'd seen and heard. She pulled on her robe, fit her feet into her husband's khussas and left the room. Outside, she approached the chaukidar who was clutching a pocket transistor radio against his ear in his nocturnal struggle against sleep. He jumped to his feet, reaching quickly for the rifle he'd carelessly leaned against his stool. He assured her that he'd heard nothing, and then shouted to the chaukidar of the neighboring house to confirm his statement.

Returning to the house, Sajida climbed the steps to the narrow patio outside the living room. She sat on a plastic chair adjoining a table stacked high with chair cushions and carefully covered each evening in the event the rains would finally come. Resting her feet on the table, she leaned her head against the back of the old chair allowing her long, thick hair to be caught in the cracks.

She considered names. *Fatima, Mehnaz, Razia.* She wondered what one named a child like that. In the fleeting glimpse of the future which had been shared with her in the adolescent form of the magical child who had just been conceived, a name was not offered.

She placed her hand on her stomach, as if it already held a kicking baby, and spoke the first words to her daughter.

"*Beti*," she said softly. The endearment became long, and Sajida marveled at the sound of the second syllable, the way it drew out her breath like the thread in a needle pulling the first stitch in a cloth.

A hint of light appeared, followed by others, until together they became the sun, the unrelenting ball of yellow so strong so early in the morning. Sajida shaded her eyes and head with her chaddar, the long shawl Hussein had purchased for her in the distant valley of Kashmir when they were first married. Wrapped in dazzling embroidery, she bowed her head to the burning Margalla Hills coming to life beyond.

ৡ

Sajida had loved Hussein since she was fifteen and had seen him for the first time when he emerged, smiling, from his mother's freshly waxed sedan in the driveway of her friend's house. Two children later, she loved him with far deeper intensity. Looking back on her teenage years, she thought herself lucky rather than wise that she'd so stubbornly cast her affections his way.

Nonetheless, there was a part of herself she didn't share with Hussein. For almost as long as she had known him, Sajida knew not to engage him in her dreams. The dreams, infrequent now, in which her mother spoke, had once been a source of contention between her and her husband. She recalled how uncomfortable he'd been one evening a few weeks after their marriage, when she sat down in front of the new sewing machine and began to stitch her new husband a summer shirt.

"How did you learn to do that?" Hussein asked one evening, the freshly pressed shirt hanging on the back of the bedroom armchair.

4

"Ma is free with sewing advice," she said carelessly, as if her mother, dead for thirteen years, lived in the house next door and was integral to their daily lives.

When Hussein said "Sa-ji-da," drawing out her name in distinct syllables in a way that became a portent for his anger, she quickly corrected herself.

"*Was* free with it. She taught me long ago."

Sajida had learned to hide this part of herself from him. When Sajida saw a strange girl dancing in the corner of her bedroom, it had been years since she'd discussed her dreams and where they came from with Hussein. She no longer wondered about whether her mother's words really did come from the bottom of the ocean, as she'd thought when she was a child, or whether her mother was speaking to her from a life in the safety of beyond.

Now a new voice, an unknown face, a yet-to-be person having appeared before her, Sajida couldn't imagine what she might attempt to say to Hussein. She'd had a dream? She'd seen their child, so different? How would she describe the 'Ammi' she'd heard and make him understand? Hussein would only think her mad.

Sajida had known immediately that her daughter would be different. But the recognition that her daughter was a thread to another world came to Sajida slowly, during the long nights of her pregnancy when she was frequently awakened by an aching bladder. Resting her throbbing feet on the cold marble floor in the bathroom, she would feel a shawl of warmth settle on her shoulders. Sometimes she remained sitting on the wobbly toilet seat for several minutes after she needed to, caressing her belly in the darkness. Awakened by the journeys to the bathroom, the baby stretched and moved inside her. Savoring the miracle of the dance, it was easy for Sajida to imagine that it was her daughter's life that provided the warmth in the unheated bathroom.

On the toilet, Sajida considered the bathroom differently. The walls were dull, not white, the porcelain tub and sink a muted orange, the crack that ran through each of them stark. The faucets were stained with age, the red for hot and blue for cold buried under gray sediment. The bathroom mat, a washed out durri, was worn and frayed at one end, its once bold lines nondescript.

Surrendering to deep sleep, Sajida's dreams grew more vivid than they had ever been. She pictured the landscape of East Pakistan—Bangladesh now—and her long-ago childhood in greens, each different from the last: rice paddies, banana leaves, palm trees, limes, sails of fishing boats. In her waking life, the rose bushes on the patio came alive, despite leaves coated with dust and an old ceramic pot un-wiped for years. When the sweet peas blossomed for the second time that year in multiple shades of crimson, she pulled Nanijaan into the short driveway and asked, "They've always looked like this?"

Inside the house, Sajida ordered the carpets washed and dried in the sun. The pattern of hexagons in the Bukhara carpet in the living room leapt up at her in deep reds and soft browns, and the tree of life in another carpet was suddenly transformed with branches of blues. Sajida saw the birthmark on her eldest son's leg, faded until it had almost vanished, again as it had once been: a raised, deep raspberry.

While Sajida's belly grew into a daughter, the lens with which Sajida saw her world sharpened to absorb a life of color as never before. No one, including Sajida, understood until much later this intimation of what her daughter would bring to her world.

During this time, Sajida could not help but recall General Z's daughter. As a rule, Sajida did not keep up with politics. But she and Hussein, who was only a year older, grew up with General Z's daughter in their midst. In the years of General Z's rule, it was im-possible not to have formed a lasting impression of the child gleaned from persistent, whispered stories. No one knew how many children General Z had, except that the boys were older and not very smart, and there was only one girl. She was a fat child, perpetually nine or ten during her father's long reign, and sat with her father at state dinners. She was known to stare at guests until they were compelled to excuse themselves to use the bathroom or blow their noses or rise from the table suddenly and without explanation, clutching at their waists, claiming that their stomachs had got the better of them. Although the child could not speak, legend had it that she had powers to see into her father's guests, make judgments about their loyalty and estimations of their lies. She conveyed her thoughts to her father through inarticulate moans and wild gestures. Under her father's order, the child was not permitted to be photographed, but people had a vision of what she looked like (small, fat, dark) and what she was: in a word, stupid.

Sajida only had her premonition of Noor, a dreamy manifestation of a child yet to be. Besides her features, slightly misshapen, Sajida knew nothing of what Noor might bring into the world. Without knowing whether she would need it, Sajida made the decision to protect her child. When she chose to make Noor her secret, she did it afraid of how Noor might be written into her father's life: squeezed into stupidity at birth or strangely flaunted, mute and dumb, underneath priceless chandeliers at a state dinner laden with heavily embossed crystal and china. The possibility that Hussein might get a head start on images such as these before Noor even arrived made it impossible for Sajida to share her secret with him.

In the slow nine months before Noor entered their world, it was much, much harder to keep the secret from dear, sweet Nanijaan, whom Sajida longed to tell. Although Nanijaan was her dadi, Sajida—along with everyone else her grandmother knew—called her Nanijaan. The day Nanijaan's first grandchild, visiting from London, mistakenly called her that, stomping her feet with conviction when she was corrected, no one was able to let it go. In the years since the name had been given to her, Nanijaan had become the consummate grandmother, having the time, energy, and love to spare for her grandchildren that she feared she'd exhausted when she was raising her own children.

Sometimes, when Nanijaan rubbed Sajida's swollen feet in the last months of her pregnancy, Nanijaan's small, flaking hands able to find aches she didn't know she had, Sajida was tempted to share her premonition.

"Have you ever seen such a thing?" she wanted to ask.

But she kept it all from Nanijaan because she was afraid, more than anything, that Nanijaan would have a remedy. As much as Sajida had prayed for healthy children when she was pregnant with the boys, she believed it was faithless and wrong to bare secrets before their time. Life was specific that way: it was best not to offer conclusions until life had unfolded as it was meant.

Left in the dark until the baby arrived, Nanijaan sensed the shift in Sajida's mood. The way she would one day describe it to Sajida was that she had set her sights inward.

"It was like you were looking inside yourself during those months, taking leave of your world. Farooq and Adel got away with murder then. They watched video after video. The driver fetched them whatever film they wanted. When I wasn't looking, the cook fed them halwa for breakfast, lunch, and dinner."

Nanijaan pampered her as best she could. She prepared Sajida's favorite foods and saved the malai the cook collected from fresh milk in the kitchen for her breakfast. Concerned with Sajida's sudden tendency toward distraction, she tried, ever so gently, to probe.

"Are you happy?"

"Yes," Sajida said, but looked away so quickly Nanijaan suspected otherwise.

"Do you think it might be a girl this time?" Nanijaan asked.

"It is."

"You'd rather have another boy? Three boys? My goodness, there would be nothing but raised toilet seats and pants in this house."

"As if there weren't already."

"Give me your feet, then," Nanijaan said firmly, setting aside her tea, sitting on the floor next to Sajida's feet.

Sajida closed her eyes as Nanijaan expertly kneaded her feet.

"You can tell me anything," Nanijaan said, trying again.

"Please, Nanijaan," Sajida suddenly said. "Stop dyeing your hair."

Nanijaan laughed. She'd been dyeing her hair to match Sajida's for more than eighteen years. She began doing so a few months after Ali, her youngest son, weak and barely recovered from typhoid, had brought Sajida back from war in East Pakistan, stumbled up the stairs, and made her part of the family. Sajida was black or, it seemed to her then, almost black. Her hair, her eyes, and the color of her skin blended into a blue-black hue absent in the girls around her.

"I'm so black," Sajida had said to Nanijaan, at first merely as observation in the full-length mirror of Nanijaan's bedroom and later as complaint.

Nanijaan explained that God knew what He was doing when He made Sajida, He hadn't dilly-dallied, He'd put all colors inside her, and she was perfect. Sajida knew she wasn't. But it helped to be told she was. Especially when her classmates came up with a new name, *kohl-ki-larki*, and she sometimes fell asleep thinking it would be best if she could bury herself in a mountain of coal and become their insult. The night Sajida confided this new name to Nanijaan, Nanijaan dyed her long white hair the deepest black she could find. In the morning, Sajida was startled by the woman hunched at her bedside, framed by an unnatural black hanging around her face, before she reached for Nanijaan and pulled her into bed.

There was another time, Nanijaan recalled, when she and Sajida had seemed almost one. A few years later, Sajida growing and Nanijaan shrinking with age, there was a month, or maybe two, when their height hovered around the same penciled line in Ali's doorway. The day they discovered this, they stood together in the doorway and Sajida, with her arms around Nanijaan, declared, "You belong to me."

"All right, meri jaan," Nanijaan broke the silence. "You're right. I'm getting a bit old for black hair, anyway."

"There isn't anything to tell," Sajida said, rolling her foot in the air until Nanijaan's fingers found the inside arch of her foot which ached so much.

"I'll help you with your daughter. She'll be beautiful like you, rani jaani. I've always been good with boys. I had so many myself. And your two . . . . But girls, I didn't know much until you came. But we haven't done too badly, have we?"

"True," Sajida said, smiling at last.

"Remember when we waxed your legs the first time? Your arms? You were too young, you know. I only let you because you insisted. Remember the quilt we stitched, the one with the horrible, holey China silk? It was a miracle, you know, how we turned it into something beautiful. The flowers we stitched . . ."

"What kind of flowers were they anyway?" Sajida asked.

"Gladiolas, tuberoses, lilies, daffodils, all mixed together. Do you think she'll like to stitch? We'll make pillow covers together, maybe she'll be the one among the three of us that masters the cross stitch."

"She might never thread a needle," Sajida said in her only hint to Nanijaan that all might not be well with the child growing inside her.

"My mother was a seamstress," Sajida said quietly, after a moment. "I must have told you. She stitched clothes in our village and several others. Her sewing machine . . . it was so heavy. Black with gold letters. The handle spun round and round. I learned to thread a needle on her machine. Ma could do it while the needle was moving up and down."

"Really?" Nanijaan said, taking note of this last fact because Sajida was not prone to exaggeration.

Nanijaan squeezed each of Sajida's toes between her fingers before pulling on them one by one ever so gently. In the stillness, broken only by the slight popping sounds of her toes, Sajida revisited her childhood, a place to which she found herself returning less and less since having her own children. The boys demanded immediacy: her presence was required in the present, from morning to night, leaving her almost without reason to look back on who she had once been.

Concentrating, Sajida thought she could make out the shape of the family hut she'd once lived in, the thatch of straw above the door that threatened to fall, the brown puddles on the floor during the monsoons, the oddly shaped piece of furniture (*what had it been?*) on which her mother placed her sewing machine that last night.

Nanijaan lifted Sajida's other foot from the floor, the one she'd already massaged snug in her lap. She rubbed Sajida's calves with both hands, trying to increase circulation to her cold feet.

"I hear her sometimes. My mother."

Nanijaan, at seventy, had lived long enough to know that voices reach beyond the grave, and sometimes they pry their way into your head. But the kind she heard, her husband's reprimands, the snickering before he beat her, were ones she could do without. So she did.

"Ma was strong. She'd carry the machine for ages. Kilometers. She didn't let me touch it." After a silence, she continued. "In one swoop. The water," she said, remembering after a long while the night of a terrifying storm. "It was as high as the hills." She waved at the Margallas beyond. "Higher, maybe. The water, it was alive. Can you imagine?"

Nanijaan, who knew she had not sought answers as best as she might have from the girl who had, by chance, become family, was honest.

"No, rani jaani, I can't. I haven't even seen the ocean!"

Nanijaan recalled that Ali had once, long ago, described Sajida as an orphan and assigned the cause. *Cyclone*, he'd said, as if her presence could be summed up in a simple word. Nanijaan considered pressing Sajida for something more but was interrupted.

"Lucky you," Sajida replied with a sigh, sinking deeper into the sofa, reveling in its solid certainty, the land on which it rested.

Still sitting on the floor, Nanijaan kissed Sajida's toes, warm by then. She cradled Sajida's foot in her small, strong hands wrinkled from accumulating age and the steady, hard work of a lifetime.

two

Hussein, a soft-spoken man with convictions that were neither strong nor weak, loved his family. He was grateful for his sons, two small beings who forced him to marvel at their world. When they were small, he would lie on the floor with them, pushing Matchbox cars up and down the designs on the carpets, minding the instructions of his sons which assigned parking lots to the diamonds and complicated highways to the tree of life imprint on the largest carpet. He'd tried to convince his boys not to play with cars missing tires by appealing to common sense (they wouldn't be able to drive anyway) but stopped when his youngest son, Farooq, announced that cars like that kept his fleet of tow trucks in business.

The day his first son was born, Hussein made no secret of his happiness. He clasped his brother in the waiting room of the hospital and whispered, "Alhamdulillah." The second time, when the doctor came to announce the arrival of another boy, Hussein repeated, in question form, the doctor's words, *larka?*, as if he were uncertain of the gift bestowed on him twice in a row.

Before his daughter was born, Hussein suspected the child would be a girl and said as much.

"She'll have her hands full with the two boys," he said laughingly, awaiting a response from a silent Sajida.

His wife behaved differently, dispensing with the peculiarities of her earlier pregnancies, a craving of tamarind and a need, every morning, for the tartest yogurt in the city. Instead, she would leave the lunch table before her sons finished eating, swiveling her cup of milky tea, staring into the steam that rose from it. It wasn't that she was sad, in fact the anticipation made her face glow and her hair bounce as never before. But she was distracted, as if the child growing inside her required all, not most, of her attention.

Sajida assumed an unexpected distance with Hussein, not waiting for him before falling asleep in bed and not sharing her dreams for the child she was carrying like she had done before the two boys.

"He will be an engineer," she'd said about the first, extrapolating from the measured kicks in her belly, the strength of which sometimes made her buckle to the floor.

"He will love music," she'd said about the second, whose somersaults she could stop with a tape recorder in her bed playing ghazals.

She said nothing about her daughter, except that she would love the child as she'd loved the others.

"Well, of course," Hussein said one day, unaware of Sajida's secret. "Why wouldn't you?"

༅

Driving to the hospital, Hussein put his hand on Sajida's belly during her contractions, feeling the muscles of her womb tighten into steel, forever amazed at how life could possibly be protected in so stretched a place. His wife hardly stirred during the contractions, breathing calmly, as if she were treating herself to breaths of cool air on a brisk morning walk. Although Hussein had never witnessed the birth of his child or any other, he knew enough to be impressed.

During the birth of his first son, he'd snuck into the waiting area outside the operation theatre where his niece stood clasping her hands, waiting for word amid a recital of moans and cries that frightened him. When a doctor swung open the door and the torn curtains on the window flapped back and forth, the attending physician gasped at Hussein's presence, insisting that he return to the men's waiting room. But he'd already caught a glimpse of the rows of beds, nurses milling about between women with their legs straddled, abandoned in the solitary task of pushing their children into the world.

Sajida's joy in her son's birth had been manifest. Her cheeks puffed in a permanent smile and her round, black eyes shone a dance when she looked at him. She was elated that she had produced life so healthy it bellowed in loud cries with its arrival. More than this, though, the new life intensified her belief in God. As much as He took, He gave much more. Love, laughter, children, second chances. Especially second chances. She believed that her big, healthy son was God's way of giving her another chance. The memories of her baby brother, the silent peace of his sleep before he was ripped from her, were always within reach. Whenever she thought of herself as lucky, like when she married a man who loved her and did not have to work to gain his family's confidence, she remembered. The helplessness, the despair, fearing that had she only been bigger or stronger, had she waved her arms and searched for him a few minutes longer, she might have saved him. So when her baby arrived from between her legs, wet and slippery, still attached to the cord, and the doctor said, "Larka hai, alhamdullilah," she heaved herself up and firmly took him from the doctor's hands.

Although she allowed the doctor to cut the umbilical cord and tie the stump into a black knot, she would not surrender her child to be bathed. Her husband was not permitted in the recovery room until the baby was cleaned because, as the woman lying in the bed next to her explained, the smell would disturb him. Sajida held on to the baby and stood, her stained kurta falling to her knees and leftover fluids running further down. She took the baby to the clogged toilet behind a curtain in the corner of the room where she urgently relieved her suddenly full bladder. With the corner of one of the towels she had brought with her to the hospital, she wiped her baby clean, starting with his belly which, next to his head, was the biggest part of him. When her husband entered the room, she was in bed, holding the not-so-slippery baby to her chest, crying at God's grace. She had difficulty letting go of her son, but she pulled herself away long enough for his father to whisper the first kalima in his ear and hold him in his arms.

"He has your lips," Hussein said. "And hands. How did you think to order them so strong? He has fingers, ten of them. Ten long nails on his toes." He loosened the swaddled blanket. "Did you see his bottom, Saji? He's got a blue spot on it, like an ink spill." He fingered the rolls of fat on the inside of the baby's knees and kissed them. "Fatoo. Look at his legs. Solid with muscles already! He has a neck somewhere, I know it." He kissed the baby's head, running his chin on the thick black curls still plastered down. He kept his face there, immediately entranced by the brand new smell emanating from somewhere in the softness of his child's head.

With a start, only just remembering, he turned to his wife. "Are you all right? Was it awful? Are you in pain?" Reaching for her hand, still trembling along with the rest of her shaking body, he said he loved her, she meant the world to him, he would treasure her sacrifice, what she had endured, to bear him a son.

Witnessing her reserved husband find expression in the scattered monologue he had just delivered, Sajida focused on controlling her desire to snatch the child from him. She wanted the baby's softness on her face, his perfection in her arms. Her need was urgent. To walk

16

on the new road her life had taken, the child firmly snuggled against her breast. To begin to demonstrate that she could do it. Entrusted with life, albeit a different one, she wanted to show the Almighty that she could hold on to it. In the face of the wind, walls of water, thundering noise, she would show Him.

Finally, with the baby asleep in his arms and the pillow underneath his wife's head wet from all the tears, Hussein found a different way of expressing his love.

"Anything. I'll do anything for you."

Immediately, Sajida asked Hussein for the baby's name. Not the baby she'd delivered, but the one who'd been swept from her arms the night of the cyclone, so that their newborn son could be his namesake. Hussein was taken aback by the request, but he dutifully pored over the scarce translations of Bengali literature available to him, read excerpts of travel brochures and poems, and scrutinized movie credits. The name was not on any of the lists he compiled, although with so many years behind her, he wondered if Sajida would know the name when she saw it. In the end, their first son had his own name: Adel.

Turning into the hospital complex, Hussein parked in the emergency lot, as he had twice before.

"I'm fine," Sajida announced at the hospital, touching her husband's cheek with her palm, letting it linger as it brushed against the nighttime shadow of his unshaven face. Less than half an hour later, without so much as a push, Noor slipped into the world.

Sajida was almost confused by the perfection of what she first saw. Her other children had been born with bruised faces, nose and mouth molded by violent contractions, head shaped like a cone. But Noor emerged from Sajida's body without so much as a mark on her, so calm and self-possessed that the doctor had to slap her bottom several times until she relented and cried.

Seeing his daughter in the first minutes of her life, wrapped like a mummy in the starched white cover they had brought with them to the hospital, Hussein was struck by her darkness. Not her skin, but her eyes were deep and endlessly black, like the abandoned well of his childhood in his great-grandfather's house. For one second, he felt like he had as a child whenever his brothers had recklessly held him above the well, threatening to drop him. His daughter's eyes were fixed on him, as if his baby girl had been born with the ability to focus, and mere moments after birth, already had something of consequence to share. Hussein lifted his daughter from his wife, effortlessly opening his body like an ocean making room for a boat. Her eyes seemed older than those of a child, and Hussein searched them for a hint of the pureness he recalled on the faces of his newborn sons. She continued to look at him with a purpose more urgent than a newborn's desire to melt into her parent's being.

Sajida stroked her daughter's head. "Noor," she said, her daughter's name suddenly coming to her.

"Light," Hussein translated into English, determined to find it in his daughter.

While Hussein went home to bathe and change into a freshly pressed kurta pajama, Ali, Sajida's father, visited the hospital. He was a real estate agent who set his own hours. He was preoccupied with plans to build a new house for his growing family, an enterprise that had left him little time to spare in the last few months. But when he'd heard from Nanijaan that Sajida had gone into labor, he cancelled all his business for the day, helped his grandsons get ready for school, and waited to be invited to the hospital. Seeing his granddaughter, he laughed at the miracle of a girl, a healthy child, and drew comparisons with Sajida.

"You. As a baby," he said simply, as if he'd known Sajida then. "She's a beauty."

But almost as soon as he spoke the words, Noor's face slowly began to change. The outer corners of her eyes fell into a permanent droop, as if the burden of sleep necessitated a physical manifestation. By the time Sajida reached to nurse her daughter again, the vaguest allusion to a bridge in her nose sank as if further deflated. Her ears, the miniscule perfections of paper-thin ridges and narrow canals of winding slopes, were suddenly out of place on her round head grown more ample in a matter of hours.

Ali, in an earlier life and another land, had seen children like Noor, a shade from black, in the hold of death. When Noor's face collapsed into what it would be, he leaned closer and, strangely, re-called something of the war he'd seen. The soiled maternity ward, new blood drying upon old, the sticky sweat of desperate work, evoked a moment in his other life. Although the day was dry and cloudless, Ali smelled a flooding pit of mud and he heard rain, unforgiving streams falling in deafening sheets. It was the roar of the monsoons, the dreaded season which stole his sleep every year. Steadying him-self, he touched Noor's face with his fingertips and let them rest by her tiny nose. He waited for her warm breath to tickle his skin and the sound of the rain to ease before he pulled away.

When Hussein returned, it occurred to Sajida that she ought, once and for all, to tell him of her premonition, the child—Noor, she now knew—she'd seen. But she wondered how she might say this, how she could convince him of the certainty of what she'd seen, and before she knew it the opportunity to say anything at all to him was gone.

"Noor?" Hussein wondered, gesturing at the baby in his wife's arms who'd looked so different when he left the hospital.

The doctor, Begum Fayaz, examined the child, and without the benefit of tests or consultations with anyone else, gave what she saw, only the first of a long list of ever-changing diagnoses that would be compiled over time.

"Mongoloid," Hussein heard, "also known as Down Syndrome," and he felt as if he'd been knocked flat.

"No," he said, when he regained his composure.

Curiously, Hussein suddenly recalled General Z's daughter. Early in Sajida's pregnancy, the general's plane had fallen from the sky without explanation. Graphic and far-fetched newspaper reports suggested the general had pressed his face against the plane's window as he plunged to his death. Hussein wondered how the general's retarded daughter was made to understand falling airplanes and her father's sudden death.

Then, Hussein recalled his own distant cousin, as old as he, a retarded child. Family folklore explained the child's affliction by claiming that the child's head had been squeezed too tightly with forceps during labor. He was reminded of his cousin's short and pudgy hands, stubs almost, when they were children.

Hussein quickly grabbed Noor's hands from underneath the blanket and pulled them away from her body. He opened Noor's tight fist and saw how long and elegant her fingers already were. "Look," he shouted to the doctor, "these are lovely!"

In the following exchange of words, Begum Fayaz, an older woman whose scratched bifocals had always worried Hussein, did not leave him with any hope.

"What the hell do you know?" he screamed at her finally, ending their relationship. "You're not even a bloody specialist. All you do is catch babies when they come out."

Sajida, however, wasn't much interested in what Begum Fayaz had to say. She paid no notice to the name thrown out that night nor would she be concerned in the future with the many different ones that would be offered by doctors in the early years of Noor's life. Autism, Rett Syndrome, Asperger's Syndrome, Martin-Bell Syndrome and more. Unlike Hussein, who read everything he could in the medical textbooks he found in old bookstores in Rawalpindi regarding the words the doctor assigned to his daughter, Sajida was not keen to wage a battle against a diagnosis, which as far as she could tell, was simply drawn from thin air. The fact of her daughter's life needed no name; it spoke for itself. Sajida loved Noor, utterly and completely, the way she did the boys.

Nanijaan understood Sajida's distaste for her child's doctors and the names they threw at her.

"She's your daughter. End of story," Nanijaan said when Sajida returned home with the newborn child. "What do doctors know of love?"

After those words, Nanijaan banned the cook from the kitchen. She emerged the next morning with plates of mithai: a collection of barfi, laddus, gulab jamuns, and more that would have put to shame the sweetmeat shops Hussein once frequented for Sajida.

At first, Hussein tried to find a way into the black depths of Noor's eyes.

He took Noor from Sajida after nighttime feedings. He tightened the diaper with safety pins and blew on her belly until she cooed. He ran his fingers through her new, silky hair, looking for forcep dents or any other marks which would explain why the baby his daughter should have been was squeezed from her.

When she started to cry, as she always did, Hussein walked with her in the dining room around the table which could seat twice the number of people in his family. He paraded the length of the living room until the roundabout movement made him dizzy. Then he took her through the swinging door into the kitchen, where the squeaking noise of the hinges and the humming refrigerator sometimes distracted her. But when she began to howl again, as was her routine, he retrieved his slippers from the heap next to the door and took her outside.

One particularly long night, he walked the short driveway charting how many of his steps amounted to a mile. Mostly, he searched for something, anything, to distract his daughter. He showed her the dancing moths gathered around a bush lit by a spotlight from the ground. He pointed out the colony of ants underneath the broken front steps which endured, no matter how often they were swept or hosed away. He poked at the colorful blossoms on the sweet-pea bushes that were about to bloom, and blew on the glistening spider webs, frantically woven in the carport during the night. He held her on her belly, her limbs outstretched like an airplane, and he swayed her low to the ground where crickets made a racket in the night. The night's noises reminded Hussein of how fitting he'd thought it was that his daughter's due date was in the spring, the cusp of bursting blossoms and loud choruses of birds.

Hussein thought he was accustomed to the frenzy of new parenthood. The sleepless nights, the constant interruptions, the single most important requirement: that the precious life that fit in the length between his palm and elbow came before everything else. In the past, it had wiggled itself between him and Sajida in intimate moments and forced them to recognize that time, which had once belonged to them, now belonged to their children. When Noor arrived, Hussein was already well schooled. He was not shocked by his exhaustion or embarrassed when, once again, he took to looking forward to the long rides to his bottle factory on dangerous, busy roads because, at the hands of the driver, they afforded him forty minutes of uninterrupted sleep.

In the beginning, he imagined that the whirlwind of doctor's appointments and discussions would settle, that a familiar rhythm of their lives would reemerge. But he was unprepared for how gravely his daughter would alter his life. No matter how bewildered he was at Noor's diagnosis, he initially believed he could overcome it. He reminded himself that his daughter had not been asked to be born, that she had been willed into life. He'd wanted her more than the boys. Maybe because she was a girl, or maybe because after two children, he thought he was ready to be a perfect parent.

But his illusions grew dimmer as the months passed. On their nighttime walks, Noor wept inconsolable sobs that tore at him. At each sound, from the shouts to the whimpers, Hussein felt himself grow more and more constricted. He wondered about the promises engendered in a new life, the hope that the life would be full and strong and loved. His realization was slow, analogous to a time in his childhood when he stared at a night sky of stars for many years before slowly seeing constellations or understanding that planets mingled in the lot of lights. Only now, no longer a child, but a grown man with tremendous responsibilities, there was no happiness or excitement to be found in his most private of discoveries. One night, roaming amid the nighttime buzz in his garden, sweet reborn fragrances of budding flowers hanging in the air, he came to see that Noor's life could not be full or strong or loved. Noor quieted in his arms, as if he had communicated this to her by the way he shifted her weight and, a hair's breadth from her face, looked beyond her instead of at her.

His belief was confirmed each time he endured reactions to the significant detail of his daughter's health. The late shift supervisor at his plastic bottle factory wanted to know what medication there was for these strangely named afflictions. The accountant helped himself to several portions of the barfi in the sweet boxes Hussein offered on the occasion of Noor's birth. Then the man whose only genius lay in numbers said, "Syndrome-shmyndrome. Can't you get rid of her?" He and Sajida cried over that one, and then Hussein refrained from sharing the rest with his wife.

"My sister's son is in a home for drug addicts. Maybe they have room there. I'll ask her for you."

"Send her to a village. They know how to deal with them there."

"It's a girl, yaar. God is merciful. He didn't land you with a boy like that."

As insensitive as all the comments were, the ones that concentrated on her sex upset Hussein the most. In fact, his sadness was greater because the child was a girl. He had two boys, each perfect and whole, but even before the second one was born, he'd wished for a girl, a child who would take longer to grow out of his love, a child who would not tire of his unconditional adoration. He saw hints of what his boys' future held for him. They were much more likely to look up from their games when their mother walked into the room than when he did. Although he read them stories every night, they fought over who would sit in their mother's lap, not his. He recited prayers with them before sleep, but it was their mother's kiss they waited for before they agreed to end their day.

These small things, however true, did not add up to his desire for a girl. Instead, he had hoped for a daughter who would, as much as possible, duplicate his wife, her laughter and beauty. He'd always adored Sajida, and he wanted another manifestation of her in this world. Greedy, perhaps, he thought, but that's the way it was.

Hussein learned to ignore the comments, expertly closing off his ears as soon as someone began making speculations or drawing conclusions. But what he could not ignore was the growing tightness in his chest, the ball of anger and frustration that intensified as he accepted blame for what he'd done. In the early months, he witnessed Sajida struggle to teach Noor how to nurse, watching her massage her breast and pull at her nipple until a watery white dripped and she put her flesh in Noor's mouth, willing her to latch on. Even though Noor finally learned, it angered him that his daughter took an age to learn what had come naturally to his sons and, in the process, required great effort from his wife. Despite the medical texts he struggled to understand, he held himself responsible for his daughter's condition, her incomplete and lacking life. As far as he could see, he had failed his child.

On Noor's first birthday, Sajida dressed her in a ruffled pink frock she stitched herself. White pearl buttons ran from the neck to her bottom and when Sajida sewed each buttonhole, she did so without considering how much difficulty she would have fastening them while her daughter wriggled to escape her reach. Sajida bought Noor shiny black shoes to wear with the outfit and as she struggled to fit Noor's wide feet inside them and buckle the strap, she wondered at the idea, given Noor had yet to stand.

The dining room was done up the way it was for the boys' birthdays. Balloons hung in bunches, streamers were taped to the ceiling, and party hats were propped on the plates. Nanijaan ordered the cake from the bakery, and Noor's name was pink like her dress across the hard, white frosting. A single candle rose from a flower bud and the boys, four and two, fought over who would eat the flower. Noor watched the candle flicker from Ali's lap as Hussein busied himself with the video camera and Sajida frantically counted twenty-eight cornflakes into Noor's white porcelain bowl.

Noor's food idiosyncrasies were something her body knew long before her mind might have began to understand. If Sajida hadn't accepted this, she might have considered unreasonable the demands placed on the kitchen. When Noor was six months old, she refused boiled chicken. Nanijaan decided that Sajida hadn't cooked it long enough and returned it to the kitchen until the soft breasts of chicken were cooked for so long the meat fell in strings from the bones. But she wouldn't eat that either. It turned out that Noor, like her grandfather, was a strict vegetarian.

Her needs were specific. She sipped at the freshly made yogurt lassi the cook made for her three times a day and poured into her orange sippy cup, the only one with a handle. The cook, who was the first to recognize Noor's desire to eat the same food for days at a time, had been too busy on Noor's birthday to count the cornflakes himself. So Sajida counted the required flakes once, and then again, while the candle burned in Noor's cake and the family sang "Happy Birthday." Sitting in Ali's lap, Noor clapped with everyone else when the song was over. Then she carefully picked the cornflakes from her bowl and ate them one at a time while the boys devoured cake and

ice cream in big, heaping bites that dribbled from their mouths and
spoons.

Although Noor, as a rule, didn't like surprises in the form of
toys or strangers, Sajida couldn't resist buying her birthday presents.
Among them was a talking baby doll, plastic blocks that connected
into oversized necklaces and, from the boys, an inflatable, plastic
beach ball. Until Nanijaan unwrapped her gift, Noor expressed no
interest in anything in front of her. Nanijaan opened the fat crayon
box and pulled out the first crayon she touched. She put it on a small
drawing tablet and brought it close to Noor.

Noor's hand, clenched like an infant's around Ali's finger, slowly
opened when she saw the crayon almost in her lap. She allowed Nanijaan to wrap her tiny fingers around the blue crayon. Then, she
held the crayon on her own, as if she'd already mastered the art of
holding a writing or drawing implement. Nanijaan clasped Noor's
wrist and gently pushed it back and forth until Noor had rubbed
color on the stiff paper. The more the paper filled with color, the
more excited Noor became. She pulled away her arm, flapped it in
the air, and squealed, "Nanijaan."

The name had been Noor's first word and when she said it, a few
weeks earlier, it was perfect and whole, as if she'd said it a thousand
times before. After Nanijaan's first grandchild, a granddaughter, provided the new name, it came to be that no one, not even Nanijaan's
children, could remember with certainty what she'd once been called.
When Noor had said "Nanijaan" for the first time, Sajida reveled that
her daughter had fallen seamlessly into the family tradition.

After she spoke, Noor squirmed in Ali's grasp until he put her on
the floor. As she was still unable, at one year, to bear the weight of her
own head, Ali propped her against the wall with sofa cushions to either side in case she should fall. Noor smelled of baby powder, hints
of chalky white visible inside the rolls of skin underneath her chin as
her head wobbled from side to side. Kneeling beside her, Nanijaan
held the drawing tablet on Noor's lap. Without help, Noor returned

the crayon to the paper. Over the next several minutes, she rubbed the crayon with more and more deliberation until it shrank and the tablet of twenty pages was almost full.

The boys had long since left the scene, putting their sticky, ice cream hands on Matchbox cars and taking their roaring chatter into other rooms. Sajida, surprised that Noor was not chewing on the crayons or tearing the paper wrappings from them as her brothers had done at her age, stared at her daughter in disbelief. She would forever remember the sound of a flat crayon scratching paper, the sight of bright wax sticking to Noor's miniature fingernails, and later, the color of Noor's pink tongue against the flecks she'd sucked from her nails. That night, no matter how hard Sajida tried to wipe the crayon from Noor's mouth with a washcloth during her bath, the specks did not budge.

No one spoke. Only Nanijaan, crouched beside Noor, holding the drawing tablet with one hand and wiping dribble from Noor's mouth with the other, had an inkling of what was transpiring. Baby Noor had a gift. Watching the same blue Islamabad sky emerge again and again on page after page was enough to convince her that Noor, different as she might be, was devoted to the vastness and complexities of colors.

In the days that followed, Noor established that her affinity for crayons and paper was not an accident. When Noor's blue crayon ran out, Nanijaan understood her wails. She went to the store to buy several boxes of crayons and when she returned home, she presented Noor with one box filled only with blues. Noor immediately stopped crying and began, again, to fill sheets of paper with the single color, slowly and deliberately, without missing a spot.

Although Sajida had known the secret of Noor for months before she was born, she was unprepared for the miracle of her daughter's talent.

"Noor drew this," she'd say to Nanijaan, both as question and as fact, trying to accustom herself to this new reality.

"Your daughter," Nanijaan would proudly answer, smiling broadly.

One year after Noor's birth Sajida remained so thoroughly exhausted, she sometimes fell asleep at the edge of the bathtub for a short minute while she waited for her youngest son to rinse his hair. In those days, watching Noor draw provided such a measure of relief and gratitude that Sajida sometimes felt her eyes fill without warning. Not because she had ever hoped for a larger-than-life miracle—that her daughter might one day wake up normal—but because she'd been granted a much smaller one. Noor, who had rejected her brother's cars, trucks, and blocks, had found something of her own to occupy her for a few minutes during the day.

But the drawings themselves, their relentlessness, began to work on Sajida. First, she was hypnotized by the color and then, by the uneven shading where Noor's tiny hands had pressed in various degrees on the crayon. One day, laying out Noor's drawings side by side until they were a carpet in the center of the living room, Sajida saw that Noor's blue was movement. Impatiently, she waited for Noor's drawings, examining and discovering a different pulse in each. Sajida could almost see ripples of water running away from the edge of a beach. She could feel the sweltering days and hear the grind of her father's fishing boat against the sand banks in the Bay of Bengal as it was pushed on land. More than anything else, she could make out fishing nets swimming and bending below the blue of Noor's crayons.

Hussein preferred not to see Noor's drawings. He stopped the video camera when Noor put her crayon on paper at her birthday party. He'd known, since the day Noor arrived, the moment he'd seen her features, freshly flat on her face, that she was abnormal. But when he saw what she made, sheets filled simply and perfectly with blue, he couldn't abide it. He believed the drawings reflected his daughter's mind, amorphous and unformed, so much so that the ugliness of what she'd spilled onto paper was the very essence of who she was. His disappointment in himself and his daughter festered until it became rage. Hussein picked up drawings scattered about the house, bunched them into tight balls, and threw them in the garbage.

Hussein could think of only one thing to do. He imagined what his mother might say if she knew. *The world is bigger than you. I brought you up better than that.* Even so, one morning shortly after Noor's first birthday, Hussein sat on the bed, shook Sajida awake, and told her what he felt.

"I can't," he began, his tone sterner than he'd hoped.

When Sajida pulled herself from her precious sleep, willing herself awake to hear her husband's urgent words, he had to repeat himself.

"I've reached the end of my line," he added.

Later, she went over his metaphor in her head and held it against him that in this most desperate of moments, he'd found a way of expressing himself that was more attuned to factory talk than feelings. *End of the line?* she should have said. *Like when a plastic bottle warps on the assembly line and is thrown into the reject bin?*

"She bothers you?" Sajida inquired, thinking about the noise, admitting to herself that her daughter's cries were difficult to endure. "Oh, meri jaan," Sajida said, sitting up and reaching for him. "It gets better. Don't you remember?"

Because Hussein was only speaking tangentially about the crying, he did not remember.

"I want her out of this room," he declared.

"It's hard for you," Sajida mumbled, tilting her cheek for Hussein's good-bye kiss as he got up to leave the room.

Sajida spent the day, or what remained of it after feedings and changing diapers, scolding herself for keeping her secret from Hussein. She'd had the nine months of her pregnancy to accept this baby; he'd only had the months since Noor was born. *Had it been a year already?* But she knew now, more than ever, that if she had approached Hussein with her vision, found the courage to describe the moments of that hot Islamabad night, if she'd had the words to describe the presence of the child that was now Noor, her husband would certainly have thought her mad.

That night, when Hussein was in the bathroom and Sajida, with Noor in her arms, was ready to go to bed, she moved the crib. She pulled it from the far side of the room until it touched the bed. When Hussein finished in the bathroom, he found the crib rolled flush against one side of his bed, and on the other side already cordoned by the intractable barrier of the wall, Sajida lay with her back to Hussein, nursing Noor.

He walked to the foot of the bed, the only part of his wife's and daughter's haven not shielded by the walls or the crib.

"I can't," he said, this time limiting himself to the boundaries he had drawn for himself.

Sajida did not look up when he spoke. He reached for her foot peaking behind the sheet. In the dim light of the room the sole of her foot was white next to her other leg. Before he could touch it, Sajida moved away in the single acknowledgement of his presence she made that night. After that, Hussein did not touch his wife for days, his child for countless more.

three

Noor learned to walk when she was thirty months old, far later than her brothers had mastered their legs, but earlier than any doctor had predicted. Her first steps, tiptoed, were upstairs in the doorway of the main bedroom. Holding herself up on a stool, she was frightened by the sudden siren of her brother's toy ambulance and wobbled toward her father. Hussein, already kneeling on the floor to retie the stiff laces on his dress shoes, caught her accomplishment from the corner of his eye. But when his daughter stumbled, first into his shadow painted on the floor by the late afternoon light, and then into his leg, he could not make himself turn around and catch her. Instead, Sajida leaped up to catch Noor before she fell. At that moment, Sajida was flush with the excitement of her daughter's step. But late at night when she lay awake, as she often did, reflecting on the absence of her husband, she understood the cold facts of what had happened. The man she might once have given her life for had found it possible to disregard a child he had helped to make.

Whatever Noor was, she could not be easily dissuaded. Despite Hussein's dismissal of her, both in practice and in fact (he did not include her photographs on his office desk where the smiling faces of the boys were frozen behind gold plated frames), she loved him just the same. When his car pulled into the driveway, she ran to the window to watch the driver deliver her father home. By the time he stood at the door, she waited on the other side, her head barely reaching the narrow window next to the door. As small as she was then, when he opened the door and entered the house, she would bend her head back with delight. She ran her eyes over his frame, loving the bigness of it, all the while, as it often seemed to Sajida, searching for some part of it she might pull from her gaze into her grasp. Sometimes, the combination of her weak muscles and heavy head made her lose her balance and more than once she toppled to the floor. But she was always happy to see him, the reservoir of her giving, remarkable as it was, oblivious to Hussein's disregard.

Since the night Hussein left his wife and child in the bedroom, his eyes averted from Noor, and when she learned first to sit and then stand by the front door in anticipation of his arrival, he did not see her there. Entering his home, he would drop his boxlike briefcase on the nearest chair. Walking around Noor, he kept his shoulders turned away from her, as if when she was in his presence, he was always making his way somewhere else. Noor would watch Hussein hug and kiss her brothers at the top of the hallway, and her smile grew wider and more buoyant with each observation, as if she gleaned some of her father's love by witnessing it bestowed on others.

Ali did not interfere. Troubled as he was with his son-in-law's behavior, he didn't raise it with Sajida. Instead, he spent more time with Noor, finding endless ways to include her in his days. As it was, when Noor was born Ali found himself utterly and immediately in love, in a way a father might be expected to embrace his own child. Ali knew that Noor, like his grandsons, was the closest he would get to the beginning of a life. But his granddaughter, her life and her love, was another story. It mattered not at all that people said Noor was *less-than* or that, in fact, she was different from the other children.

Ali loved the circle of her face, her ears, perfect in each curve, and her hair, the only thing straight about her. What others held against Noor, Ali relished. He delighted that Noor did not reach milestones as quickly as the other children had—that she didn't speak or walk in a hurry and would still need to be rocked to sleep when she was three. Ali loved that the child, so patient, knew enough to grow up slowly.

Long before Noor's arrival, Ali had sought to move his family out of his childhood house. The rented house was cramped and old, and no matter how often the walls were painted, they always appeared in need of a fresh coat. Sometimes, when Ali thought back on the day Hussein and his mother had come with a marriage proposal for Sajida, he chuckled a bit shamefully. He'd insisted Hussein and Sajida live with him and exaggerated his plans to build a larger house, though he had been in no position to do so. He lied in the midst of a heated discussion, knowing full well in his heart that he would say and do whatever was necessary to hold on to Sajida. Nevertheless, he always intended to move himself and his family into a bigger house. He began to prepare for it as soon as he'd made himself a father. When Sajida was still small, he stumbled on an affordable real estate scheme through his work as real estate agent and bought a plot of land in the most remote sector of Islamabad.

Over the years, he visited the plot. He would drive his car in wide circles, imagining the kitchen and dining room, bedrooms and bathrooms, the lounge and foyer, beneath the car. Since the day Ali bought the land, the sector on the far edges of Islamabad had remained empty except for rough roads, the barest foundation for a sector market, and one other semi-structure. This structure, a house, intended to be grand, had been deserted in the midst of construction. The bottom floor was completed before work stopped, except for the gaping holes where windows should have been. The top floor was only a frame, but curiously, a finished, wide marble balcony ran around it. Trees had been planted alongside the outer wall of the house, and over the many years they grew to shade it, making it unclear from a distance whether the house was occupied or not. Like everyone else in Islamabad, Ali assumed that the partly built houses scattered around the city, which existed in a strange tandem of being there and not being there, belonged to East Pakistanis, dead or alive, who hadn't claimed them after the war.

Although the years accumulated and put more and more distance between Ali and the months he'd spent in East Pakistan, he knew better than anyone in Islamabad where these houses were located. As a real estate agent, driving his clients through the city, he went out of his way to avoid them. But when he couldn't, he turned away his head in dread of what they were: stark, scattered reminders of where he'd once been.

When Sajida became pregnant with Noor, Ali collected all the money he'd carefully saved from his real estate commissions and hired a contractor to build a house on his plot big enough for parents and children alike. Before Noor could walk, it had been possible to whisk her in and out of the gates and take her on outings. Daily, Ali strapped her to his back at the construction site where together they would survey the continuing work. But by the time the roof was finally put on, Noor had outgrown toddlerhood, learned to walk, and made it clear that she would not be moved.

No one, least of all Ali, was prepared to risk Noor's fury. Her cries were deafening. She screamed as if she were being tortured and made to bear excruciating pain. In those early years, servants ran away and neighbors pulled closed their windows and called in their children at the start of her scenes. Noor's brothers, who during better times spent hours making her laugh, fled from her presence at the first shriek. If Sajida was nearby when the crying began, she would sit on the floor and intertwine her arms with Noor's, gently soothing her daughter as they rocked together.

Quite by accident one day, Sajida discovered a remedy. She was running a bath for the boys when Noor began to cry. She scooped Noor into her arms and ran to the bathroom. At the sound of the water, Noor's cries lessened. When Sajida turned off the bath faucet, Noor's crying intensified until she was once again shaking and shivering with her own screams. In a trial of on-and-off Sajida confirmed that Noor was calmed by the uninterrupted sound of running bath water. From that day onward, Sajida carried Noor into the bathroom at the first hint of a wail. With their backs against the bathtub while it filled, Sajida waited until Noor's shrill cries and deep sobs abated. And, as if Sajida were being divinely compensated for her tremendous effort, the hours the two of them spent in the bathroom resulted in Noor being potty-trained earlier and more easily than either of the boys.

Even though it became possible to soothe Noor, the sheer intensity of her early, most desperate cries would never be forgotten by anyone in the family. It was natural, then, that when Noor decided to limit her universe to the house or draw herself borders within its confines, no one, including Ali who was busy with his construction site, rose to contradict her.

Nanijaan saw the new house for the first time when Ali announced it was ready to be occupied. All along, she made it understood that she considered Ali's ambition for a bigger and better house nothing less than wasteful. When she toured the house and recognized how in the senseless architecture her son had turned his back on the mountains, the only beauty on the otherwise empty horizon, she declared that even God's mercy could not fix his new found tendency toward waste.

"God can't do the work for you," she said. "You need to fix yourself. In the mean time you need to fix a place on the roof for me."

The move to the new house was delayed while Nanijaan insisted that Ali build her a set of spiraling steps to the roof of her bedroom so that perched above, she, at least, could relish the majestic view.

Once or twice in the years ahead, sitting on her aluminum folding chair with the Margalla Hills forming her horizon, Nanijaan would suspect that her son's choice of house spoke to the dark secrets all men of war shared. Contemplating the outdated architecture of his house (*who'd heard of a modern house with a courtyard, after all?*), she imagined that Ali had fortified the inner sanctity of his home with rooms on all sides in the same way that he'd fortified himself against marriage. Just as his courtyard could not be seen from the street, he would never have a wife who might come to know whatever it was he'd seen in those months in that distant, wretched land.

The house was a simple square. The first visitor slapped Ali's back and shouted, "Yaar, you've gone and built a sector house." Over time, because of the neatness of its shape, the house came to be known to people in Islamabad and Rawalpindi alike as Ali's Sector. To a population imprisoned by the whims of questionable urban planners, the name seemed perfect. The planners had rigidly dictated the square sectors in which the carefully designed city at the foot of great mountains was to be built. It wasn't surprising that the suffocating sectors of the city eventually found their way into the architecture of someone's home. Once Ali accepted the parallel for himself, he placed a cement sign noting the house's name and street address at the top of the driveway. The sign was in good humor and very accurate: the narrow white slab with blue lettering mimicked the proportion and lettering of the city's street signs.

Ali's Sector was a single-story building, a series of high-ceilinged, adjacent rooms. There were two bedrooms on one side, the kitchen and overly generous dining room on the other, the living room and lounge on the third side. On the fourth side, which would one day face the servants' quarters of a neighboring mansion, there were three large rooms for Sajida and her family. One of the design peculiarities was that from the road the brick house, without the benefit of a roadside garden or a narrow strip of tended land, appeared stark and uninviting, a virtual fort. There were few windows in the outside walls. In the kitchen there was a long one flanked by exhaust fans which ran noisily day and night, through the hot, cool, and rainy seasons alike. But even this window seemed intentionally misplaced. The cook bent over the long and spacious granite counter on the opposite side of the room, his back permanently to the window. Oddly enough, only the bathrooms had generous windows but these were enclosed in iron cages which impinged on the view of the Margalla Hills.

On the day of the move, Sajida gave Noor two doses of cough medicine and waited until she was in a deep sleep before putting her into the car and transferring her to their new home. She put Noor into the master bedroom, a room Ali had built in pretense for Sajida and Hussein. Next to the bed, Sajida leaned a box of crayons bought for this occasion against paper propped on a child's easel. Although Sajida knew Noor never used the easel, she suspected her daughter might draw comfort from her art supplies if they were in immediate sight when she awoke.

Sajida waited for the effectiveness of the cough medicine to wane. When Noor opened her eyes to her new surroundings, Sajida let the bath water run while she softly explained where they were. Moments later a plumbing difficulty required the water supply to be turned off and the faucet sputtered until it was dry. In the absence of running water, Sajida could do nothing but hold Noor in her arms while the child screamed and cried as never before. Ali cursed the workmen for their shoddy work which resulted in the plumbing crisis, and took the boys back to the empty house for a night without beds but blessed with precious silence. Hours later, Noor fell asleep and Sajida, wet with perspiration at her marathon effort, followed suit. When they awoke the next morning, Noor appeared to have forgiven Sajida the trespass of her boundaries. She bounced from the bed in her recently acquired gait to peer from her new windows. It was another week or two before she widened her new boundaries and could be coaxed from the room.

In the beginning, the rooftop getaway was Nanijaan's solace. Because the house lacked neighbors, the unimpeded scenery in all directions was expressly hers for the taking. Nanijaan would call the boys or Sajida to the roof, and in the evenings they would watch the stars rise and the moon and planets shine above the fading outline of the hills. But within months after shifting to their new home, neighborhood construction began in earnest. Nanijaan was not alone in recognizing that the sudden growth of the neighborhood corresponded to a plague of bank scandals involving the new democratically elected government. Much to her dismay, her expansive view shrank even as she moved her folding chair from one place to the next to hold on to glimpses of it. Finally, when the surrounding architecture became massive pillars and mansions—some that strove to duplicate the style of the faraway White House on the other side of the ocean—Nanijaan's vista was devoured.

One of Nanijaan's biggest complaints had been that the house was flush with the boundaries of the plot, leaving no room between itself and the road or the imminent neighbors' houses.

"You're as greedy as the rest," she'd said to Ali, irritated. "You've filled it all up with concrete."

When the double- and triple-story monstrosities went up around Ali's Sector, filling each inch of the surrounding plots with solid houses, she blamed him for the scramble of homes overtaking her view.

"You started it. What do you need a house so big for? Sitting on the edges of your property? Instead of planting a vegetable patch or some flower gardens, you've gone and planted excess in everyone else's head."

One morning, a few months after the move to Ali's Sector, Noor climbed on an empty, manual cement mixer at the entrance to the driveway. The machine, almost entirely covered with hardened gray cement, had been abandoned by Ali's contractor. Perched atop, Noor's plump, hour-glass legs, hung loosely from either side. Swinging them back and forth, Noor caught one of her legs in a handle. While twisting to free herself, she fell to the side. Her leg did not move with her and she hung from the machine with her left leg bent in unexpected ways.

Turning into the street after grocery shopping, Sajida saw Noor hanging from the cement mixer before she reached the driveway. She jumped from the car and ran to her daughter, only to find Noor, her eyes wide open and staring at the sky, utterly still. With help from the driver, Sajida lifted Noor and gently slipped her broken leg free. Except for Noor's contorted leg, there was no evidence of the tumble. Wrapping Noor, so quiet, in her arms, Sajida felt something new. For the first time since Noor's birth, she was afraid.

Initially, Sajida had been comforted by the fact that Noor seemed not to notice physical pain. As much time as Noor spent crying and fussing when she was born, it seemed a gift that she did not notice a pinch or scratch here or there. When Sajida accidentally scraped Noor with a safety pin for the first time, a few days after she returned from the hospital, Noor was oblivious. During her immunizations and endless blood tests, the doctors remarked with concern on her inability to feel needles pricking her body. When the boys poked Noor's foot with a small nail to extract blood to add to their own in a childish sacrament that would bind them together forever, Sajida considered calling the doctor because Noor sat unbothered by the fuss as her foot bled through plenty of bandages before it stopped. Rather than finding any of this worrisome, Sajida was grateful that Noor was tougher than the rest of them.

But the realization that Noor did not feel excruciating pain after suffering a severely broken bone made Sajida shake with fright and sadness. Trying not to surrender to her emotions, she did her best to relax her shoulders and ignore the cramp in her stomach. She brought her face close to Noor's ear, her lips grazing Noor's tiny lobe.

"Meri jaan," Sajida whispered. "You're far too brave for us!"

It took three people, Sajida, the driver, and Ali, to force Noor into the car. She screamed at an unforgettable pitch when the car reversed down the driveway and beyond the universe she'd made her limit.

At the hospital, despite her dangling leg, she kicked at the doctors and bit the nurse before a tranquilizer was administered. The doctor, a young, burly man, pumped the child with morphine, unconvinced that Noor did not feel the pain of her leg broken in five places.

Her leg was stretched, twisted, X-rayed, set and bolted with steel pins before Noor spoke. She strung together more words than she ever had, completing for the first time, not one but two sentences at once.

"Don't feel sad," she said to Sajida. "Noor is brave."

"What?" Sajida asked, startled, cupping her ear.

Noor repeated herself in perfectly enunciated and thoughtfully intoned words.

It was, Sajida would explain to Nanijaan, as if her four-year-old child, so different, had been speaking for years.

For several months, Noor's leg was in a full-size cast. The huge plaster mold added to the imbalance of her body's proportions. Along with tiny ears and slanted eyes, delicate fingers and bracelets of fat on her wrists, her broken leg was immense against her frame and the good one suddenly thin and weak in comparison. Every so often, Noor would be returned to the hospital for her leg to be checked and her cast to be sawed off. She could no longer be convinced to take cough medicine, and therefore kicked and screamed through the entire visit. The progress was far slower than the doctors had hoped and her still-broken leg, withering and blue, was covered in a new cast three times.

During those months, Ali added to his plans for the courtyard. Because the house was set on the very edges of the property, the courtyard had seemed ample at first. With minimal effort, it had been transformed from the barren land on which the house was built. Grass seed was sown early and coaxed into a thin carpet by the garden hose and the gardener, who was as young as he was eager. Ali had planted a cactus that he cajoled from a store owner who was reluctant to part with the large and thriving plant. Brick walkways wound around the courtyard, spreading into a landing of sorts next to each door that opened on it.

But when Noor broke her leg, Ali had new ideas. In one corner, he pitched a steel pole into a deep hole filled with a bucket of cement. From it, he hung a gigantic wrought-iron birdcage that he'd ordered from a famous iron furniture maker in one of Karachi's busiest shopping districts. The cage arrived by truck in a wooden container that had to be stripped away board by board. It had several doors, each with its own latch, and numerous rods where a large number of birds could perch and play.

Ali went to the market in Rawalpindi to find birds lovely enough to live in their courtyard. He selected the most colorful birds, all of them parrots. Some had bright yellow collars around their necks and maroon shoulder patches. Others had black and rose-pink collars with blue wings and yellow tips on their tails. When he returned home, touting a collection of birds in the back seat of the car that might have impressed the most serious of bird collectors, he followed the storekeeper's advice and added the specimens to the big cage slowly and one at a time over a few days. Eventually the parrots were comfortable enough to make their calls, and these early morning concerts of *keeak-keaak, tooi? tooi?,* and *chee-chee-chee* became the background noise of Ali's Sector. Ali thought himself fortunate that the birds rarely sat still, because Noor, enchanted by the birds, was never able to determine how many lived in the cage. Until Ali found the perfect combination, he would simply remove and replace dead birds with whatever was available when Noor was not looking. Finally, when the birds began laying eggs and multiplying on their own, Ali was saved the chore of replacing them, for by then even he had lost count of the population.

Although the parrots helped distract Noor, she developed a new affliction while her leg was in a cast. With unnatural vehemence, Noor began to fear lines: of walls that marked the property, the doorways she was forced to pass under, the cracks on the brick walkways, the miniature blades of dead grass, short, brown and broken that she was convinced lay beneath the green grass carpet of the courtyard. It was the boys' idea to plant badminton nets, a veritable fence, with extra wickets along one of the walkways. They invented games for Noor which had her rolling the ball from between the lines of the brick walkway on one side of the courtyard to the boys whose net-fence prevented the ball from trespassing the flower beds and walkway lines. Most exhausting, Noor also required of those who moved her from place to place that they not violate the lines. Every day, her back aching from a child made unnaturally heavy by a full-length leg cast, Sajida strained to fit her bare feet inside the edges of bricks while Noor, peering down, supervised her every step.

Finally, and without confiding in anyone, Ali went to a marble factory on the outskirts of Rawalpindi, thirty-five minutes away. He bought Noor a slab of polished white marble with fading purple veins Sajida imagined spreading out like the winding trails in the Margalla Hills beyond. Before he allowed the marble to be set in the courtyard under Noor's watchful eye, he dug up the grass beneath it where lines of any type might have been hiding. Then, as three grown men heaved and groaned lowering the flat, generous stone, he supervised its placement on the dirt.

Over time, Noor graduated to drawings of more than one color and one shape. The marble was large enough to accommodate Noor and her ever growing art supplies. Whether she chose to draw in a sketchbook, on narrow rolls of paper, or on the taut pieces of canvas

Sajida constructed for her, and whether or not anyone chose to sit beside her while she drew, the stone was large enough.

Regardless of the season, it became routine for Noor to begin her mornings on the marble. In the spring and summer, when the family thought it too hot to allow her to bake outside in the heat, Noor shouted and cried until she was allowed otherwise. Although it was difficult for others to accept, Noor took as little notice of the weather as she did of physical pain. When temperatures soared outside and others dripped with perspiration merely crossing the courtyard, Noor did not require ice in her soft drink or a fan in her midst. When temperatures dropped and others walked about with sweaters and chaddars wrapped around their shoulders, Noor dressed in the short-sleeved, cotton frocks she wore in the heat of summer. Only when her drawings and supplies were threatened with rain did she agree to spend her days indoors.

So it happened that every morning while the boys rushed to get ready for school, Ali and Hussein finished their last cups of tea before leaving for work, and the sweeper finished brushing dust from the driveway beyond, Noor would sit near the parrots with her pail filled with crayons, pastels, chalk, ink, and pencils. When Noor's cast was finally taken off and left at the hospital, Nanijaan watched as Noor began her day by falling to her knees on the marble every morning. She folded her good leg beneath her and the other, bruised, withered, and forever stiffened by steel pins, lay flat and extended behind. Her long hair tied in pigtails high on the sides of her round head, and tiny diamond earrings painlessly put in the s of her earlobes, Noor hurled herself into her work. While Noor bowed low to a paintbrush, the birdcage swayed above and crayons and paints rolled on the stone. It was as if, with Noor sitting atop it, Ali's shiny piece of marble was a magical place no one else, even sitting on it beside Noor, could hope to reach. Feeling this, Nanijaan imagined more than once that the child had found her own special way to commune with God.

◌

Noor's first drawing on Ali's marble slab was her first foray into paints. She found the small tubes of oil paints Nanijaan had stacked for later use in a cupboard, and she painted on a poster board Sajida had bought for one of the boys' school projects. Like the sheets of single color with which Noor had begun her drawings, every inch of the poster was saturated. She used a brush the width of one of her feet. The painting was multicolored: reds, blues, purples. Vague, swirling shapes drawn with generous brush strokes began in the right corner, before swooping down to the bottom edge and becoming even less distinct as they traversed Noor's canvas from right to left. Three splotches of crinkled silver were scattered over what Noor had drawn. They were sheets of vark, paper-thin sheets of edible silver intended as special decoration for Nanijaan's famous sweets. An afterthought, sitting on forgotten lumps of oil paint, the silver lent Noor's first painting a touch of extravagance.

Nanijaan saw the drawing first. She dared not blink her eyes as shapes emerged from the colors. She was so taken with what she saw, she was forced off her feet. Sitting on the floor, she held the painting by its edge. Wet, sticky paint rubbed off on her fingers. She recognized in Noor's creation a beautiful, calligraphic version of one word: God. The "Allah" seemed all the more miraculous to Nanijaan because of how she feared He was treated in her home. He was ignored by a son who'd forgotten how to pray since returning from the war, and He was abused by a son-in-law who could not find enough love and gratitude for Him to stand beside his wife and their daughter.

Using her fingernail, Nanijaan scratched the silver and tasted the crumbs of metallic color. In her bedroom, she checked the vark she kept locked in her dresser. The packet, normally tied with a ribbon in a felt envelope, lay open. Silver shreds littered the drawer, leaving behind fairytale dust. The next day, Nanijaan stood on a ladder and hammered the painting into the wall above the front door. Every day, when her eyes sought it out, she confirmed her belief that Noor's drawings were invocations to God. Nanijaan suspected that this meant something of beauty was unfolding, although even she could not be prepared for the significance of it.

When Sajida saw Noor's painting standing against a wall, curling slightly in the corners, she received her daughter's gift—as she always did—with surprise and pleasure.

"Lovely," she said. While hugging Noor, she wondered how her daughter had learned to trust her paintbrush and the muse which directed it. It was the kind of thought she—in natural reflex—thought to share with Hussein before recalling with returning disappointment and surprise that she could not. Without Hussein beside her, she'd learned to be more direct about everything, so she simply asked Noor. "How?" she said. "But *how* do you do it?"

Noor only shrugged and giggled, carrying herself away from her mother and the painting, her withered and still bruised leg trailing behind.

Sajida concentrated on the contours of what was hidden in Noor's splash of colors. The curves were well drawn, as if they were intended to be exactly what they were. Walking around the painting, inspecting it from various angles, it occurred to Sajida that the twists and turns might be the very beginnings of letters in a child's head. Despite the ever-changing medical diagnoses of her child and their invariable limitations (*she'll never learn to write, she'll never be able to look after herself*), the painting prompted Sajida to take action. Armed with undivided love and the perseverance she'd gained by teaching her sons how to read and write, Sajida decided to teach Noor the alphabet.

In the evening hours, sitting with Noor in their bedroom underneath the humming ceiling fan with their backs against the bed that had been a wedding gift from Ali, Sajida attempted to persuade Noor to draw the words she spoke. In the beginning, Sajida offered words in alphabetical order in a muddle of Urdu and English, apples and anar for alif, bananas, boats, bakri for *b*. But Noor had no patience for the rigidity of either alphabet, and before long, picked and drew random words from these sessions with Sajida. In the corner of each drawing, with great care, Sajida printed a caption, the single word Noor had chosen to illustrate.

Ali was the first to showcase Noor's drawings. When Nanijaan presented Noor with her first box of crayons and Noor, struggling to sit, filled sheet after sheet of paper with single colors, Ali chose an orange one (flat and long like sunsets he'd once seen) to hang on his door. Early on, when Noor's ability to draw still elicited surprise, Ali once remarked to Nanijaan that sometimes, when Noor was not drawing, her eyes seemed vacant.

Nanijaan had just laughed at her son. "You wouldn't know vacant from occupied," she'd said, as if Ali were still a young boy. "Your granddaughter has more going on in her head than any of us."

Ali called Noor's new drawings of the simple words, mostly objects she drew so easily, still lifes. The collection grew into piles around the house until Ali began to paste the drawings onto a wall in the courtyard. He used Sajida's notations to arrange them alphabetically into a gallery. Ali thought of the drawings as beautiful because they were Noor's, but he also thought of them as evidence of what went on inside Noor's head. The more letters Sajida taught Noor, the larger the collection grew. Eventually, it wound around the walls, the *p*'s interrupted by the kitchen door and bedroom windows, the *z*'s floating around the electrical fuse box and washed away with the heaviest day of rains during the late monsoons of one particularly hot summer.

Ali selected a few of his favorite drawings, asked Noor's permission, and took them to be framed. Ali came upon Hussein as he stumbled, as if by accident, and dropped his heavy briefcase on the freshly delivered bundle of frames lying near the door. The glass shattered and some of the frames broke.

"Be careful," Ali said, expressing irritation, but nothing more, with his son-in-law.

Rather than dispense with the drawings, Ali hung them anyway, their lopsided frames awkward on inside and outside walls alike.

"You made these," Ali said to Noor as they walked together amidst the drawings. "Allow me," he said, proudly bowing to her. "The family *artiste!*"

She put her hand in her grandfather's. The two walked around the courtyard as if they were in a museum together, Ali pointing at things she'd drawn—apple, orange, pomegranate, banana.

"Alif comes first, you know," he said, waving in the direction of drawings for the beginning of the alphabet. As an afterthought, he touched one and pointed to the word in the corner: *aam,* mango. Noor had hung the drawing herself, helping Nanijaan cut short lengths of tape with her heavy sewing scissors. Noor had drawn the plumpest variety of mango, the family favorite. After looking at it, Ali relished mangoes even more because of the exquisite detail scripted into Noor's miniature fruits.

When Noor's drawings began to clutter the walls of Ali's Sector, Hussein tried not to, but couldn't help take notice. Some days after Ali began his gallery, Hussein secretly tore a drawing from the wall. It was one of Noor's original sheets of blue he so despised. He was unable to silence his suspicions that Noor's drawings, no longer limited to sheets of color, were continuing evidence of her muddied, broken mind. He shredded the drawing into pieces and had enough foresight to pack the scraps in a separate bag and bury it in the week's garbage. The next morning, when the household was preoccupied with trying to coax from Noor the reason she'd torn the drawing from the wall, he left for the office without saying a word.

Noor's drawings continued to disappear from the walls. A day, a week, or sometimes as long as a month later, the drawing would suddenly reappear in the empty space where it had once hung. Everyone in Ali's Sector would become perplexed, again, at why Noor had taken the drawing from the wall in the first place, where she'd hidden it while the house was searched, and why magically, like the drawings themselves, it reappeared on the walls without the slightest crease or hint of where it had been. Only Hussein, almost entirely committed to looking beyond his daughter, noticed that the drawings which replaced the ones he removed were perfect reproductions of those he'd destroyed.

ৎ

Ali's Sector was young and loud. Ali loved the boys, their howling and wailing, their silly bickering, and as they grew, their banter and unruly cricket matches. Even the rattling sound of screen doors opening and falling closed, along with everything else, made Ali happy. There was peace in the noise, a stillness in the day-to-day uproar of which Ali was most proud. He hadn't known this when Sajida was small. Her friends jabbered on and on, squeaking and screeching through stories, giggling and laughing, but the din they made was different from what presently filled his house.

Some days, Ali was overcome by the marvel of the children. He'd contemplate his family and know that there was nothing on earth he could have done to deserve this sort of fulfillment. When he'd first returned from the war, still sick, Sajida in tow, he'd wondered sometimes at what he was doing: snatching, as if from thin air, and coming up, quite suddenly, with a ready-made family. But as the years passed, first with Sajida's marriage and then the birth of her children, Ali recognized that he'd secretly longed for what followed: the voices, the love, the little bodies, the giddy, uncontrollable laughter, the childhood illnesses even, glands swollen with mumps, throats and feet alike ransacked with chicken pox. All of it was evidence to Ali of how life should be lived: in the moment, full and whole, everything else cast aside, to the past or the future, dissolving or as yet unmade.

That was what his ready-made family had done for him. To live, again, where he was sitting, rather than where he'd been. Once in a while, when his new house was pierced with a shout from one of the boys and Noor was asleep in his arms, he feared that what he was so proud of, this peace and noise the same, might not in the end be something of which he was worthy.

He was twenty-three. It was winter, he remembered. Nineteen-seventy. He was an officer in the Pakistani Army.

"I'm going," he told his mother during leave one day. "I'll fight for my country. You'll be proud."

"There's a difference, you know, being in the army here, in West Pakistan, and fighting there, in East Pakistan," his mother said, pointing out what seemed obvious to her.

"I'm worthy of this," he insisted.

"You're worthy of whatever you desire," she replied matter-of-factly. "But war is vicious. . ."

"It's not war," Ali interrupted.

"It will be," Nanijaan said, annoying Ali with her habit of making exaggerated predictions. "War is an animal gone mad. It happens to you," she added, fearing for her son's life.

Ali requested the posting, and begged his company commander to move him up in the departure order. At the Karachi airport, he fought for his seat on the overbooked flight. The soldier whose seat Ali took was given a reprieve and he didn't reach East Pakistan until a few months later. One day, Ali met him on a road outside Tangail, his jeep lying to the side of the road in at least as many pieces as its driver. "If I'd been on that plane, I'd have been here months ago and I'd already be dead. Then I wouldn't have lived to see this," he said.

Ali understood being posted to East Pakistan as a precious opportunity to live life on his own terms. He was young then, but already believed he had been constrained by life. His grandmother had committed him to marry his cousin before the girl had been conceived, much less born. He was four when the pronouncement was made, and his aunt would have one more son before she had the daughter destined to be Ali's wife. In one family album there was a photograph of the entire generation of cousins, and Ali was holding the girl, still a baby, her diaper peeking from beneath her ruffled dress. But a few months before Ali turned nineteen, the girl was dead from meningitis and he was free to make life decisions on his own. He put his arms around his aunt at the funeral and cried along with her. But he couldn't help anticipating the freedom he'd suddenly been granted.

"I've lost one child already," his aunt said when she heard his plans. "Please come home."

He went to war, strong and brash as the next. He worked hard and imagined he did his work well. His job, more often than not a night shift, was to accompany retrieved and inventoried remnants of blown-up bridges to storage locations. He returned to Islamabad nine months later, battered by typhoid and the staggering facts of the war, clutching a child of five or six in his arms.

Ali loved his mother. But his love for Sajida, his daughter, this beautiful child who seemed, in fact, to be life itself, overwhelmed him. When she landed in his home (for that was what the years had done to sum up the event) and he carried her, her spindly arms wrapped around his neck, into his mother's room, he ceased thinking of her as someone else's child. He made her his on the short walk from the front door to his mother's upstairs bedroom. On the stairs, against the banister which steadied him when his leg buckled, it somehow happened. It was as if her presence, in a sudden burst, breathed meaning into his vacant self. What he had witnessed, what he had, in fact, been part of, death and its astonishing variety of deliverance, had emptied him. Ali slipped at the top of the stairs, and the girl's grasp around his neck did not waver. Her cheek fell into his, and he felt her warm, barely moist breath on his skin. *Daughter,* he'd thought, *she is my daughter.*

"Nanijaan?" he said in the hallway.

His mother, small and pale as he remembered, appeared in the doorway. Her head was covered, and out of a deep-rooted habit so stubborn, her lips continued to move while she finished the whispered prayer she'd begun before she heard his voice. Without letting go of the girl, mother and son embraced each other. In the months that Ali had been away, the size of his feet, the length with which they filled the floor faded for Nanijaan, and she stepped on them three times while reaching for her son.

The relief of seeing her child alive made Nanijaan's heart quicken almost as much as it had those mornings (and they had always been mornings) when she pushed her babies into the world. She'd received scattered reports of his well-being, the last from a friend of his who'd phoned her from emergency duty in a communications tower in Dhaka.

"He's fine," he shouted into the line. "He's fine."

"Who?" she answered, wanting to hear her son's friend say his name.

But the friend didn't say it and in the tangle of suspicion and dread, she'd imagined that the phone call was a bad omen. She feared, almost expected, her son's death.

Ali stood in front of Nanijaan and she scarcely saw the girl in his arms.

"It *is* you," she cried. "You're alive!"

It was only after Ali sat down, put his feet on a footrest, and unwrapped one arm from the child to intertwine his fingers with his mother's that Nanijaan, from the low stool she'd set next to his chair, turned to him and said, "Beta, who is she?"

"Sajida," he said, as if it were perfectly normal to introduce a new member of the family without any explanation whatsoever.

"Her name is Sajida," he repeated less matter-of-factly.

"Who *is* she?" Nanijaan asked again, the presence of an unknown child not enough to deter her wide and glowing smile.

"She says she's fiveandsix. Little girl from East Pakistan. She'll stay with us."

"Fiveandsix," Nanijaan said after a pause. "What's that? A little girl from East Pakistan, you mean, and she's going to stay with us?"

"Yes, Nanijaan."

"Where's her mother?"

"Now may I have some tea?" Ali asked.

"Allah," Nanijaan said, rising to fix her son his tea.

Although Ali was at home, alive, and had brought her a child as evidence of this, Nanijaan sometimes checked for herself. She'd wander into his room at odd hours when Ali was expected to be sleeping and observe her son who, if somewhat of a stranger to her, had returned home a man. She'd stand at the foot of his bed for a minute or two before straightening the bed sheet over his feet as if he were a baby again. When she stood in his presence, his eyes would be closed, but he followed her every movement as her shadow fell on his eyelids that came and went with the hall light when she opened and closed his bedroom door or walked around his room.

In the first two or three years after his return, there were times when Nanijaan's ritual was far more elaborate. She would stand near the foot of his bed for hardly a moment, before she circled Ali, gently squeezing his hands and shoulders, kissing his forehead, running her fingers over his neck, touching his fingernails. *Taking inventory*, Ali thought. Ali didn't like his mother touching him so tenderly, but he lay in bed pretending to sleep because he was her son and, after all, it seemed a small thing to which he could acquiesce. She mumbled prayers Ali couldn't make out, offering thanks for the various parts of him she touched. It was when she touched his fingers that Ali required the most control. He was tempted to clutch her hand in his. Once or twice, he almost pulled his mother onto his bed, thinking he would tell it like it was. *What in God's name would he say?* The thought had made him chuckle and he stirred as if he'd coughed.

Now—twenty years or more later, Noor asleep in his arms—as then, Ali refused to remember everything. He recalled returning home, tired and dirty, his child, Sajida, in his arms. But he never dwelled on what he'd done afterwards, far into his first night home, when he was all alone.

The child had long since been sleeping, along with Nanijaan. Ali had locked himself in the bathroom, fancying his head a wall-sized cabinet of drawers that could be nailed closed. He accomplished his feat in the solitude of the windowless room of his childhood home. Enveloped by steam so hot it seared his nostrils, he sat on the edge of the bathtub, slowly forcing his body into the water. Many years later, when the war had long since been forgotten and he wondered aloud why he had once thought he could cleanse himself so privately, perspiration dripped from him as easily as it had in the foggy bathroom.

He submerged his feet, and just like that, he relegated the screams to one drawer, the pit of dead bodies and their scattered twitching into another. Kneeling into the tub, the scathing heat turned his knees pink, and he put the rich color of blood disappearing into a pit of mud into its own compartment, as far back as possible. Of all, it was the most difficult to contain. By the time his genitals were burned and blistered by the boiling water, the color bled. He was reminded of the penises his commander had pierced with a bayonet and the confused officer whose lobeless ears trembled as he trailed behind, obeying orders to sever genitals with nothing but a blunt kitchen knife and his own hands.

Ali stood, coughing in the suffocating steam. The second time he lowered himself into the water, he fortified the drawers with more nails and the color of blood, deep and dark as it remained even when he had seen it swallowed by mud, stayed inside. As he worked soap suds into his chest, the lather painting his black hair white, he focused on the image of a woman's breasts.

She'd had a face too, in the beginning, but Ali had never seen it. He'd been overwhelmed by her breasts, round and beautiful, despite the children who suckled from them. One was full with milk for the baby who had been torn from her and the other was hidden behind the coarse cloth of her sari. The commander pushed her to the floor. He pulled and stretched the breast that was large and firm until it sprayed a stream of milk. He laughed, called her a whore and much worse, stopping only to lick drops of her milk which landed on his lips. Then he forced his rifle into her mouth, tore her sari, and sat on top of her. When he was done, he stuffed his belt between her legs letting the oversized buckle catch and tear, laughing at how cleverly he had leashed her. The baby was dead by then, thrown to the side of the room with other corpses. After the man pulled the trigger, what was left of the woman's body, milk still leaking from her breasts, was kicked into the same heap. Overcome with nausea, rinsing away the bitter, yellow liquid from his hands in the bath water, Ali resolved that he had thought of this woman for the final time.

The last of him to be immersed was his head. He'd shaved it already, and tossing his thick black curls into the toilet, he wished that the war flushed away as easily. Ali let his bald head, freshly smooth and without stubble, fall back. His ears dull with water, he put away the very last of the memories. A young child plunging through sheets of rain into a brimming pit of mud. Ali told himself that the girl (had she been the only child?) was no different from the others—sinking, drowning, dead—within her reach.

Finally, he rose from the tub and, for several minutes, stood in his private cloud of steam. Despite what he'd lost, his frame thin, ribs like ridges in sand, he felt strong. Bending to put on his underwear, his muscles tensed, and he was reminded of the years when he'd played field hockey, his whole body firm and hard. His legs remembered winning. His calluses, dry and raised buttons at the top of his palms, were yet to fade. Rubbing cologne on his face, he considered the order he'd made inside his head. He imagined his story, the sum of horrible details, so neatly stored away, he'd done away with any reason to retrieve it. Ever.

And that was how Ali had planned to return to life.

four

When Noor tried sweetmeats for the first time, Sajida joked that she had found a soul mate in her daughter. Like Sajida, Noor craved sweets as a necessity. When Noor indulged she did it in a measured way, eating neither too much nor too little, but a balance that Nanijaan considered unnatural for a young child. "Don't be so grown," Nanijaan would say to her granddaughter when she served her sweets. "Have all you want."

Sajida, on the other hand, could not help but succumb to her weakness. She had tried to teach her children otherwise, and had been successful with her boys. But when Noor arrived, an infinite supply of sweets arrived with her. While Noor was spared party invitations, she was showered with the finest confections in the country. Once in a while, watching offerings bestowed on Noor, Sajida recalled General Z's daughter, forever nine or ten, forever fat, and understood why his child became so wide.

Noor ate confections slowly, licking her lips clean of the sweet, rose-watered rasgulla syrup and running her tongue along her teeth for the last bits of pistachios from specialty gulab jamuns. She ate what she desired and, if the portion was too large, she lifted it from the plate if it was barfi or returned them to their package if it was Chicklets or Smarties and tucked them away in secret hiding places for the following day. Unable to endure uneaten sweets in the house, Sajida sometimes searched their bedroom while Noor slept. Although Sajida tried her best not to make a habit of it, it was difficult to resist sampling Noor's secret store hidden underneath her bed or inside her shoes.

Sajida and Noor were sitting in the lounge, a box of mithai from the most exclusive sweetmeat shop in Rawalpindi open on the table in front of them. The confections were a gift from a neighbor whose daughter had recently become engaged. The shiny silver box had been wrapped in red cellophane paper that crackled to the touch and was kept in place with a broad gold ribbon. Noor rested her weak, scarred leg on the table and touched the cellophane wrapper with her toes. A plastic bucket of crayons and pastels, her select favorites, was on the floor, with two or three drawings rolled up in spools poking above its rim.

"Do you know," Sajida was saying, "when you were born, Nani-jaan made the mithai herself?"

"Alone?"

"She threw the cook out of the kitchen. He was making biryani—it was ruined—and he was very angry with her. She didn't come out until the next morning. I ate her laddus for breakfast. You slept."

"Raisins in biryani?"

"I've never tasted such laddus," said Sajida, not answering, remembering the coconut-tinted delicacy.

Noor finished the sweets on her plate and licked her long fingers. After Sajida served herself another helping of the fudgelike barfi decorated with paper-thin sheets of silver vark, Noor closed the box with the remaining sweetmeats and carefully retied the ribbon.

"Not good for you," Noor said, moving the box away from Sajida, repeating Sajida's frequent reprimand to the boys. Noor put the box on her sketchpad and traced its shape. She slowly began to fill the roughly penciled square with perfect rows of the sweets she'd eaten. Later, when Ali found the drawing lodged between cushions in the sofa, he took it to the printer and had it reproduced on heavyweight, glossy paper as the family's annual holiday card.

Nanijaan, her dupatta held perfectly in place by the thin bun of hair on her head, entered the room with a tray of teacups.

After a minute, Noor looked up from her work and asked, "Aba eats gulab jamuns?"

Sajida had done her best to lock Hussein from her life, but at moments like these she couldn't help but recall him as he'd been. She remembered when they were young, how Hussein had licked crumbs and confectioner's sugar from her fingers. She'd pulled her dupatta to her face, embarrassed and thrilled at what he was doing.

"I don't know if he does anymore," Sajida said quietly. "He used to, though."

"Why of course he does!" Nanijaan said, a bit more loudly than she intended. Turning to Noor, she added, "Not so much. You see, he has to watch his belly."

"And Nana?" Noor asked, wondering about Ali.

"No, he doesn't eat sweets anymore," Nanijaan said with authority. *Not since he came back*, she finished to herself. "He used to love them as much as your mother, though," Nanijaan suddenly added.

"He did?" Sajida asked. "When?"

"Before," Nanijaan answered.

"Before what?"

"You," Nanijaan said to Sajida. But Noor and Sajida had both looked up at her before she answered, and for a moment Nanijaan was confused, thinking she could just as well have meant either of them.

୬

Years earlier, Nanijaan encountered Hussein the first time on an evening when the black sky was filled with tangled necklaces of stars. Nanijaan's last cup of bedtime tea was disturbed by unfamiliar sounds. With an ear attuned to all murmurs of life, especially the unexpected, Nanijaan rose from her bed to investigate. Before long, she stood outside the house, not considering the possibility of a thief, murderer, or plain goonda, as good-for-nothing ragamuffins were called. Instead, she suspected Sajida's involvement in the nighttime disturbance, but exactly why she couldn't say. The noises were intermittent, but the clicking of new shoes on concrete was easy to follow.

From her hiding place behind some shrubs, Nanijaan listened to the two children, able to identify Sajida's frenetic whisper before discerning an older boy's more quiet and controlled one. In the hushed staccato tones, there was a music, and before announcing her presence, Nanijaan had a premonition that the concert of the overheard conversation was the beginning of a shared lifetime. Notwithstanding, and because of a longer-than-necessary pause that followed her thought, Nanijaan jumped from behind the shrubs and pounced on Hussein. She frightened him so much that the three of them almost fell off the patio. If Hussein and Sajida had not had at least a foot to spare between them, Nanijaan might have thrown him off the edge herself. Instead, she chased Hussein from the grounds, taking note of his fine Italian shoes, muttering her abuses rather than shouting them, in consideration of her sleeping son.

Sajida had never seen Nanijaan, an old woman by any standards, so agile. If Sajida were not in such serious trouble, she might have laughingly shared her observation. But she was in no position to say anything, caught with a boy, in the dark, in her father's house. The chase left Nanijaan unamused, and when she returned to the house, she disparaged that Sajida had surely lost her mind. She pulled the trembling girl into her bedroom and, after a moment, guided her into the armchair. As always, it was only when Sajida sat and Nanijaan stood that the shrunken frame of the second stood taller than the first.

In the long silence that followed and terrified Sajida, Nanijaan was absorbed by issues far more serious and complex than the conversation for which Sajida was bracing herself. But Nanijaan, who had had many sons and no daughters to guide her, was uncertain how she might proceed. She started several times in a stop-and-go that confused Sajida, although she listened intently, with complete respect, even nodding in agreement once or twice.

"Boys shouldn't be in the house."

"We can't trust you anymore."

"No good boy will want a loose girl."

"Did you think you could keep the secret from your father?"

"You must keep your honor, child. It's all you have in life, you know."

It was the invocation of honor that made Nanijaan realize that the only way to convey the urgency of her advice was to speak the truth. Because the truth was not always foremost on everyone's mind when they dealt with Sajida, it was hard for Nanijaan to begin all that she felt required to say.

She sat on the bed next to Sajida's chair, on a razai the two women, one so young, the other old, had stitched together in a playful game of splashing the heavy sheen of silk with lavishly embroidered trees and flowers. It wouldn't be until Sajida was pregnant with Noor and Nanijaan had given names to the flowers they'd stitched—*tulips, carnations, lilies, pansies, daffodils, tuberoses*—that Sajida could run her fingers over the embroidery and identify them herself.

The razai made Nanijaan recall Sajida's first night in her home. Nanijaan's bed was a simple charpai with a variety of razais stacked on it, and a separate bundle at her feet from which to choose. With few words and many gestures, she invited Sajida to select her own razai from the two piles. When Sajida was wrapped in the thin quilt and after Nanijaan had kissed her, the little girl whispered, "Alhamdulillah," giving praise to God. Nanijaan's first thought was, *Where did she learn that?* Before the thought was complete, she was ashamed. East Pakistanis, Bengalis, were Muslim, too, she knew. But somehow hearing the words spill from the child's mouth made it true for Nanijaan as it hadn't been before.

Sajida reached for her wrinkled hand and, without thinking, played with the extra fold of leathery skin on her thumb.

"Allahu-akbar," Nanijaan mumbled, calling on Him for strength before retreating to the sad certainty of what had once been her life. She sifted through her memories, and when she could not quickly find what she was searching for, she began, as she would later admit she'd done, to dig at the dirt. The effort was laborious and when she was done all of her ached. Especially where her fingernails and fingertips met, the tender spots accustomed to a different type of excavation, more typically called upon to transform a large head of cauliflower into tiny florets for one of her special curries.

She took Sajida back to when she had been a bride, a girl younger than Sajida, without any experience in a world that was not connected to her parents. She could not recall ever being allowed to stray anywhere without a family member. Her marriage was an arrangement between her parents and her husband's parents, she said, adding apologetically, "This, of course you'd know." Nanijaan had liked him though, whatever that meant for a sixteen-year-old who still didn't understand that a woman had three holes between her legs, not one as she'd thought when she was a child, or two as she'd suspected when she was older. "Remember, I told you?" she said to Sajida, trying to establish the kind of intimacy her advice would necessitate. Nanijaan had birthed her first child before she'd realized that her monthly blood and her urine did not come from the same place. "Donkey's brains," she'd said in mock horror to Sajida, tapping on her head. They'd chuckled together because Nanijaan had felt responsible for teaching this intricacy to Sajida long before she even began menstruating.

Finally, like the reality itself, the confession was thrown into the air.

"He beat me."

Sajida, just sixteen herself, and someone who had never witnessed so much as a spanking in her family or any other, assumed that Nanijaan was saying something different.

"Beat you at what?"

"Hit, you silly girl. He hit me."

"What for?" said Sajida, a little too quickly.

"Being his wife," Nanijaan replied.

"He didn't like you? What did you do?"

"When he hit me?"

"No. What did you do to make him hit you?"

"You're still so young," Nanijaan said, not accusingly. She climbed in next to Sajida, and between both of them, they filled the ample seat of Nanijaan's arm chair.

Ever since Sajida had entered the family, Nanijaan had attempted to do her best to prepare the child for life as a grown woman. She'd taught Sajida the specifics of her body and, now, having discovered Sajida's relationship with a boy, was compelled to teach her about the more complicated matters of the heart. Nanijaan would not allow Sajida to duplicate her own mistakes, and with this thought in mind, she confessed.

Nanijaan shared what she could remember. The first time, the blow was unforeseen. It was morning. The children were still sleeping, all three of them, in the coolest room of the house, the living room, where two ceiling fans worked side by side against the heat. He was in the bathroom when the plumber arrived. Nanijaan searched the house for him and by the time she reached the bathroom, her calls were impatient.

62

"The plumber has come," she'd said. "Please hurry."

Ali's father hated to be rushed. The only thing he hated more was being nagged. Between his wife and his children, it seemed the only things being uttered by his family were demands. Whether or not they were couched with respect and "pleases," they were all the same. He'd had money, then he'd made more, lots of it; why should anything more be expected from him?

When Ali's father didn't answer, cigarette and bathroom smells seeping from under the door announcing his certain presence anyway, Nanijaan knocked.

"Please come. The plumber is here."

After a minute, the door flew open, and the depression the door knob made in the wall remained whole and perfect forever after. Nanijaan had turned her back to the bathroom and was absentmindedly wiping dust from the glass doors of a cabinet. She could hear the murmurs of the plumber in the driveway. Nanijaan jumped at the sudden noise of the door banging against the wall. Before she could recover, her husband had grabbed her from the back, twisting her shoulders around, until her face was level with his. He wrapped his hands around her neck, squinting his eyes, biting his lips, shouting out of his narrowed mouth.

"Kutti," he said. *Dog.*

His grip became tighter and tighter until Nanijaan expected something in her neck to crack before he let go, allowing her a quick, short-lived breath of air. And then he punched her, slamming her face against the wardrobe, knocking all the knickknacks from their places, shattering one of the glass doors and leaving the other hanging from a broken hinge.

The servants were in the kitchen, and having started early on their cooking for the day, were caramelizing the onions for garnish on the lunch chicken pulao. On the other side of the house, Nanijaan, covering her head with her hands, was certain they hadn't heard. But the plumber and the chaukidar, how could they not have heard her husband's lunacy? Nanijaan pulled herself from the floor and waited until he had finished. He said some more things which she couldn't recall except that they were nasty like his blows.

The worst, she told Sajida, was how lonely it was. She couldn't tell anyone. The fear she lived with was that someone else might guess, let on, and then he would certainly take her life.

"One day, you'll not be so lucky," he'd said, at last.

Then a servant came, and Ali's father used his gentlest voice to ask for help for his bleeding wife who, he said, had run into the cupboard, *squarely, imagine that!* By the time the children awoke, the ice had eased the swelling and she'd wrapped gauze around her wound so her boys, the dear little ones, would be spared the sight of her blood.

That was the first time. Then there were other beatings, countless others, most of which took place in the bedroom when the children were sleeping, the servants were resting, the old, blemished walls her only witness.

"You didn't leave?" Sajida asked, giving away her age, again, by assuming Nanijaan might have done what she desired rather than what was expected.

"In the end, God took him," Nanijaan said, something Sajida already knew. Ali's father fell to the floor one day in the middle of a rage, and died. *First he was bellowing,* Ali had once told Sajida, *and then he was quiet. One second to the next.*

Nanijaan pulled Sajida so her eyeglasses pressed against Sajida's cheek.

"You must be sure that Mr. Italian Shoes is not like that. Before you marry, you must make him promise he will never hit you. Do you understand?"

"Nanijaan!" Sajida exclaimed, doubly astounded. First, that Nanijaan could ever conceive of the man in the shadows of the patio capable of raising his hand in a gesture other than love. And second,

64

that Nanijaan knew what Sajida only suspected: that one day she and Hussein would be married.

Dissatisfied, not because she expected Sajida to say anything different, but because she understood, perfectly, the limited range of a sixteen-year-old heart, Nanijaan resolved that when the time came, she would seek this promise from him herself.

"What's his name?" she said. "His full name."

"Hussein Ahmed. Son of Ahmed Aftab Fareed."

"Well, Begum Hussein, you mark my words."

It was moments like these which muddied the truth and had Sajida fleetingly believing in the certainty of the ground beneath her feet: she was, indeed, Nanijaan's granddaughter. Ever since the beginning, when the two lay side by side on Nanijaan's bed, examining finger nails and toenails, assessing arm hair and leg hair, it had been easy to believe that Nanijaan was related, however distantly, to the voices inside Sajida's head, her dreams, and her long-ago family swallowed by water. How else could sweet, wise Nanijaan know the future when she saw it?

By the time Hussein and his mother appeared with a marriage proposal for Sajida, Nanijaan had already softened towards Hussein. Sitting on the patio from which she'd almost pushed him, she couldn't summon the furor of the night he'd trespassed into her home. Instead, Nanijaan witnessed that the sweets she had prepared for the occasion competed with Sajida for Hussein's attention. Aware of this, Nanijaan tempted Hussein, bringing the plates of multi colored sweets close to his nose when she served him, enjoying the warnings his mother gave under her breath to observe a more modest appetite.

It was a beautiful day, as every September day was, the air no longer expectant with summer heat, but comfortable enough to sit on the patio for tea without the use of the heavy pedestal fans that

were put away in storerooms at the end of summer for a few months
each year. Hussein and his family sat on the freshly dusted chairs.
Tea was served from Nanijaan's best tea set, white porcelain with blue
flowers, a wedding gift from a European business acquaintance of her
dead husband.

Nanijaan studied first Hussein's mother and then Hussein, trying
to determine how much of one was in the other. She liked Hussein's
soft face and, especially, the line of his chin. It was solid and, she
believed, it foretold of the will life required from successful people.
His hands were more delicate, but Nanijaan tried not to notice that.
Remembering her husband, she knew that the stories of people were
not written on their hands but in their hearts, safe from view and difficult to read. Nanijaan was dressed in one of the white shalwar kameezes she'd taken to wearing over the years, a lightly embroidered,
sheer dupatta covering her head. As much as life had taught her to
see otherwise, she weighed the young man's complexion. He was as
fair as a Pathan, which meant, Nanijaan could not help noticing, that
he was as fair as Sajida was dark. When Sajida had entered the house
for the first time so many years ago and Nanijaan recognized she'd
come to stay, she had accepted the deep color of her granddaughter's
skin. But on the day of Hussein's marriage proposal, the contrast was
stark enough for her to notice and she found herself wondering what
combination of Sajida and Hussein their children might be.

"Of course," Ali said, shaking his future son-in-law's hand, drawing him into his embrace in much the same way the two were being
pulled into each other's lives. The bigness of Ali's embrace required
Hussein to return it and the two men, sharing little else than a love
for the same woman, became family.

"Certainly," Ali said, when the proposal was made by Hussein's
mother. Then he announced his condition: the newlyweds would
live with him.

Later, Nanijaan thought that Ali had been so steadfast with his
condition because it was fall and his mood was still slightly agitat-

ed as it always was for several weeks following the monsoon season when, exhausted, he could not sleep because of the rain.

Hussein's mother, a woman with a vast education and a successful civil service career, had not counted on any conditions, much less one that would tamper with her ideas of family. As she listened to Ali speak, she bristled with the thought that he had no idea how much she'd already compromised in giving her son permission to marry a girl much shorter and darker than she would have liked.

Hussein's mother interrupted Ali. She explained that an architect had looked over the floor plans of her house and decided that an annex, yet to be built, would be large enough to accommodate all the bedrooms the newlyweds would ever need as their family grew.

"Sajida is joining our family," Hussein's mother said. "She'll live with us."

She made this announcement with a big smile on her face and it wasn't difficult to believe, like Hussein did, that she was merely expressing pride at the prospect of extending her family to include a bride. Ali, furious that the accepted marriage proposal was giving Hussein's family liberty to already claim his daughter as theirs, couldn't bring himself to say that Sajida would always belong to him.

Finally, because Nanijaan was old enough to be mother to all who were seated, she said exactly what she wanted.

"Sajida stays here. Hussein may marry her. Of course. But she stays in this home."

Later, in private, Nanijaan scolded Ali. "It would have been a good time, beta, to let her go. You can't hold on to her forever," Nanijaan said. "She deserves her own life," she added, as much to herself as to Ali.

She didn't say what she intended, that Sajida did not belong to Ali, because she didn't want to speak of her granddaughter in words better suited to land and war. But mostly she did not say this because in a vital way she secretly held on to the notion that Sajida belonged to her. The daughter she'd never had. In some ways, appearing out of the blue without the nine months of consideration, Sajida was a child more real than any she'd had.

"She'll be a mother one day," Nanijaan said. Because she did not have the love of—or for—her own husband as a point of reference, it did not occur to her that Hussein might have already claimed the largest piece of Sajida's heart. "And, you'll *have* to share her," she added.

Even though Ali was a grown man, nearing forty by then, his mother was sometimes able to enrage him like she had when he was a child.

"I shared her with you, didn't I?" he asked.

༙

When Noor asked Sajida and Nanijaan, instead of Hussein, her own father, whether he liked sweets, Nanijaan was outraged that Noor couldn't simply ask him herself. Noor's question brought into focus the charade her family had been living for the last three years. Nanijaan saw her family as if it were the subject of a cheap movie and, all of a sudden, she wanted nothing more than to switch it off and turn on the lights.

Nanijaan had been the first to know when Hussein moved out of Sajida's bedroom. She heard him rummaging through the linen closet for the first time in his married life, looking for pillows and sheets. She'd almost risen from her bed to help him. Later, when they moved to Ali's Sector and Hussein took to sleeping in the dining room and using the guest bathroom as if it were his own, no one needed to bring this to Nanijaan's attention. Lying in bed against the wall which she shared with the dining room, she listened to Hussein readying himself for his mattress on the floor. From the noises that

68

traveled through the walls, she came to know, almost to the minute, when he took his nightly bath, flushed the toilet, and dimmed the lights.

Nanijaan knew now she'd been mistaken not to seek his word, as she'd threatened Sajida she would, on the very day that Ali had accepted Hussein's marriage proposal. She should have taken him aside that day, whispered in his ear, made him promise. Afterwards, she'd still meant to do just that, but during the wedding preparations Sajida was so wary of Nanijaan's presence around Hussein, she hated to make Sajida even more uncomfortable. More than that, the two children, giddy and blushing in each other's presence, seemed so in love. Their love lasted through the birth of one child and then another, and Nanijaan finally dismissed her fears and came to believe, as Sajida did, that raising hands or leveling fists would never be a reality in Sajida's life. But when Hussein moved out of Sajida's bedroom, Nanijaan knew he'd found the surest way of knocking his wife cold and she resolved that one day she would tell him that she'd been mistaken not to demand his promise.

Now, with Noor's question ringing in her ears, Nanijaan found she could no longer spare Sajida or Hussein. That night, a few minutes before she knew Hussein would enter the dining room for the night, she gathered herself from her bed and stationed herself in the courtyard. In the shadow of the parrots' cages, in full reach of their flapping wings and clipped, nighttime squawks, she waited. When Hussein passed her, carrying his clothes for the next morning under his arms, she stepped from the shadows and called to him.

"What will it be next?" she demanded.

"Excuse me?" Hussein stammered, recovering from the fright.

"It's been too easy for you. You gave up God, your wife, and your daughter all in the same breath."

"What?" Hussein asked.

"It's true, isn't it? When was the last time you talked to any of them? I don't know what's happened, Mr. Italian Shoes. This is what I see: your daughter cannot ask you if you like sweets. Can you imagine? Not only can she not ask, *Do you like gulab jamuns? Do you like laddus? What's your favorite barfi?* She can't even ask you whether you like sweets! You've done such a good job of ignoring her, she believes you wouldn't hear her if she asked, just like you don't see her. You don't understand—despite how rotten you are towards her—how she loves you. By the grace of God, she may forgive you one day. God, forever merciful, will forgive you. But Sajida . . . "

"Please, Nanijaan. I had a long day at the office," Hussein interrupted.

"Your problems with bottles at the office are nothing compared to your problems here."

"It's very late," Hussein said.

"I warned Sajida to tell you before she married you. *Tell him,* I told her, *tell him to swear that he will never beat you.* She said, *Oh, no!* She couldn't, she said, because of the *bara* understanding she had with you. And look at you, now. Look at what her great understanding with you has gotten her. You've gone and done much worse than put your hands on her."

Hussein opened the dining room door.

"Shame," Nanijaan said quietly before the screen door and then the wooden one closed behind him.

Nanijaan didn't sleep at all that night. Neither, she could hear, did Hussein. It came to her that she ought to throw Hussein out of the house. She imagined hiring thugs to do just that. She considered filing a false report of adultery against him at the police station. She weighed suggesting divorce to Sajida. She was tempted to consult Ali and demand he do something. Nanijaan cursed herself. *Ullu ki patthi. Bevakuf.* Why, she muttered to herself, had it taken her so many years to confront Sajida's husband?

That was as close as Nanijaan came. Except for that night, she did with her anger what her own marriage had trained her for, what she knew best, what she'd been doing all along. She harbored her anger toward Hussein silently. She chose to maintain form, above all. It wasn't right, she convinced herself, to add to the humiliation already meted out to Sajida. And drawing attention to Hussein's shortfalls, despicable and obvious as they were, would only tear away the pretenses which Sajida and everyone else in the family needed to believe in. Hussein was still a father, a husband, a son-in-law, the owner of a bottle factory. Regardless of how he was lacking, these facts were still true.

Life in Ali's Sector continued. As always, there were shared meals on the dining table, large block structures built jointly by boys and men alike in the bedrooms, cricket matches on their street after school and work. There were special Friday outings to ice cream parlors, birthday celebrations at restaurants, Eid prayers in the spaceship-like King Faisal mosque at the very foot of the Margalla Hills, school festivals and family parties. It was as it had been before, only a different tenor than the earliest days when the undercurrent of Sajida's and Hussein's love for each other marked the family Ali had made.

All the while, Nanijaan watched Hussein carefully. Every night, she heard him make his bed on the mattress roll he kept stowed on the top shelf of the dining room closet that even he, tall as he was, needed a chair to reach. As disappointed as Nanijaan remained in him, he was still the father of her grandchildren. So on laundry day Nanijaan's anger momentarily ebbed and she ordered the cover of his razai stripped, washed, dried, ironed and replaced by the servants within a few hours of his departure to the office. Every Wednesday, Nanijaan could not help but be amused that Hussein could secretly stow away the same bedding every morning for so many years without wondering why his sheets and covers didn't simply rot away. It was a secret Nanijaan and the servants guarded between themselves.

five

Noor was five when she began to paint her dreams.

In the early Islamabad morning, Sajida stood in front of the full-length mirror in the corner of her bedroom, applying eyeliner and lipstick, watching Noor in the reflection. Had she been standing, Noor would have reached Sajida's thigh. Noor was losing some of her baby fat and although she would always be round, she appeared to have shed the extra bracelets around her knees and wrists. At five (and earlier than her brothers), she'd already lost baby teeth, the curved gaps quickly filled with bone-white teeth too big for her mouth. Crouched over her drawing and her orange bucket of sharpened crayons and pencils, the angle of Noor's back reminded Sajida of her husband, Hussein. As much as Sajida once loved him, she thought it unjust that her daughter, forsaken by her father, should have any physical likeness to him at all.

Noor, focused as neither of her brothers ever seemed to be, drew quickly and deliberately, her hand slipping from her paper and marking the bedsheets. Before Sajida pinned her hair and sprayed her favorite cologne on her neck, Noor had covered the bed with pictures.

Sajida was more lenient with Noor than with the other two children. Not only because of Noor's condition (the names, the ever-changing diagnoses of her mental state irrelevant, Sajida believed, to her beloved but different child), but because she'd learned that marks on bedsheets could be washed away, there was always more paper to be had, and certainly, the peace of mind gained from a few uninterrupted moments was worth whatever mischief Noor came up with to fill them.

Sajida collected the pictures strewn around Noor, hardly paying attention to what covered them.

"Look," Noor demanded.

Without looking, Sajida murmured, "Bee-uu-tee-ful."

Attuned to lapses of insincerity more than the boys, Noor made her demand again.

"Look," she repeated until Sajida sat on the bed, her freshly ironed dupatta wrinkling under her weight.

"Show Ammi what you drew."

Noor took the stack from Sajida's hands and shuffled them. The first thing Sajida noticed was that all the pictures, except for a few scribbles here and there, were identical. It wasn't, however, until Noor pointed to the sharply outlined shape which curved at each end and inquired, "What's this?" that Sajida suddenly recognized the shape. It was the staple of a previous life she'd lived on the edge of a sea, a different country now, miles away.

"I don't know," Sajida said, keeping what she saw, the boat, to herself. "What did you mean to draw?"

"Noor is not mean," Noor said, alarmed.

"Of course not. What did you want to draw?"

"Don't call names in the house," Noor answered, mimicking Sajida's frequent reprimands to her sons, unable to let go of the insult she suspected her mother of directing towards her.

"This is . . . fish in a boat," Noor finally said, intentionally smudging one of the surprisingly clean drawings with her fingertips. "Fishboat."

Sajida took the drawings from Noor and saw that she was right. Sajida recognized the similarity of her daughter's word, "fishboat," with "fisherman's boat," a word she'd heard used many, many years before in a different language—Bengali—which she'd long since lost. In this other life, Sajida's younger brother or sister (she could no longer remember which) had used it to describe the boat her father and uncles used in their daily work to bring home fish from the Bay of Bengal.

Sajida reached for a pencil and printed Noor's word, "fishboat," in the corner of the drawing. Noor wasn't much interested in shaping letters or even identifying them yet, but she enjoyed the certainty of Sajida's printed captions. Sajida wrote slowly and meticulously, each letter the same size as the one which preceded it. She felt a vague sense of anticipation, as if with the unexpected familiarity of a memory that wasn't her own, Noor was launching mother and daughter on a journey yet to be named. Sajida hung Noor's drawing in its place on the courtyard wall. Over the next few weeks, Noor drew the fishboat scene over and over again, sometimes a dozen times in one day, until it was filled with great detail.

Then one night Noor had a dream of a tree with two fingers that rose into the heavens, a boat drenched in silver nets perched in the shadowed crook in between. Upon waking, Noor rushed from her bed into the bathtub. While others in the house slept, she scrubbed and scrubbed her feet, because the grains of sand between her toes tickled when she walked. She had difficulty reaching the foot of her stiff leg. She tied two washcloths together, hooked them around her sole, and rubbed back and forth.

"It was a dream!" Sajida said when she awoke to Noor's frantic trips to the bathroom. But try as she might, she couldn't make her daughter understand that dreams, in all their magnificence, despite the taste of salt and texture of sliding sand, were not real.

"Hear it!" Noor answered, pretending to run into the ebb and flow of imaginary waves.

An hour later, the boat in Noor's latest drawing was brimming with dead and rotting fish. Sajida stumbled on the drawing on her way to the kitchen. She missed a step and leaned into the wall, as if it was required to keep her upright. More astonishing than the exactness of Noor's rendering was the startling truth that Sajida was again staring at the dead, rotting fish in silver fishing nets that she had seen as a child wound around a tree.

When Sajida could finally speak again, she asked Noor where she had taken the idea for the drawing. Noor's capacity for language lagged behind her age by some years. But her response was immediate.

"From my head, Ammi." Pinching closed her nose, coating her voice with more of a nasal hum than was her habit, she added, "Smell the fish?"

Sajida nodded.

"Dreams," Sajida was explaining to Noor, "They're pretend."

Sajida was making it up as she went along, never having had to explain the difference between reality and dreams to her boys. They'd known about it from the beginning, a miracle similar to their ability to distinguish sounds of Land Rovers from taxis and minibuses.

"I like dreams," Noor offered.

"Of course. Sometimes you can go places you wouldn't otherwise," Sajida answered. "Like the sea. I couldn't take you to the sea. But you went there in your dream!"

"Why you won't take me?"

"I don't like it."

"Why?"

"Big. Loud. I like the ground better."

"When you were a snake-girl, Ammi. On the tree. You scared?" Noor asked softly.

Because Sajida had been wrapped like a snake in the tree and plastered with mud near rotting fish in torn nets, she understood Noor's question. Staring at her daughter, she wondered why Noor had omitted this detail in her careful pictures. In the gallery of pictures that hung from the walls of the house, there was no place to hang pictures such as these. Where would they go, anyway, Sajida wondered. With *m*'s for memories? Or *p*'s for past life?

"No," Sajida lied softly, "I wasn't scared." But she felt a shade of fear when she lied, as if the past and present of her life were shifting course, and were—inexplicably—rushing towards each other.

When Noor was no longer a child, and the family's stories had been woven into knots and tangles, Noor brought up the drawing of the cyclone, her omission of Sajida in a tree.

"Didn't want to. Draw you scared," she said, as if she'd known the truth all along. "You're my Mamma."

ॐ

Noor brought the cyclone back for Sajida. Sajida, then, had been the same age as Noor. She lived within walking distance of a sea full of fish on the shores of what was once East Pakistan but had since become Bangladesh.

All except Sajida's father had slept deeply that night. Before the cyclone, he was riding the sea in his boat. He prayed for a large enough catch in the dangling fishing nets so that when the sun rose again he might earn respite from the water. Miles away, in a tiny village a few minutes' walk from the coast, Sajida's mother put her six children to sleep after dinner to the soft patter of rain on their matted rooftop. In between their bedrolls, puddles sprang like islands from the carefully swept ground. In the land of East Pakistan, as much water as earth, Sajida liked to climb the only hill and watch the water recede. The young child knew the places her father's fishing boat could reach when waters were high: the paved road in the distance, the bicycle shop where rickshaws, bicycles, and car tires were patched, and beyond, the low-lying bridge swept away with the rain of the season.

By the time her mother awoke, the new baby already in her arms, it was not possible to distinguish the sound of the wind from the noise of the sea. Astonished, as always, at how soundly her children slept, her feet searched the ground for her plastic sandals. She found her voice and startled her children awake with her shouts. With one hand, she reached for her black sewing machine and when she set it on the small wooden crate, the only furniture in her home, the wheel next to the faded gold letters that spelled S-i-n-g-e-r spun back and forth like it did when one of her children played with it.

No one thought to run. Their lives were conditioned by the force and speed of water on their flat, flat land, and they knew they didn't stand a chance. Once out of their house, the children—including the thirteen-year-old boy who'd recently begun to resent looking at his mother when she spoke to him—tried to cling to her clothes. The smallest ones cried, frightened by the unearthly roar that sent thunderclap shivers into the ground they stood on. Her mother passed the lone acacia tree which in drier months blossomed in tight yellow flowers that her girls threaded and braided into garlands. While others in the village scrambled onto the roofs of their feeble houses with the help of bamboo ladders and each other, she pulled her children toward the road in the distance where she knew a single metal pole was cemented into the ground. In a flash of lightning, she found the pole. Before instructing the older children to spread their arms around the pole, she kneeled down to secure the younger children and gave Sajida the baby, warning her, Sajida would forever remember, to be careful.

After the worst of the water had receded, when Sajida was found alone, her body and clothes torn and battered by the fury of the sea, no one knew how long she had been there. She did not make a sound when the relief workers approached.

In striking distance, their legs knee-deep in the mud and water that ravaged the roots of the only two trees to be seen for miles, it was not any easier for them to trust what their eyes revealed. An old, splintered tree with a trunk no wider than one of the men's waists held, in the fork of its twisted branches, an unscathed fishing boat. The name, printed in black and in English, graced the sides: *Freedom*, bold and deliberate, as if it had been painted in oils the previous day. The tree carried the boat like a trophy, thrusting it into the sky as if each inch of branch had grown for this purpose alone. It was after the men accepted what they saw that the stench became overwhelming. The boat's silver fishing nets, filled with rotten fish the color of brown bleeding into black, hung from the tall tree. The nets shimmered in the gleaming sun like a lace curtain.

Two pink men made white by the sun. By the time Sajida saw the approaching men through her tearing eyes, she'd been hugging the tree with her body for so long it seemed to be doing it on its own. It was only because her body had joined the tree that they had such difficulty extracting her. She wanted to help, to make a sound, but her limbs, like her throat, refused.

One of the men touched her. The girl's skin, nothing like bark, gave way like that of the fresh corpses he had lifted, carried, and set aside. The girl's body was wrapped around the branch as tightly as a snake's, and when they found her head by the trunk, facing the sky, they did not expect to find life. But the soft, weak breaths drawn between her swollen lips and tongue suggested otherwise. The two men, first flabbergasted by the reminder of life in one tree and now by the existence of it in the other, used all their strength to pry loose the girl. They took turns carrying her, a meager child whose bones at the ankles and wrists jutted from sores on her body as if her insides were spilling out.

With mud in their boots and an almost-dead girl in their arms, the two men somehow managed to find land that did not sink beneath their feet. As they carried her to dry land, her head near one of their armpits and then another, Sajida smelled their skin, traces of unfamiliar soap and sweat made sweet because of it.

In the relief camp, piled with blankets, her body shook all night. In her nightmares, she heard her mother's voice rising from the bottom of the sea. At first her mother had spoken the simplest and most common of daily reminders: *move the hair from your eyes, take your thumb from your mouth, take the laundry bundle to the river.* After a few nights, Sajida was addressed like an adult in her communications with her dead mother. *You make shalwars*, Sajida was told, in anticipation of the place in which she would spend the rest of her life, *by cutting the cloth in two arm's-lengths, exaggerating the width of the man's legs, and sewing the seams on the inside before stitching the cuff's border for decoration.* Sajida was tempted to believe that her days were dreams and her nights, spent in the company of her mother's clear voice, were not.

ॐ

Noor squeezed her last "fishboat" on the wall, in between "fan" and "farmer." The difference with this drawing was that when Noor passed it, she held her nose as if her fishboat brought its stench into the courtyard of her grandfather's house.

Some days later, Sajida awoke to a picture on her pillowcase. She saw an animal, *a buffalo?*, grotesquely bloated, his head that of a different, more kindly beast. As in Noor's very first pictures, every inch of the paper was covered with color. This time it was brown, exactly the right brown-black of the mud after the cyclone, and the buffalo sank in it. Sitting up, Sajida lifted Noor's work from the pillowcase. In Noor's drawing, Sajida saw a young girl, clothes ripped from her, clumps of hair plastered to her forehead and her neck. Her small hand disappeared into the buffalo's monstrous body. In the corner of the drawing, there was an outline of a baby. *The longest of lashes,* Sajida noted, eyes drawn perfectly closed. The recognition of this detail more than any other made Sajida's hands go cold.

When Sajida had her boys, she would sometimes hold on to them *for dear life!* (as Hussein would say), overwhelmed by the memory of the baby Noor had drawn. After their bodies outgrew their need for her, she'd find the boys in the courtyard or sitting at the table doing their homework and wrap her arms around them and squeeze as if her life depended on it.

Sajida's mother had handed Sajida her baby brother. There were so many children, and only one pole. Then the sea was before them, in a wall so high Sajida could not tell the bottom from the top. Light, all of it, lanterns, flashlights, candles, fires, lightning, vanished, and the blackness was a hole of dizziness and terror. The wave lifted Sajida from her feet more easily than her father could sweep his children into his arms. The pole slipped from her grasp as if it had never been there, but she held first the baby and then her breath, the way she'd learned from her eldest brother when they'd jumped in water to keep them cool. She was thrown so high, so far, so deep, the baby was wrenched from her arms. Flailing, her hands struck something solid. She dug into the hardness while her body, desperate for air, was swallowed by the sea. When she awoke she was holding on to a dead buffalo. Swollen, floating like a boat.

Except for the baby, Sajida's recollections were scattered.

Her mother's last "Bismillah." Broken into pieces and thrown back by a wall of water. *Freedom.* Her eyes trained on the sea for the shape of her father's boat, his silhouette at the edge of it. The camp, old men, voices without strength or inflection. Imagining bits of her mother floating through dark valleys near the ocean floor, scraping rocks and shells in the pit of the sea's belly where sound, like light, did not reach. Dreams filled with demons and gods who were equally cruel. Later (*but how much later?*), she'd kept herself steady on the side of a road, one palm flat in the air, the other on her knee, as a makeshift chair of a man's arms lifted her from one place to another.

Sajida didn't remember all the details, the rhythm of the story, how it ran one way and then another and then back again, like water rushing about. Hearing her daughter scratch on her drawing tablet at the other side of the room, Sajida blinked and studied the drawing: the eyelashes, long and curled as she was certain they had been. Noor, she thought, this child, so sweet and magical, born not of this world, but of another.

For years, Sajida and Noor slept together in Sajida's marriage bed, a king-sized bed the family carpenter had built for her. It had a high headboard with several panels of woodwork, rows of intricately carved flower buds that blossomed from one panel to the next. She'd gone to the bazaar by herself to order the bed. The carpenter gave her a cup of tea, and while she sipped the sugary mixture he sketched examples for her on the faded newsprint of old dailies. She wasn't keen on big furniture, but it seemed natural to her that her marriage bed should be an exception. She toyed with the idea of posts and canopies, footboards and odd, pull-out night tables she'd seen in a home decorating magazine. Then the carpenter transformed a thick piece of wood with his chisel into a lily before her very eyes. She lifted it from the carpenter's hands and held it near her nose, half expecting it to exude the fresh, after-rain smell she loved so much.

When Hussein moved out of her bed (and their life) onto a mattress in another room, she stopped thinking of her bed in the same way. The flowers were simply the headboard against which she lay while she nursed and rocked her daughter to sleep. Later, when Noor no longer required her embrace to sleep, the headboard, now useless, was virtually forgotten. But Sajida became increasingly mindful of the parameters of the bed and she wondered how a bed that was large, even for two adults, could be so cramped. Her nights were interrupted by Noor's restless dreams in which the child traveled from the foot of the bed back up and from one side to the next, without regard for her mother's presence. Often, Sajida's side was bruised where Noor's legs, the strong one and the weak one, left their marks on her.

But the day after Noor left a drawing on Sajida's pillow, and through what Sajida could only attribute to a miracle, Noor was overcome with a newfound and urgent need for privacy.

"*Noor ka bister,*" Noor said one morning, pointing at Sajida's marriage bed and making it her own. "Where is Ammi's bed?" she continued, holding her hands up, as if another bed, her mother's, might suddenly appear.

It took Sajida a moment to respond, unprepared that after all these years she was being released by her daughter, if only for a few hours each night.

"I'll fetch another bed," she finally said, gently lowering Noor's hands to her side. "My bed is coming."

Sajida did not think twice about relinquishing her bed. She poked her head in the storerooms near the servant's quarters and from the second one retrieved a single bed. The cot was nothing but woven jute loosely strung on a simple frame, but Sajida was not interested in the specifics. The servants forced the bed behind a divider of faded velvet curtains into the tight space of the dressing room, a narrow, dark alcove of sorts that had never been put to proper use. Sajida took to the itchy cot in the claustrophobic room, as Nanijaan would have said, like a fish in water. Sajida loved her child, utterly and completely, but the fact was that Noor had encroached on her nights even before she was born.

Alone, Sajida slept more deeply than ever, night after night surrendering to a deep slumber filled with dreams that had beginnings and endings. She no longer rose with the light of the day as she had her whole life, even when her children were infants and her nights were exhausting hours of rocking and feeding. Instead, Sajida slept through dawn in the darkness of her alcove. Sometimes, she was awakened by Noor. Noor would draw open the discolored curtains in an impatient rush, and the clatter of the metal rings running over the rusting curtain rod delivered Sajida into the next day.

Once in a while, with streaming sunlight behind Noor, the disheveled girl, in a rumpled dress she'd refused to exchange for nightclothes, appeared more a vision than a child. On those mornings, Sajida marveled at the God who'd made this special child her own.

Ali came across Noor's drawing while he was tidying some newspapers in the lounge. It was caught between the morning and afternoon dailies, a burst of energy tucked in black newsprint. On principle, Ali liked anything Noor drew, although he was partial to the foods she managed to illustrate so exactly he sometimes found himself with an appetite after looking at them.

The drawing Ali held in his hands was slightly different from what Noor usually drew. It lacked a caption from Sajida: no "storm" or "rain" or any other description. More importantly, the brown-black of the background, the images of torn, upside-down trees and shattered boats, were drawn from an odd perspective, as if from above rather than *inside* the scene. Yet there was a special mist of gray that ran across the picture—so certainly, Ali knew at first glance, that of East Pakistan's monsoons. The contradiction that struck Ali was that one had to be inside the rain, feel it beat down steadily to know the color, the length of the sheets. Nothing less would do. He knew this unequivocally. Now, whenever the monsoons arrived, planting a roar inside his head, he lay awake in his bed recalling the symmetry of falling sheets of rain, the pounding of the drops, the sinking mud.

Ali thought of the last monsoon season in Islamabad and re-membered, with a start, how he and Noor had stood in the middle of the courtyard one suffocatingly hot day when the skies emptied with rain and steam rose like smoke from the fine marble slab and the red bricks of the house. The two of them danced and slipped on the drowning marble, celebrating like poor, unclothed children in the alleys of a Rawalpindi bazaar before Sajida put a stop to their fun.

Was it gray like that? Ali tried to recall, suddenly able to smell the mud and rain, months later, on a day in April when the sky held nothing but a brilliant sun.

The drawing stayed with Ali, and he finally understood where it belonged: with the *c*'s for cyclone. Late at night, lying in bed with a sheet pulled to his chin, hands next to his sides, palms flat, ready, as had been his habit in the army, he recalled what he'd seen.

From above, in the airplane, there was no question. East Pakistan was beautiful. Lush and green the way West Pakistan never was, even during the monsoons. Snaking rivers and endless tributaries flowing like life itself through the rich fields. The earth so fertile it hardly needed seeds. The land is black like the people, someone had said, only not as lazy.

The flight lasted hours. It circled around the tip of India and, when the plane couldn't land in Dhaka because of the fighting, back down again to wait in Sri Lanka. Twenty-one hours later, again morning, it landed in Dhaka. Dried mud was preserved in the most unlikely of places—tops of trees, airplane hangars, tin roofs of the barracks. Who hadn't heard about the cyclone? East Pakistan, it was said, always and forever unlucky in the mouth of the Bay of Bengal.

By the time I got there, the bloated buffaloes had long since fed the crows and the flies. Carcasses crumbled across the land. The air was heavy, but not with rain. Everything, living or not, seemed alive with hate. The roads, the trees, the bicycles, the bharis. The first night, walking the streets of Dhaka looking for miscreants, I scarcely dared to breathe. Within hours, I was gulping at the air greedily, as if, already then, to prove I was still alive.

Come back home, Auntie had said. But right then, it was so far away, it might have been another world. If it existed at all.

Did you know that?

Sitting in his armchair, glancing at the newspaper headlines, Ali heard Noor dragging her bucket of supplies across the brick path in the courtyard. Along with the slight limp of her once-broken leg, keeping her bare, flat feet inside the rectangles of the bricks, never on the lines, resulted in slow going. Some minutes later, she presented herself in front of Ali for her morning embrace in a freshly starched dress while the cook readied her plate. Noor was in a cucumber stage, and for the second time that day, the cook had scraped out the seeds and carved what remained into identically sized triangles. The cyclone lay on the cocktail table, next to the cucumbers.

"See?" Noor asked, picking it up.

"My *artiste*," Ali said, and although he was sitting, he attempted a waist bow. Noor squealed with delight.

"Bow to the queen!" she exclaimed, standing, the ruffles on her frock suddenly appearing regal.

"*Kya?*" Ali said, asking Noor to identify the animal she'd drawn.

"Buffalo," Noor said. "Fat."

"Fat, indeed!" Ali said.

Noor picked up the salt shaker. She unscrewed the cap, took out a pinch of salt, and sprinkled it on the tens of tiny triangles on her plate.

"You've seen a buffalo?" Noor asked.

Ali studied the drawing, looking beyond the mist. He looked at it from different angles, tilting the paper this way and that, examining the animal, eyes bulging, *gone maybe*, the head small compared to the immense belly. *Fat and stiff. Dead.*

Startled at the details of the drawing, he looked from the buffalo to his granddaughter.

"You've seen a buffalo like this?" Noor asked again.

He let a few minutes pass.

"People like this," Ali said so softly he wasn't sure Noor heard him above the crunch of the cucumbers.

six

Sometimes, at dusk, the marble slab in the courtyard caught the sun setting into the Margalla Hills and colors danced on the polished surface as if it were water. The wrought iron cages hanging above swayed back and forth as the parrots' evening songs climbed to their crescendo and dried bits of grass fell through the bars to the ground. No one took notice. In the rush to put dinner on the table, a clamor of dishes and pots rose from the kitchen, along with the tempting smells of chapattis puffing on gas burners on the stove. The boys dashed from one place to another, one practicing newly learned kung fu moves perilously close to the other, and the second issuing defensive screeches that brought Sajida running.

One such evening, sitting on her marble, Noor drew a side profile of a man's shoe. Elegant stitching ran in a U on top of the foot. Identical stitches connected the body to the sole. The tongue of the loafer rose slightly above a narrow leather band. A square buckle lay flat against the polished side of the shoe. In the kitchen storeroom, where shoe supplies were kept, Noor rubbed her long fingertips into a cake of shoe polish and ran the neutral color along the edge of the stiff, leather sole she'd drawn.

Hussein found the drawing taped on the back of the driver's headrest in the car the next morning. His instinct was to rip it from the headrest, much as he had done with some others from the wall. But the shock of seeing a perfect replica of a shoe he'd once worn prevented him. He stared at the drawing as the car bounced on the rough roads to his factory, sunlight streaming in through the rear windows and playing off the grains of what Noor had drawn.

After some minutes passed, Hussein took his white handkerchief from his pocket and reached for the drawing. He touched the handkerchief to the edge of the shoe's sole, reproducing the gesture of a night so many years before, when he'd bent to the floor to polish just such a shoe on his foot. Hussein recalled, then, what he had never forgotten: the night of anticipation, murmurs and whispers, the scent of Sajida's lovely skin, despite the arm's length between them, and the frightening moment when Nanijaan sprang onto the patio. He'd stumbled as he ran. The shoes were large on him; the next day his feet would be blistered. They'd made noise against the patio and then the driveway as he left the house. He'd cursed them as he ran, regretting that he hadn't been more modest and worn tennis shoes instead.

Leaning back in his seat, he closed his eyes as he had done when his children were very young and he stole sleep in the car. He allowed himself to remember the night he wore those shoes, knowing, as he put them on, that his fate was sealed to Sajida's. He was only seventeen then, secure in the belief that he already knew everything worth knowing. Now it embarrassed him how absurd such thoughts had been. A confluence of luck and fate had brought Sajida into his life. He'd been blessed. Until Noor, anyway. When he tried to recall the night he'd left his wife and crying child, he could remember how certain he'd been, how sure of what he'd decided, but he could no longer remember what he'd said to Sajida before he'd walked away from the room and the life that had been theirs.

Touching the edge of the sole with his finger, rubbing the shoe polish into the shoe, Noor's drawing wasn't frightening, like the others. He'd loathed the sheets of blue and the simple words that hung from the walls of his house to remind everyone who saw them how far Noor had yet to go. But the one taped to the headrest of his car was not like that at all. Was the drawing a coincidence? His shoes had been exactly like that. *God, had they been noisy!* Hussein clicked his tongue to reproduce the noise of his shoes on the pavement, a steady beat the driver mistook as accompaniment to the car stereo. He turned the volume higher, drowning the beat of Hussein's memory.

Halfway through the journey to his factory, Hussein recalled the day of his marriage. Fires exploded in ripping roars across the city. Later, he'd heard Nanijaan tease Sajida that on a day so momentous, the heavens rained fireworks on her celebration. In truth, it hadn't been fireworks at all. The facts had been so fantastic that standing there, watching the show from behind the hotel windows, no one could have dreamed up the explanation. Hussein watched Ali, his father-in-law, run to the window, an electric shaver in his hand, towel around his waist, run to the window. While everyone else seemed confused, Ali was transfixed. Hussein imagined that the possibilities running through Ali's mind were no different than what others were guessing, except that because Ali had already seen war, he'd know what they meant. *War. Again. The Indians.* Their wedding reception cancelled, lying in bed together a few hours earlier than they'd dared to hope, Sajida told Hussein that at first she thought he might be responsible for the racket, a wedding prank, some unexpected, storybook way of serenading her.

On their wedding day, an overstocked ammunition depot had exploded a short walk from their hotel. Missiles rained on Islamabad and Rawalpindi in a mad show of colors and noise that landed ammunition in various stages of explosion on moving cars, unsuspecting pedestrians, roads, alleyways, bazaars, construction sites, tea-stalls, and the houses of rich and poor people alike. After the noise had settled, people were buried and the edge of fear was blurred, jokes abounded among those unscathed. The one Hussein heard Ali share was that the explosion of the depot was the first time the country sought to evenly distribute its wealth.

Hussein remembered thinking of General Z the day missiles and shells rose from the same place in the skyline, beyond the hotel, before whistling and plunging in every direction. The general wasn't hurt. It would still be five years before his airplane, without explanation, would fall like one of those missiles from the sky, plummeting him to his death. But on that day, General Z and his daughter were safe, and this made Hussein suddenly consider the rumors he'd heard. *Of course.* The general was safe because of a daughter who must have known.

Of all the diagnoses that were offered for Noor, none suggested that she might know more than anyone else, much less that she might know what others had forgotten. *How could she?* Shaken by the question, Hussein took the drawing from the headrest. He carefully put the leather loafer he'd worn in a previous life inside a pocket of his briefcase.

That night, Hussein returned home early from work. As always, he dropped his briefcase in the chair by the door without acknowledging Noor, who waited nearby, having long since forsaken the window for the opposite corner of cushions. While Hussein was in the next room, masterfully wailing along with the sirens of the boys' toys, Noor reached for Hussein's briefcase. It was a heavy leather bag, capable of holding several boxes of sweets and chocolates, gifts that were a routine part of his homecoming even if he'd only been gone one night.

Noor never touched these sweets. As much as she would have savored them, she wanted even more that her mother have a larger portion. Sajida's craving for sweets was family lore, parts of which had been repeated to Noor, at her insistence, countless times.

When Sajida and Hussein were first married, he'd brought her tea to bed every morning with a silver papered square of the city's finest sweetmeat wedged on the saucer.

"But how did he know?" Noor would ask, her big eyes always filling with tears at the miracle of her father's love.

"Before we were married, we ate at sweet shops together," Sajida would say. "I ate until my tummy ache made it hard for me to stand."

"Sweets are not good for you," Noor would add, imitating what Sajida told the boys when they, too, caved to excess.

"Don't tell them," Sajida would call out in well-rehearsed play while Noor ran to find her brothers and do just that.

Since he hadn't returned from a trip, there weren't any sweets in Hussein's bag. Only hundreds of papers, some of them packed in colored rubber bands and others squeezed into folders that made the bag awkward and heavy. Noor carried the briefcase into the lounge.

True to her deliberative nature, Noor emptied the many compartment sleeves of her father's briefcase, one by one, in order. But then, in an after-the-fact motion, as if she was unsure of her next step, she tossed the sheaves of paper into the air in a jerky movement that took her by surprise. She watched as the drawing of her father's Italian shoe rose to the ceiling and then floated to the floor. By the time Hussein came in to use the bathroom less than ten minutes later, his briefcase was unrecognizably flat, the insides scattered as much and as widely as if they had been offered to the ceiling fan.

Noor stood waiting, her hands on her hips, in a pose of defiance no one had ever seen. He stopped before he'd fully entered the room, allowing the screen door to bang against his heels in a quickening rhythm: one, two, three. Despite the fact that Hussein had mastered being blind to her, this time Noor stood in front of him in stark relief. Hussein was struck more by the silhouette of his daughter in the far corner of his eye than anything else in his view, especially his floating papers. For the first time, and because she was demanding his attention rather than asking for it, Hussein was unable to refuse. Slowly and tentatively, he allowed his eyes to meet hers, managing until the very last moment not to turn his head in her direction.

Later, when Noor spoke to her mother about what happened, she joked that she should have made her father angry much sooner. At the time, standing in front of her father, she'd wanted to make the moment last. She stood completely still, only moving when the fist at her hip fell asleep and the tingles prickled so much she was forced to take a step.

Mostly, Hussein was unprepared for Noor's face, the pull of her hairline and the bones falling below her ears. But that was once he could move beyond the blackness, the depth of which had frightened him so when she was a baby. Her eyes had seemed without end, then, a pool without a bottom. He contemplated her big eyes, strong beyond belief, and it occurred to him, all at once, that they might be a refuge. He wasn't sure why he wasn't afraid—they were even deeper and darker than he remembered—but he wasn't. And once he'd established that, he took in the face of his daughter.

Beyond Noor's particularities—the slants, the flatness, the proportions, the gap of another lost tooth—the sum of which announced her presence to him and others as alarming, he discovered the most unexpected. *Sajida.* Noor's hairline was his wife's. At the tip of the imaginary line from her nose to her hair, the line peaked in a tight point. Sajida hid hers with light bangs on her forehead, but Noor's was precise, the hair gathered into a single ponytail high on her head leaving the certainty of it for all to see. Had Hussein spent time imagining Noor's face in the many years since he'd last looked, he would have remembered it as round with baby fat and a double chin. But as he now saw, her contours were his wife's, especially the curve of her lips, the prelude for almost all the words she'd ever exchanged with him. The fact that Hussein had finally found his wife in Noor made him see that it was so: Noor was his daughter.

He spoke her name.

What was left of Noor's pose dissolved and she broke out in giggles that came from her belly. Despite her stiff leg, she skipped a perfect hopscotch over Hussein's fallen papers until she reached the door. Too late, Hussein stretched his hand. With Noor already gone, he only caught the rush of air before the screen door fell back, again. One, two, three.

Right then, Hussein had a vision of his family.

Whole, like a tree.

That night, like every other, Sajida carried out her responsibilities. After making sure the boys had completed their homework and had their baths, she checked that their lights were out. Surprisingly, Noor had fallen asleep on the sofa in the living room, and rather than wake the child, Sajida covered her with a shawl and let her be. In the other corner of the house, she supervised the cleaning up of the kitchen. She sent the cook to Ali with his nightly tea, but she took Nanijaan's herself. She spent longer than she usually did with Nanijaan in her room, listening to daily stories of friends and distant relatives.

It was close to midnight, after the kitchen floor was swept and the servants had bolted the gate, when Sajida paused in her daily duties as mother, daughter, granddaughter, and wife, and pulled open the screen door of her bedroom. As was often the case after everyone was asleep, all it took was the cool touch of the handle to irritate her: so many years later she seemed unable to escape the fact that the room had once belonged to both of them. As she straddled the tiny step, the door began to close on her. The perfume, not a skein, but a full-bodied gust, rushed toward her and, as she would always believe, fairly knocked her from her feet. The unexpected fragrance was so thick she put her hands to her face to protect herself from the bouquet. Seconds later, on bruised knees and loosely trapped by her dupatta—one end on her shoulders, the other caught in the screen door—she gasped at what she saw.

There before her was a man-made mountain of flowers. It prompted her to recall each and every rose Hussein had given her what seemed like a lifetime ago on long and lazy afternoons of secret courtship. After Hussein and Sajida were caught together unchaperoned in a car by Hussein's sister and his mother forbade him to spend time with Sajida, she persuaded Ali to teach her to drive. Subsequently, she and Hussein took to secret meetings on little-traveled, unpaved roads that cut into the Margalla Hills away from the city.

During each of these meetings, Hussein had presented Sajida with a rose. Often, he'd put himself at some risk finding one. If roses weren't available in the bazaar, he gave her one secretly plucked from his mother's garden. When that was not possible, he gave the family driver or cook a few coins and enlisted help in searching the neighbors' grounds. Because of one ruse or another, not one visit passed without this gift that Sajida treasured as much as the soft brush of Hussein's touch when he put the flower in her hands. Always, as much as she longed to take it home, put it in a vase beside her bed, and awaken to its sweet fragrance, circumstances would never allow this. Instead, while driving home from their visits, she plucked the flower bare, petal by petal, letting each hint of velvet be carried from her car window. But she could not resist saving the last piece of the flower and dropping the lone stem in her wastebasket at home. Until the servant emptied it the following morning, she was thrilled to have in her room the only real evidence of forbidden love, a mere arm's length away.

In the backdrop of Islamabad, a few miles from Ali's Sector, among the mountains of shrubbery and streams that broke so abruptly from the plateau, their future took hold. As a sixteen-year-old, when she gazed at the low-lying hills beyond her home, she could hear the trickle of the hidden streams which accompanied the most anticipated moments of her life. But when Hussein chose to leave her bedroom, the melody of the hills ran dry and Sajida came to regard the certainty she had felt for Hussein with the ripe eye of maturity, and began to think of it as nothing more than schoolgirl nonsense. Everything had changed. The Islamabad hills, Sajida noticed, were no longer as quiet as they'd been. Paved roads ate into them, and scattered patches of brown grew on the crests where trees and shrubs had been pulled for firewood and furniture alike.

In the silence of the night in her bedroom, while Sajida recalled the first roses, their feel and their perfume, her sadness was compounded. She touched her blue-black hair only recently speckled with strands of gray.

No piece of furniture was spared. Their bed was laden, as was her dresser and mirror, the antique chest and the corner tables of lamps. It was, she thought with a start, as if the assembly of flowers Nanijaan and she had stitched on a quilt when she was a child, had multiplied and come to life. Gladiolas, tuberoses, pansies, lilies—red, pink, and the pale colors in between—covered every inch of her room, hanging from the edges of bookshelves and draped from the ceiling fan, transforming it into a billowing chandelier. While she stared at the immense bouquet so lush it might have been a dream, she could not help recalling the single-stemmed roses Hussein had given her in the months before they married. There were eighteen of them. She remembered how the thorns on the first one pricked her thumb, the second one the palm of her hand, and the last, notable because Hussein had shaved off each thorn with his own razor that morning, felt as smooth and perfect as their love in those ancient days.

Overcome with the scene and true to her past, her instinct was to tear the petals, one by one, from the thousands of blossoms in her midst. It took her a long time, enough to collect close to one hundred bare stems, to absorb the reality. Her husband had been in her bedroom. He was responsible for the perfumed air. It could only mean that, finally, he had something to say. In a shiver of impatience, Sajida stopped peeling the blossoms and flung them, whole, behind her.

That was how Hussein found her. With Noor asleep elsewhere and the boys in their own rooms, Hussein wandered back to the wife and bedroom he had forsaken, in that order, years earlier. He knocked on the door and opened it without waiting. When he saw Sajida kneeling in a pool of petals, he felt the rumblings of a love he'd intended to bury so long ago.

"Saji," he said once, and then again.

In a lap full of bare stems, he laid down his head. Sajida's hands were bleeding, and when she touched his face, he could feel the splinters of thorns in her palms. She noticed, all of a sudden, that boxes of mithai were spread between the flowers. The boxes were open, their lids tucked at an angle behind, the elaborate sweets carefully displayed. The boxes were wrapped in cellophane paper, gathered and stapled in a decorative twist to the side.

"You deserted us," she began calmly, unaware that the anger and confusion she had stored over the years was so complete it spilled out in sentences more exact than the array of accusations she had anticipated throwing at him. "You woke up one morning and decided. There was no warning. Her love was too strong, too precious, too real. You could not bear her crying. That's what you said! You didn't even have the courage to be honest. You could not allow her into your life, because you believed that if you did it would reflect *your* weakness. Instead, you burrowed in ignorance, you've drowned in it, you've embraced it at the expense of everything else. You did not make her. God did. And in the face of Him . . ."

Sajida paused. A rush of rage flushed her face and the wide veins in her forehead pulsed. She struggled to keep the dams inside her closed; the shouts and wails that had been building for what now seemed forever. But when she continued, her voice did not so much as tremble.

"In the face of His love, you ran. For five years, you behaved as if she didn't exist. You shut us both from your life. You gave up on her, on us, on life, on God. You let her fall taking her first steps. Not once did you greet her, let alone kiss her, when she waited for you at the door. She's spent her whole life trying to make you love her. Why do you think she pulls the chair for you at the dinner table night after night even though you never acknowledge her, much less her kindness? She gives instructions to the kitchen about the meals to prepare and on Fridays, when you are home, she makes sure the menu fits your tastes. And she's so bright she knows all that better than anyone. No one else in this house likes bharta. Do you hear?

"The boys love her. They kiss her, hold her. Have you seen Farooq's eyes when she walks into the room? The boys . . . the boys love you, but she adores you. And you won't even talk to her. What kind of a father are you? She came from our bodies and if I can love her, why can't you? Because you're stingy with your love. It doesn't have foundation. You don't have enough love inside you to do battle with your anger. Angry at God? Who the hell are you to be angry with God? Look at your life. You've never lacked for anything. The first day I met you, you were wearing Italian shoes, for God's sake! At sixteen or seventeen you had more shirts in your closet than most people will see in a lifetime. Your mother gave you the money to start your own business. She sat down one afternoon, pushed aside her biggest tray of crystal, and wrote you a check above and beyond what you'd asked for the bottle factory. I was there. And, after all that, after all that love and luck and money, when God puts a challenge in your arms, when He asks you for something, when He asks you to show Him, you toss away your baby. Who are you? Good God, who are you?"

In the minutes Sajida took to speak, the sound of her own voice filled her so completely, she did not hear Hussein. But when she stopped, it was sounds from Hussein that needed acknowledgement. They were familiar to Sajida, even if she hadn't heard them in years, since the night she and Hussein had held each other and, together, she'd thought, shaken the grief from their souls. But tonight his sobs were his alone and they emanated from his chest in a rasp entirely other than the one she once loved in his deep, beautiful voice.

"Who are you?" she insisted, again.

"My name is Hussein," he answered in a small whisper. "Your husband. Noor's father. I have disgraced myself. And God."

The two of them sat in the bedroom, on the cold floor of a November night, smothered by a blanket thick with spoken words and the sweetest of fragrances. For hours, neither spoke. He, uncertain they might rise beyond, and she, afraid they would.

You should have killed him, Sajida's mother said to her in her dreams that night, speaking in murmurs from the bottom of the ocean.

He did not sleep in here, Sajida tried to defend herself.

Think of Noor. Forgive him? Have you forgotten? her mother insisted.

It was the opposite, in fact. Since the moment Hussein's head had fallen into her lap, the ledger of his misdeeds and trespasses, something she hadn't realized she'd been silently accumulating with precision over all these years, exploded. She knew that all of it, every single detail, amounted to betrayal. But it was liberating to give her anger shape, to remember how unprepared she had been for his behavior and remind herself that she'd been entitled to closing him from her heart, and not the other way around.

In the end, when he knocked on her door, the years of silence between them were no match for the profound emptiness that filled her insides. It had been hard to believe, she'd often thought, how the emptiness, the dead weight of it, could be so heavy, beyond comparison to the pounds she'd carried day after day during the three intervals in her life when she was making children.

So she let him in.

When he laid his beautifully shaped head in her lap, she recalled immediately the curves of it as if she had stroked his forehead, his neck, and the astonishing arc of an angle in between, only yesterday. Her voice may not have quivered, but her hand, cupped as if in prayer, did. His tears made the colors in her embroidered new kameez run, and the mishmash of orange, green, and purple reminded her there was nothing tidy about life.

So she let him in.

Until her mother mentioned it from the bottom of the ocean, she had not thought of forgiveness. She was not sure she knew what it meant. She'd never lived in the face of such tangible wrong before. It was one thing to lose her family as a child, with the culprit—water, God, destiny—so much greater, so much bigger and so completely beyond her reach. It was quite another to live in the same house with a husband who had rejected her and their child because of an unexpected, unfamiliar celebration of life. But just as she had not had the audacity to forgive God and His elements, she could not do it for Hussein. Instead, she accepted him for what he had become, for the remorse he had shown that one single night, but more so, she knew, for the next morning, when he kissed Noor's forehead. His eyes closed. It was he who was begging for love. Because of that, mostly because of that, she let him in.

Some years later, when Ali—her father—started speaking to her, really speaking to her, when his story rolled from his tongue, she recalled that night with Hussein and knew that in some vague and insufficient way, she'd been preparing for what was to come. As her father spoke, she appreciated the tenor of what forgiveness might mean and that life's pain, just like its love, was infinite and uncomprehending. That holes and emptiness were only one manifestation of sadness, and not even a great one at that. And, finally, that love, in its eternity and sincerity, its God-awful trueness, could be more exacting than anything she'd believed. Or dreamed.

seven

A few months later, Hussein invited Noor to join an outing to his factory. Although he promised she could sit in the front seat of the big truck, Noor could not be persuaded to stray from Ali's Sector. Instead, she helped Sajida supervise the picnic lunch that was put together for the occasion. Noor added a thermos of sugary tea for Hussein and bottles of 7-Up for the boys. Nanijaan made a stack of parathas and rolled the bread in newspaper to go with the aloo ki bhujia, the current staple of Noor's diet. Hussein, not a fan of potatoes or other vegetarian dishes, made allowances for Noor, and when she told him what she'd packed, he smiled as if he relished potatoes and mustard seeds.

"Thank you, lovely," he said.

Noor clapped her hands together, jingling the thin, sparkling glass bangles Hussein had given her a few days earlier. When Hussein presented them to her in a package of tissue paper, Sajida recalled wearing glass bangles when she was Noor's age. She'd often cut herself and cried as she bled when the cheap, multicolored bangles broke into sharp pieces. This wasn't a problem for her daughter who did not notice physical pain—*brave*, as Noor had said, describing herself years earlier.

It took a while before Hussein's tenderness towards Noor stopped startling Sajida. But she always noticed it, and when he said *lovely*, mother and daughter giggled together with pleasure and surprise at the endearments he'd taken to using.

"You're invited, too, you know," Hussein said to Sajida.

"Now what would I want in all that dust?" she responded teasingly as if she were sixteen again.

While Hussein and the boys were getting ready, the driver carried Noor into the courtyard. Early in the morning, the sweeper had hosed down the brick walkways, deepening the color of the bricks and making the lines between them too difficult for Noor to negotiate. With Hussein in the shower and Sajida's back weak from all the carrying she had done when Noor was smaller, Sajida had instructed the driver to carry Noor over the still-wet walkway into the courtyard.

Noor had recently shed dresses in favor of shalwar kameezes. Instead of a dupatta, she wore a folded sash hung over one of her shoulders and tied in a knot by her mother at the opposite hip. Noor's shalwar rode up from her ankles as she was carried. Her dark leg hair was visible, especially near the whitened scars on her thinner, weaker leg.

The parrots had grown and multiplied over the years until they required more than one cage. Ali had returned to the same iron-smiths in Karachi who'd made the first cage, and ordered two additional cages smaller than the first. The trio hung from more than one pole. Looking at them closely, it was possible to see the barest hint of green, the only clue that the cages once sat in the salty air of a city by the sea.

Noor stood close to the parrots. As if it were still night, one of them roosted upside down, hanging from a bare branch someone fixed into the cage. Some sidled on the floor of the cage, two toes pointing forward and two behind. Others perched on their rods, but all were silent and unperturbed by Noor's familiar presence.

Recently, though no one knew exactly how, Noor had learned that parrots could be trained to talk. *Like us*, she insisted. She clung to the idea with passion, even after Ali explained to her that his parrots, *not very smart*, were unlikely to do so. But Noor persisted, and took to speaking to the birds as if she expected them not only to respond but also to magically repeat the different words she spoke to them every day.

Standing in front of one of the cages, knocking on it to get the birds' attention, she tried again. She said, slowly, *crayon, yellow*. She was met with silence. Then she rubbed the crayon on her paper and held it up to the cage. *Picture*, she pronounced a little louder, while the parrots shrank away from the noise of paper crinkling on their cages. Eventually, when the bricks had dried in the sun, Noor skipped between the lines of the bricks, ran to the kitchen, and retrieved what was left of the previous night's dinner. She scooped food onto her fingers and thrust them in the cage. *Chholeh, raita*, she said in a rush, chickpeas and yogurt falling in clumps from her fingers. The parrots did not take the food, nor did they speak any words. They pecked harshly at her fingers.

"Donkeys," she screamed, losing patience with the parrots.

Her brothers, entering the courtyard on their way to the truck, shouted in unison, because this had happened several times recently. "*Tote*, Noor. Parrots, not donkeys!"

Frustrated with the parrots and her brothers, Noor threw her bucket of art supplies at the cages. The bucket hit a cage with such force that a tiny door popped open. One of the boys ran to close it before any of the birds could escape.

Alerted by the noise, Nanijaan hurried to Noor and wrapped her arms around her granddaughter. She wiped away the tears and stroked her hair, until Noor was calm again. The cook picked up

Noor's art supplies, dusting them before returning them to the dented bucket with a newly broken handle.

After Hussein and the boys left, Noor bruised her knees crouching on the marble slab the rest of the morning. She sifted through her art supplies, crayons, pencils, pens, and brushes, hitting the stone and rolling over the edge, until she settled on what she needed. She laid out the oil paints and delicate brushes she'd found and bent over her work until her face almost touched it. Once in a while, Nanijaan could make out the furrow of Noor's thick eyebrows pulled tightly together in concentration. But she could not make out what Noor was drawing.

After a few hours, it was complete.

A snapshot, four by six. A pyramid of tin barrels. Thirty-six of them lying on their sides. The barrel tops round like faces, spouts for wide-set eyes. The rows of tops looked like an oddly-shaped palette of paints with colors gone awry: dirty green, aqua blue in brown, orange-yellow in white, reds, dark and without punch. The barrels were knocked out of shape, dented and scraped as if they'd been lifted and dropped dozens of times. The sidewalk underneath crumbled, the curb shed rock. Bricks were missing from the whitewashed wall against which the pyramid of barrels was built. Electric wires and tree branches hovered behind. The sky was heavy with the city's dust.

The trip to the factory had been an annual outing ever since the boys were toddlers. Early on, Hussein enticed them with a truck ride and a chance to examine the controls on impressive machinery in the factory. They were known to come home with barrels of discarded plastic molds that had, through some defect, not turned into the precise bottles the machines were known to manufacture. The boys' favorites were green, unformed bottles of 7-Up, which they took home with them and used in their building structures or as tools for digging. But now that the boys were older, father and sons discussed cricket matches, studies, and plans for the future. Adel, as Sajida had always known, planned on being an engineer. Farooq, too distracted by music at ten, thought only of extending his cassette collection. Although Hussein had always been very generous in this regard, Farooq wanted a job in his father's factory to pay for his hobby. "You wouldn't last a day!" Hussein pointed out.

When they got to the factory, Hussein proved his point by leaving Farooq with an inspector who tried to teach him the difference between bottles that were defective and ones that were not. The conveyor belt moved too quickly for Farooq and the differences in bottles remained unclear to him. By the time Hussein returned, the inspector had pulled out a few defects while Farooq stood next to him, empty-handed, with a perplexed look on his face. Laughing, Hussein embraced his son.

Hussein recognized some of himself in his empty-handed, confused son. He'd felt like that dozens of times in the last several years as he'd struggled to run his business. As far as he was concerned, two incompetent prime ministers, one a woman and one a man, shuffled places between leading the country and leading the opposition in a far-fetched game of politics. In the charade that pillaged the country, rules and regulations for business changed at whim from one day to the next in the form of long and complicated promulgations and codes that were impossible to decipher, much less comply with. He spent many late nights at the office with his new accountant, a young man with good connections, struggling to make sense of tax schemes, but, in the end, he resigned himself to fate the way an empty-handed Farooq did the day of the factory outing.

When the boys returned home, they filled in Noor and Sajida with the latest developments. The factory was loud with the new air conditioning in the main chamber. They liked the design of the new bottles for mineral water the factory had recently begun producing. They brought a box of bottled water home for Sajida, who had given the water its name, *Natural*, and composed the description on the label which made it appear as if the water ran directly from the highest snow-capped mountains in the Himalayan mountain range, cascaded down the Margalla Hills, and magically arrived at Hussein's factory.

Late that night, when Hussein was waiting for her in their narrow bed in the alcove behind drawn curtains, Sajida found the drawing, the smallest Noor had ever made, on a side table in the lounge, propped against the lamp she always turned off before she went to bed. Sajida picked it up, momentarily mistaking it for a postcard. She turned to see if something had been written on the other side. In her hands, the stiff paper was glossy, tiny ridges covered the back, and Sajida recognized it as the insert that had lain underneath the lid of Noor's latest gift of chocolates. Briefly glancing at what Noor had painted, Sajida made a mental note to ask the boys what they had shared with Noor to prompt the intricate collection of old, multicolored barrels.

Sajida bent down to prop the drawing against the lamp. Midway, she froze. She drew in her breath quickly before letting it out in a hiccuping gasp. She was certain she'd seen those barrels. In fact, she knew how many of them there were. "Thirty-six," she said to an empty room.

She studied Noor's oil barrels. They were stacked like a pyramid against the dirty white of the wall, only slightly distinct from the hazy sky, a different white, above. She wondered, more than ever, how Noor mixed colors so precisely. Sajida rubbed her thumb on the face of a barrel, letting it linger on the slight bump, absorbing a hint of heat.

She knew Noor's barrels were meant to be hot to the touch, just as they had been the day she had touched the large, empty tin barrels as a child. In Noor's drawing, there was a smudged imprint on the wall and greens behind the brushstrokes. It took Sajida only a minute to see beyond the brushstrokes. She knew what had been there. *Joi Bangla*, Hail Bangladesh. She knew this even though, when she'd seen it for herself on the wall behind the oil drums, the box-like script had been unclear. Sajida wiped her eyes with her fists, as if she were no longer in Ali's Sector, but in Dhaka, a city far, far beyond, rubbing away the exhaust from trucks and buses on a street with a crumbling sidewalk. She pulled at the shoulder of her perfectly tailored kurta as if, almost twenty years later, it was big and loose and hung from her bare shoulders like it had on that day in Dhaka.

There was no question now. Noor's drawings were no longer simple words to be alphabetized on a wall. They were windows into another world, far away and distant, which might have ceased to exist without Noor. Sajida had always expected that her children would humble her with their lessons; she hadn't considered that one of them would teach her the past, bring it back and put it in front of her with an exactitude that was astonishing.

Sajida sat down in Ali's chair. She could only remember snippets, if that, of how she'd come hundreds of miles from her village, drowned by the cyclone, to the big city of Dhaka. In her recollection, there was a white Land Rover, big and tall off the ground. Pale blue writing on it, UN. She was helped to her seat. She sat next to the window. They tried to feed her. Biscuits from tins. Rectangles with sprinkled sugar stuck on top. She'd taken a bite and tried to pick up the sugar granules that fell into her lap. When she cried, the woman next to her put the tin in her lap. She remembered, quite certainly, she had not been hungry.

The roads were high like hills. She looked down on the fields and the people beyond, and thought she must be flying. The roads, stretching out endlessly, made her think of the water, and she remembered her father, the fisherman on the ocean, a pole in hand, pushing the sand underneath the boat. *He'll find me*, Sajida still believed. The Land Rover bumped over roads full of holes, thankfully leaving the smell of the sea behind.

Then there was the city: Dhaka. Crowded. Buildings stretched into the sky. Frightening, the bustle and noise. She was taken to a bungalow lined with flowerpots. She was spoken to in a language she couldn't understand. She knew now that they must have been foreigners, relief workers. She was given clothes. In the mornings, she remembered someone trying to alter her clothes with safety pins. The bungalow was busy—*was it a hospital?*—and people gathered around it.

Early one morning, while a line was assembling outside, Sajida wandered from the house unnoticed. She walked the road, wide like a river, a few blocks beyond. It was almost empty. The already baking pavement hurt her bare feet. In front of her, to the side of a small length of sidewalk, a mountain of tin barrels stood against a wall. She wanted to jump inside them, curling up to fit, but the openings, like the spouts on the cans of cooking oil her mother used at home, were too small. The barrels lay on their sides on top of one another, rising in smaller and smaller rows. They were bright and rusted at the same time, a medley of blues, whites, greens, reds.

Sajida stopped reminiscing to confirm the memory of the barrels. She counted them on Noor's drawing in her hand. *Thirty-six. Blues, whites, greens, reds. Oranges and browns, too.* Noor was right. She'd drawn what Sajida had forgotten.

She'd picked up a small rod, heavy, lying on the curb of the road, and hit the tin barrels. The noise that answered made her jump back. She fell on the side of the road and sat where she'd fallen, against a crumbling curve, her elbows burning. She stayed there, squatting, hiding from the racket.

Joi Bangla was on the wall. *In green?* Although she had yet to read, she'd known the call, like everyone else, young and old alike. Those days it was everywhere.

The rod was still in her hand and she kept her head down, studying it. It was rough, rusted, hollow, but heavy. A truck sped by, kicking up dust and gravel, but she couldn't move. When the jeep pulled up from behind, she was scraping her thumbnail against the rod's winding grooves. A man got out of the jeep. She heard him, but she didn't turn to look. She was suddenly exhausted, so overcome that when this man—Ali, Aba, her father—picked her up (*with one arm or two?*) from the side of the road, she let him.

Was it like that? Sajida suddenly wondered. *I could ask him*, she thought, imagining Ali attempting to provide her with answers. He'd lifted her. And just like that day in Dhaka, the faces of her father, the fisherman, and Ali, the man who'd found her by the side of the road, blended into one.

Sajida stood and put Noor's drawing on the armrest of Ali's chair. Afraid he would knock it down while he sat, she changed her mind and placed it on the cushion instead.

That night she fell asleep on top of Hussein and dreamed the way it had been.

The body of the airplane was deep like a river and its wings were longer than anything Sajida could imagine would fly. There were no seats, just some belts woven with square buckles, harnesses almost, attached to the sides. At the top of the stairs, the door in the belly, Sajida balked. Unschooled in the whims of children, much less those who'd seen what she had, Ali hadn't considered she might panic. But his reflexes were trained from practice, and as soon as she tried to run, he had his hands on both her shoulders. He picked her up like that, her back to his stomach, his arms swathed around her body like oversized clothing.

They were among the first to board (Ali's papers bought them that), but they couldn't choose their seats. The force of the crowd behind pushed them forward until they were flat against the back of the plane where the handle of an emergency door jutted out.

Surrounded by people she did not know, flanked by people she could barely tell apart from the others, Sajida cried.

"Ma," her body shook with dry sobs.

From above, the land was scattered and random, as if God had shaken out the earth from an almighty salt shaker and watched as the specks fought to find some bearing in an all consuming ocean.

Weeks later, in her new country, after Nanijaan had calmed the shock from her and Ali had befriended her, he made a request.

"Call me Aba," he said.

She did, and made it final. Ali was her father.

In the morning, still lying next to Hussein in bed, Sajida wondered if she honestly knew these things, whether any of her memories from those days were really hers: the water (so high), the men (so pink), the fish (so dead). She'd been so small. She could have formed the pictures in her mind just as easily from overheard descriptions and partial conversations in the camps. But who would have thought of pink men besides her? As a mother, she now knew firsthand about a child's tendency to incorporate most everything into her own world at the cost of truth. She'd been in shock, after all; her head unreliable, like the sea that had finally released the land. *Freedom*, the name of the boat perched in the tree. How had she remembered that when she had yet to learn to read her own language, much less someone else's? Did she really remember anything from the camp after the cyclone? Was it really near a pit of mud so large people swam in it? So much was unclear. Had there been bodies there? Dead?

Whether her memories were accurate or whether the tale she constructed for herself was merely imagined, it was of little consequence when pieces of the story came to her. They tended to come suddenly and quite unexpectedly, like the day Noor drew dead fish in silver fishing nets or rusty barrels on the side of a Dhaka road. Or the morning, long before Noor, when she was bathing her youngest son and nearly dropped him because something about the lather in her hands recalled the nurse who'd given her her first bath in the relief camp. Until then, she'd only known her mother's hands on her body, working the lather from her hair down to her feet before rinsing her with a bucket of cold water.

But Noor's drawings were lending Sajida's memories an unexpected clarity that was different. It made her think of General Z's daughter, fat and silly, the faith placed in her gestures, her moans. Noor wasn't like that. But Sajida knew when Noor was nothing more than a dance inside her that she was connected to some other world in a way that no one else was. As the years passed, Sajida came to consider Noor's drawings—the depictions of things she shouldn't have known—as evidence of this. They gave Sajida pause. Every so often, with a slight hint of concern, she wondered what Noor might draw next, if she might reveal anything Sajida didn't already know.

Hussein stirred next to her and Sajida put her hand on his soft, smooth back and sighed. She felt relief that her beginning, at least, was crystal clear. The cyclone, the baby torn from her arms, the water, so great, so big, so loud. She recalled Nanijaan's home that first night. The first Urdu word she learned, *razai*, for the stack of quilts at the foot of Nanijaan's bed from which she was allowed to choose. It was Adel's first word, too, and Nanijaan, who was keen on coincidences, clapped with the thrill.

Or was her beginning so clear? The image of oil drums stacked in a pyramid below a hazy sky worried Sajida. It jumbled her memories of the cyclone with something else—a wide avenue in a big city, a large airplane, endless mud and rain, Ali.

Sajida left her bed and went to Ali's armchair to check on Noor's drawing. It had been brushed aside and was lying on the floor. She picked it up and set it on the table, weighing it down with a corner of the lamp. She returned to her bedroom to bathe and dress before she started her day.

Half an hour later, when Ali finally saw it, he handed it to Hussein.

"Why so many barrels at the factory?" he inquired.

"But we don't have any there," Hussein answered. "What are these?" he asked, pointing to the pyramid.

"Oil drums?" Ali answered with a question.

"Noor's?" Hussein asked, examining the postcard-sized rendition, taking the sheet of paper that had once graced Noor's latest box of chocolates. He turned it over and looked for Sajida's handwriting, an explanation in a single worded caption. After a moment, finding nothing, he softly added, "You know, you might ask Noor."

"Yes," Ali said, aware that Hussein was right. "I know."

eight

The morning Noor awoke in bedsheets spotted with blood, her cry sent a shiver through her grandfather, unable to sleep in his room across the courtyard while the monsoon rains drenched Islamabad.

Sajida and Hussein were asleep in the cramped dressing room. Hussein's feet hung over the edge of the charpai and Sajida's hair, still thick and beautiful after three children and one on-and-off-and-on-again husband, spread like a fan over Hussein's chest on one side and her own on the other. The two lay like spoons in a drawer in a bed that would have been too narrow for either of them even if they'd slept alone. They awoke with the scream, but much to Hussein's surprise, Sajida did not jump from her bed. She lay still, listening to the breadth of her daughter's cry, wondering, for a moment, if in the fullness of it there was something familiar.

Ali appeared in the bedroom without knocking. He bent over Noor before Sajida rose to her feet. She sat on Noor's bed, one of her knees touching her father's. Noor was shaking, thrashing at her bedcovers, kicking at her mother and grandfather. Ali saw the blood first. A small spot to the side of Noor's waist, and when she lifted her bottom to move away from it, there were other spots on the sheet, others yet on Hussein's old kurta, which Noor had taken to wearing to sleep. Ali touched his granddaughter on the inside of her knee, which was smeared with blood.

Knowing exactly and immediately what it was, Sajida tried to put her arms around her daughter. She whispered into Noor's ear. "*Na, na, beti.*"

Hussein arrived at his daughter's side to see his father-in-law touching his daughter's blood and his wife trying to restrain a child grown bigger than she. Sajida was managing, it seemed, and Hussein was thankful he was not needed on Noor's bed. When he'd seen Sajida in the hospital, after the children were born, her sheets had had splotches of blood on them too. The spots were multicolored, the reddest, darkest ones from his wife, the rust-colored stains from other patients.

Over the years, Hussein had not spent time with Noor in the bathroom while the bathtub and sink overflowed with water and the soothing sound finally calmed her. In the past, before he'd reconciled with Noor, he'd thought of this routine as wasteful, especially in the summer, when he had to pay exorbitant amounts to truck drivers to deliver and pour water into the house's depleted water tank.

That morning, however, Hussein knew enough to take the few steps to the bathroom and open the faucets. He and Sajida carried Noor into the bathroom. Noor's kurta, pulled above her knees and her underwear, girl-like in thickness and cut, was stained with menstrual blood. Their backs against the cool bathtub, their feet on the tile, just as Noor liked, the screams lessened, the sounds quieted, and it was possible to understand what she was saying.

"Dreams, Aba!" she cried in Hussein's arms. "Red like the river."

"That's only a dream, meri jaan," Noor's father said. "Dreams aren't true."

"Ammi has them."

Sajida looked away quickly, uneasy with Noor's intimation of her dreams in which, only Sajida knew, voices spoke to her from the bottom of the ocean.

"There's no river," Hussein declared.

"A river of what?" Sajida asked Noor.

"Reddishness."

"Radishes?" Sajida repeated what she thought Noor had said.

"Red blood," Noor corrected her.

"Don't be afraid, meri jaan. It's only a dream. Dreams aren't real. Don't mind the red. Red isn't only for blood. It's for cars. Convertibles. Your brothers' pedal car," Hussein said to Noor.

"I don't like cars, Aba."

"I'm so sorry, meri jaan."

The water comforted, as it always had, and after some minutes, Noor's cries finally stopped.

"Why is the river red?" Sajida suddenly asked.

"Fat people," Noor said without explanation.

"Fat people?" Sajida inquired.

Hussein, who'd hoped the conversation had ended, registered his unhappiness with this question by glaring fiercely at his wife.

"It's all right, beti," Hussein said, holding his daughter's hand. Noor's slender hand, the one she used to make crayon drawings from her dreams, disappeared in between Hussein's palms.

Although she'd just been rebuffed by him, Sajida observed the father of her child, Noor's head in the crook of his neck, his shoulders opened and curved, as if they were a refuge for Noor, and for a moment, Sajida imagined that Hussein's arms had always been as open and safe and sure for Noor as they were right then.

Sajida stood, and while Hussein held his daughter on the cool bathroom floor, she sponged Noor's legs with a washcloth. She hid the blood in the crumpled washcloth in her fists until, with her back to Noor, she ran water on it in the sink, unplugging the drain, allowing the pinkish water to be carried away.

Suddenly, Sajida recalled the buffalo of Noor's drawing. The one for which she had let go of her baby brother. Or was that afterwards? Small as she was, the buffalo was bloated to an immensity that when she let go again—of the animal for the tree—almost drowning in mud and water, the size of the buffalo startled her. The jaw of the animal stretched so wide, and inside, the swollen, monstrous tongue.

Fat, Sajida thought.

Dead, she remembered.

ഗ

There wasn't much blood. As a teenager, Ali had read about menstrual blood. A few tablespoons a day, if that. And the children's shouts were one thing, as were their wails—especially when they were much smaller—but a shriek as shrill and hollow as Noor's that morning wasn't what Ali was accustomed to. The blood between Noor's legs, her crying on the other side of the bathroom door, made him think (in spite of himself and what he had resolved against) of his river. The one behind the officer's house, the darkness of it, in midday, the brightest of afternoon suns spilling from the sky.

We took the train south. I remember thinking that Bengalis may be dimwits, but they certainly had a lot of water and their fields were damn green. It was February, then, the rains were months away. The journey was only a few hours. At the train station, there was a woman, she was young, you could see that from her face, parading up and down the platform. She had a wrap around her bottom half, you see, nothing on her torso. It was hard to tell what she was, at first, with the train pulling in slowly. But then she was virtually in front of us, and there were two huge pink infections oozing pus, yellow, where her breasts should have been. Chopped off, they were. What kind of knife? I wondered.

The officer insisted we take the woman from the train station. We had orders to wrap her in a blanket and bring her to headquarters. But she got wilder the closer we got—we didn't have chloroform—and the officer slapped her to keep her down. Once there, she collapsed on a cot, eyes bulging, and didn't move. We washed her wounds, I picked maggots from them, first with my fingers and then with tweezers. She was bandaged with the best we had.

She slept for three days. We changed the sheets several times until one of us, not me, noticed blood coming from between her legs. It wasn't much, but it dirtied her, red on her thighs, the insides of them. The officer washed her and put a rag there. When she woke up, she talked. She rattled off story after story. None of us knew if any of it was true. "Yes, go on," we said, so she would know we were there. When I could, I listened. How couldn't I? The stories were packed with detail, down to the smell of a man's breath: acrid like rot. A story of a family that was slaughtered in broad daylight with a scythe. Another about a baby thrown into the air, caught by a bayonet. Oh, that's the dagger at the end of a rifle. Men forced to eat their cut-off penises. By then I'd seen the penises. I believed that one. Do you know what they look like with blood drained out of them? Nothing to hang from? Handful, or less, of flesh. That's all.

Even the officer, when he wasn't out doing his job, listened. We called her Auntie because he did. She couldn't have been much older than we were. The worst was in the middle of the night, when she thought she saw her children. We'd light the lamp and repeat what she'd told us. "God's looking after them now." It calmed her. Every time. The officer thought she'd pulled through. The bandages on her chest, finally, were stiff and dry. She could keep down the thin, watery dal fed to her with a spoon. She liked the flat, plastic one. We took turns. After a month of storytelling, she stopped. "Talk to us, Auntie," we'd say. "Tell us a story." But she didn't answer. She lay on the cot, a white sheet tucked in on all sides, we made sure, the pink openings, big like hands on her body, now maggot-free, hidden beneath. "Tell me about the cricket match," I said, but she didn't tell us again. One morning, she shouted, "I see Him," and then she was dead. Immediately. Like a bad Hindi film. The glimpse of the Almighty was enough to stop her heart. She was twenty-four.

The lawn behind the barracks sloped to the river. The river, in the sun, without haze, was dark. With dead bodies, not just that day, but the whole time we were there. They floated like paper boats. What is the physics of this—no sinking? Dogs swam out to pick at them. Birds flew low. Digging the grave took a long time because we had to dig deep enough to protect the body from the animals. We did it twice. The first time a dog dug at the grave and stood still while we threw stones at it. Then we dug the grave again and covered it with rocks. The dogs, crows, didn't bother the grave after that.

Oh. Even after she died, her wounds oozed. Her nose bled, too, then, and her ears. We stuck cotton swabs in them. Between her legs, the blood still ran. The body rids itself of fluids after death. Left to its own devices. I should have known that. I'd been told. Not at the Academy. The blood's still warm. For a long time. Did you know that?

ॐ

Noor stayed in bed for the three days her flow of blood was steady. Sajida pampered her with hot water bottles, as if Noor could feel the cramps. Although Noor did not draw during her convalescence, her broken orange bucket sat on the floor beside her bed, full to the brim with paints and brushes, crayons and pastels, and Nanijaan added to it with a new collection of ballpoint pens and thin-tipped markers she found at the market.

One afternoon, Ali visited Noor in the bedroom. She was no longer a young child, a menstrual pad between her legs and the beginnings of breasts inside her kurta. But she seemed small again, lying alone in what had been her parents' marriage bed, her head propped against the carved lilies in the design and glass bangles covering her wrists.

"What can I do for you?" Ali asked as he pulled a chair next to the bed.

"Tell me a joke," Noor said, clutching her stomach and pretending she was in pain.

"I don't know many jokes," he said. "Shall I read to you?"

"No," Noor replied. "Jokes. Please."

"All right," Ali said, struggling for a selection. Then he recalled one he'd known years before and, without warning, it fell from his lips. "Why are Bengalis so weak?" he asked. Then he answered himself. "Because they can't tell rice from grass!"

Effortlessly, as if he'd learned them yesterday, Ali remembered several similar jokes. *How can you tell a Bengali from a fly? Bengalis smell. Bengalis are women with small penises. Bengalis are such cowards, God help them, they turned to the Indians for help! What does independence mean for a Bengali? Not having to be told to wash his hands after having a shit.*

"Not so funny. Tell me a story, Nana," Noor said.

Ali thought for a moment. "Hmmm. Just for you, all right?"

"I didn't know anyone in East Pakistan," Ali began. "In the Academy, I had a course mate, a Bengali. Everyone made fun of him. This fellow, about this tall," Ali said, and raised his hand. "They're very short, you know, and almost black. He wasn't posted to East Pakistan anyway. Bingos weren't trusted to keep their people in line, so he'd gone to some place—I think Baluchistan—where army officers promised to make a man out of him. He was my roommate. When I was posted to East Pakistan, the fellow gave me an address and asked, if I was ever able, to please look up his family. It so happened that a few months into my tour, I found myself a few miles away from the address. More out of curiosity than anything else, I drove by the house. The second time I drove by, the driver stayed in the jeep and I knocked on the door.

"The man who opened the door didn't look anything like my roommate. He was a large man, especially for over there. Also fat—not so common, you know.

"'Sir,' the man said, as if he spoke English.

"'My name is Ali,' I said. 'I'm a friend of your son's. We trained together at the Academy back home . . .' But before I could continue, an old woman, henna in her hair, a glass in her hand, charged to the door. There were children in the room hiding behind the sofa. Her English was very English," Ali said, and then added in a heavily drawn-out accent, "'If you please.'

"The woman barked . . ."

"She was a dog?" Noor interrupted.

"No, no. 'Get out of my house,' this woman said. 'No one from your army could be a friend of my son's. Look what you people have done to my family, my house.' She threw her glass at me and shouted, 'Murderer!' I stepped away just in time. The glass hit the door. The man waved at the woman, chattering urgently in a dialect I couldn't understand. The woman paid no heed and the man turned to me and whispered, almost apologetically, 'English teacher.'

"The next morning, early, after I got my ration for the week—food, mosquito repellent, things like that—I drove by the house again. It was early, I shouldn't have been on the streets. I didn't get out of the jeep this time. I stood on the seat and threw the ration into the bolted window. I used to have perfect aim in those days, you know?"

Ali was thinking of another joke he hadn't shared with Noor. *Bengalis are so stupid they can't appreciate what they've been given. He'd heard that one a lot.*

"What's a Bengali?" Noor suddenly asked.

"There used to be an East Pakistan, long, long ago. It's a part of Bengal. Those people, we used to call them Bingos."

"Who?" Noor asked.

"You know," Ali said softly. It was suddenly important that Noor should know. "Your mother—she's really from Bengal."

"Bingo's also a game," Noor said quickly, sitting up. Ali remembered he'd introduced her to this foreign board game he'd found in a bazaar years earlier when he'd tried to teach her numbers.

Sajida walked into the room, her arms full of books and magazines to entertain Noor.

"Bingo!" Noor said, pointing at her.

"What?" Sajida asked, oblivious to the word that had just been thrown in her direction.

ॐ

Sajida took to washing Nanijaan's white hair when Nanijaan's arthritis precluded her from lifting her hands above her head. Their evening ritual had been established years earlier, when Noor was a baby and massaging Nanijaan's scalp had helped Sajida feel less exhausted and alone at the end of a day. Nanijaan would sit in her own bathroom on a dining room chair piled with cushions to make her taller and lean her head into Sajida's hands.

Sajida was never in a hurry and could wash Nanijaan's hair more than two or three times in one sitting. Hussein, who knew better than to interfere with their time together, learned anew that he had to wait an hour or more before these sessions came to an end and Sajida came to bed. Sajida's hands lingered for a reason. When the mirror was clouded with steam and the lather peaked with drifts, stories flowed easily and abundantly from Nanijaan.

It had been during an evening like this that Nanijaan came

around to sharing the details of her wedding night with Sajida. The confession began with a joke after Hussein ended his absence and returned to Sajida's bed. The house had buzzed with talk among the servants after Nanijaan had instructed one of them to remove the bedding from the dining room cabinet and return it to the family linen closet.

"Better than the first time for you, I hope," Nanijaan said, having grown bolder with the years, making reference to the night she imagined Hussein returned to his senses.

Sajida insisted that nothing, in fact, had happened the night Hussein plucked every flower in Islamabad (or had the servants do this for him, as Nanijaan informed Sajida) and put them in her bedroom. But it didn't matter what Sajida said.

"Don't expect me to believe you," Nanijaan said, her eyes closed and her shoulders relaxing as Sajida rubbed her head.

Then the words rose from her before she could stop herself, and Nanijaan carried on to tell Sajida about her wedding night, how she'd cowered at the edge of her mattress when the man she hadn't laid eyes on until that morning had sat on the bed and ordered her to move closer, and when she hesitated, raised his voice and pulled her arms from her chest. She'd done what he said, finally, because she knew no better, and when it was over, she bit her lip and cried without making a sound until she fell asleep. The next day, her mother had run out and bought her dark lipstick to hide the marks on her lips.

"You wouldn't know about this," she said as Sajida rinsed her hair. "You had done things you shouldn't have done *before* you got married," Nanijaan said and giggled. "But then fireworks rained from the heavens that day for all of us to see, and what could have happened between you two on your wedding night to outdo that?"

Sajida had been surprised at Nanijaan's frankness, but the two of them laughed so hard, Sajida had to sit on the bathroom floor for a moment. Although she was a grown woman herself, Sajida loved it when Nanijaan confided in her, when they spoke to each other more like confidants than family. In the years Hussein was absent, Sajida depended on these moments of intimacy to pull her from one day to the next. Although Hussein had returned to her life, she found that she had no desire to curtail these moments spent with Nanijaan. This is why, on the Thursday after Noor got her period, Sajida was washing Nanijaan's hair in the bathroom sink and the two of them were discussing Noor's entrance into womanhood.

"But she's only ten!" Sajida said, frustrated that she hadn't prepared her daughter better for the eventuality of menstruation. "Who would have thought?"

"As much as you love her, even you underestimate her sometimes. What did you think? She'd stay a child?"

"No, I just didn't think."

Compounded with the thought of her child menstruating was the inescapable image Noor had planted in her head. Fat, dead people in a red river. It made Sajida want to ask Nanijaan about a beginning, and she'd saved her question until she was elbow deep in shampoo bubbles and the creases in Nanijaan's forehead smoothed with the respite.

"Did you wonder, Nanijaan . . . that night, long ago," Sajida started, summoning the memory of the night she'd entered Nanijaan's family. "Did you wonder where I'd come from?"

After Nanijaan established what Sajida meant, she answered, "Your father told me. He brought you from Dhaka. You told me about the cyclone, when you were pregnant with Noor. Remember?"

"What do you suppose would have happened if he hadn't found me?"

"I don't know . . . . It was war."

"Many died. Millions, maybe," said Sajida, unsure of how it was that *millions* rolled from her tongue rather than something different.

"That many?" Nanijaan inquired, never having thought to attach a number, any one number, to the war. "People die. That's what happens in war."

"Children."

"Everyone, rani jani."

Leaning closer towards Nanijaan, careful not to catch Nanijaan's gold hoop earrings in her fingers, Sajida said, "My family was already dead. Before the war."

"Because of the cyclone."

"Afterwards, bodies were everywhere. I couldn't find them. I tried."

"How could you, my love? Of course you couldn't."

"I never found anyone I knew."

"What do you mean?"

"There were bodies everywhere. First, near the camps. Afterwards, in the city. Dhaka. I saw them."

Sajida rinsed Nanijaan's hair, squeezed the water from it, and began to lather it up again.

A few minutes later, Nanijaan asked, "When were you in Dhaka?"

"I don't know. Summer. When Aba found me."

"June? Just a minute. The cyclone was in November," Nanijaan said, counting on her fingers, "just before Ali left for East Pakistan." Nanijaan held out her hand, her thumb resting on the center of her middle finger, where it had landed after counting the months from November to June in the three almost-even spaces each on her pinkie and ring fingers. "But people who died then . . . during the cyclone in November . . . their bodies would have been gone by the time you got to Dhaka in June."

"What do you mean?"

"In six months," Nanijaan said. "Buried. Rotted. Gone."

"I suppose," Sajida said.

"You're sure you saw bodies in Dhaka?"

"In the river," Sajida said. "They float, did you know that?"

"It was war, meri jaan. You see?"

"The bodies in the rivers, they were from the war?" Sajida asked.

"Must have been."

"You know," Sajida said and stopped before starting again, finding it difficult after an absence of years, to recall one detail. "Sometimes, their hands were tied together in the river."

"No," Nanijaan declared, while Sajida toweled her hair.

"The river changed color. Pale. Pink, sometimes. Who were they?"

"I don't know."

"Who killed them?"

"I don't know."

"Aba knows?" Sajida asked.

"I don't know," Nanijaan whispered as if she were responding to the same question for the third consecutive time.

"He wouldn't know, though," Sajida said. "Would he?"

Sajida wrapped Nanijaan's head in a thick towel before they walked through the courtyard into the dining room, where Sajida had fixed the professional style, stand-up hair dryer into an electrical outlet intended for the air conditioner. When Ali built the house, Nanijaan had refused to allow the electrician to install one in her room, insisting that she had no need for unnecessary appliances like air conditioners.

In the stillness of the courtyard, broken only by the soft flutters of parrots, Sajida considered what she knew. She knew she'd lost her family in a cyclone near the sea in what had been East Pakistan. That was in November. Months later, in June, miles from her village, she was rescued from the side of a Dhaka road by Ali, the man who became her father. Sometime in between, there was war. In Dhaka, already summer in March and April, she'd seen corpses floating in a muddy river.

The two women were startled when the quiet was broken by

the calls of hyenas from the Margallas. Sajida imagined the hills, the mountains hidden behind, and the mountain ranges beyond those.

"I like the mountains," Sajida said to Nanijaan, opening the screen door for her. "It's my favorite thing about Islamabad."

"None of us used to look at them until you got here," Nanijaan replied, suddenly exhausted, her body heavy with the need for sleep.

nine

The first drawing Noor made after the bleeding stopped and she agreed to leave her bed was of a river. The river was wide, the banks, black and rich, were wider yet, the land flat. The river was full, despite the shadow that hung above it and foretold of monsoons yet to come. In the daylight of Ali's Sector, the river was divided into two parallel streams. Half the river was pink, the other half gray. The pink was watercolor, the rest crayon. The textured banks of the river were oil paints squeezed roughly from a tube and gently patted down by Noor's delicate fingertips.

After eating lunch with Ali, Noor held out her river and asked him how to spell it.

Over the years, Ali had become accustomed to Noor's talent, but at some point a difference emerged between the drawings she created on her own (most of which hung in her gallery) and those like the one Noor was waving in front of Ali, which she was able to pluck from someone else's head. He couldn't remember exactly when the change had occurred. Had it been when she drew the buffalo? Since then, when he looked at her drawings, he braced himself for what they might be. Always, he tried hard to keep his reaction even, lest he frighten her with his surprise.

"It goes with the *s*'s," Noor said, giving Ali a hint, gesturing towards her private gallery on the walls of the house.

Ali didn't require her help. He needed only the briefest of glances to recall the way the river had sounded. He put his hand to his ear, as if he could muffle the memory. He remembered burying the no-breasted woman. The river, cumbersome, almost heaving in its downward flow, the water pushing against banks, thuds more than anything else, as they had worked to dig the grave once, and then again. The humming breeze was, for a split second, a welcome reprieve from the heat. But when Ali looked up and saw the shadow, he knew otherwise. It was a swarm of crows, thousands of them, wings flapping in a loud hum as they circled lower and lower, in unison, above the stinking water of the river.

"Nana!" Noor insisted, bringing back Ali's attention.

"*Sitalakhya*," Ali slowly answered, a word he hadn't imagined he'd mention again. He wrote the river's name in the corner of the drawing, as Sajida would have done. All the while, Ali couldn't take his eyes away from the parallel streams in the river, recalling how striking it had been to see in person. And, as if the difference needed to be emphasized, he took Noor's pencil from her long fingers and drew a line to separate the pink from the gray.

"In case there's any confusion," Ali mumbled.

"What, Nana?" Noor asked.

"I was just saying, it's important to be specific, my *artiste*. You don't mind, do you?" He ran his hand over her head, the shape of her mother's, covered with the same thick, blue-black hair.

"You try," Noor said, offering him her orange bucket and a piece of paper.

Ali shook his head. He hadn't any choice but to draw the line, Ali thought. One side was the river, the other something entirely different. Noor, her head full of pictures, her beautiful hands eager to render them, didn't need to know that.

It occurred to Ali that Noor's drawing was a manifestation of what he'd locked away so carefully years ago in the cabinets of his mind. In the presence of a granddaughter he loved so much and her meticulous drawing of the Sitalakhya the day he'd buried a woman, he understood what had happened. His past had arrived. Soon it would be its own gallery, for all to see. However faint, there was a measure of relief in that. Looking at the walls of his house, considering how neatly Noor's drawings were ordered and hung, he knew he'd been wrong in the scalding bath on his homecoming to think he could pack it all away.

With a sinking feeling, Ali hoped that the life he'd been living since the day he returned to Nanijaan's house with a child in tow had given him what he needed to confront what lay ahead. Noor sat on her marble in the courtyard, her head bent over a new drawing. However things might unfold, whether or not he'd still have the family he'd made. *Well,* Ali thought, *that remained to be seen.*

ৡ

The next time Sajida washed Nanijaan's hair, she didn't wait until she'd worked up a lather to begin her questions. She helped Nanijaan stand on a stool and settle on the dining room chair piled high with cushions. While Nanijaan's feet were still swinging above the floor, Sajida picked up where she'd left off a few days earlier.

"How long was he gone?"

"Eight months, one week, two days."

"I can't imagine Adel or Farooq being gone so long. Not knowing if he'd be alive. You worried about that, didn't you?" Sajida said.

"I told God that I'd give up anything for him to come home alive."

Sajida massaged Nanijaan's scalp, gently kneading it with her fingertips. She'd learned from Nanijaan. As a child, Sajida would walk on her back and legs, following her instructions. After Sajida was married, Nanijaan returned the favor by rubbing Sajida's feet and back during her pregnancies, especially during the last, when she put her hands to use in the hope of making Sajida seem less remote.

"Did you?" Sajida asked.

"No, I didn't. Ali gave up meat and marriage, when he came home."

"How long was he supposed to be gone?"

"Two years."

"Why did he come home early?"

"Typhoid," Nanijaan said. "He got it there. From dirty water. He came back so weak. He could hardly carry you." She was grateful beyond compare for his return and, she told Sajida, she didn't think it was her place to pry. "He was tired," she said. "First he couldn't sleep. Then he slept so many hours every day. Do you remember? His days and nights were undone. All that mattered was that he was home."

When he'd walked into the house one afternoon with a child in his arms, Nanijaan thought she was seeing an apparition, the ghost of her son informing her of his death. But she'd kept on praying, in the name of the Almighty, and suddenly, it was her son.

Opening her eyes, watching Sajida imagine herself as the child in Ali's arms on top of the landing in the other house, Nanijaan admitted to herself that her son *had* died in the war. The one that had come home was different. He didn't pray. Every so often, she would watch as his face was gently transformed, and she knew, even without the details, that it was the weight of remembering. Of what exactly, it wasn't her place to ask.

Nanijaan relaxed into her chair as the warm water rushed over her head and Sajida worked carefully to prevent the shampoo from running into her eyes.

"You've noticed? He can never sleep during the monsoons. But you . . . would you really have wanted to know if it had been your son?" Nanijaan slapped her forehead with her hand and shook her head. "Stupid, stupid war," she said again, only repeating to herself what she had declared before it even started. "He was different, though," Nanijaan said. "He'd learned to love. He loved you immediately. He'd have done anything for you then. He found joy in the smallest of things. We picked you up the first day of school and when he saw you with your friend . . . Rifaat, remember? . . . holding hands, his chin, I swear to you, trembled. The day we rushed you to the hospital when you dislocated your shoulder, he cried when they put you underneath the X-ray machine. The doctors said they'd never seen a father cry over a daughter's injury before and let him stay in the room with you.

"Suddenly," Nanijaan continued, "he was an ocean of patience. You know what he'd been like? This boy who, when he was a child, would scream and wet his pants rather than interrupt his play! Grown, he'd wait until eleven for dinner guests who should have been here at eight-thirty and then meet them in the driveway without a grumble, as if that was the appointed time. 'Oh, don't you mind,' he'd say if they tried to apologize. The driver took advantage of him. They all did. He'd leave Ali in the car while he fetched groceries. One time, and I made sure it was only once, after an hour of waiting, Ali went to find him—out of curiosity more than anything. The driver was chatting with a friend. Ali drew up a chair at the music stall. The friend ordered tea, played a string of cassettes for him, and hours later when they came home and I demanded to know where they'd been, Ali said, 'Never mind, Nanijaan, it was the music that did it. Don't be angry with the driver.' I *was* angry with them. Both of them. I'd missed my tea party.

"He was a boy who never had time for food: he gulped it down, fingerfuls wrapped in chapattis, legs of chicken, biting and eating the bones, effortlessly, as if it were all white meat. But after he returned, he ate slowly, so slowly that the cook would be bringing me my tea and he'd only just be ordering his second phulka. I'd sit there with him, after you were in bed, watching him put food in his mouth. I thought at first, alhamdullilah, he'd learned to eat properly! I imagined he would savor every bite of chicken pulao and saag gosht, as it deserved. Instead, he gave up the bones, the meat, everything. And the food, even soft dals, sat in his throat and it was hard for him to swallow. He dwindled. I changed his stock of shirts several times. He was once a sixteen-and-a-half neck size. He played field hockey when he was younger, he ran the fastest, hit the hardest. His coaches would joke about him being on the Olympic team. When he returned, he'd lost his shoulders. People thought he was weak. He was thin. He wasn't the same at all."

Sajida's hands stiffened and stopped, as if she might say something, but she didn't.

"But, oh my goodness, could he laugh! Before, he'd had a small laugh and he didn't use it often. But when he returned, it was fuller, heartier—a booming laugh. In the beginning, when you were a small girl, he'd take you and your friends to the park, over a few houses, and I'd sit outside and hear him with you. It made me put the newspaper down, that laugh. And when you came home I'd ask what was so funny, but none of you could ever remember."

When Nanijaan stopped speaking, Sajida wrung the water from her hair. Before she was done, Nanijaan lifted her head from the washbasin and turned to Sajida.

"What *was* so funny? Can you remember now?" Nanijaan asked.

As Nanijaan spoke, the bathroom door opened. Noor, dressed for bed in another of her father's kurtas, skipped into the room, her limp almost gone. Her developing body wasn't hidden by the thin kurta, and she wore her hair coiled into a bun on the top of her head, a recent trick to appear taller. Sajida was about to scold her for running about without a robe or anything on her feet, momentarily forgetting that Noor was immune to heat and cold alike.

"I know!" Noor interrupted, giggling. "Hands tied together, birds of a feather, goes on forever, awful weather . . ." she said, stopping to think of what else might fit in her nonsense rhyme.

෯

If Nanijaan hadn't already suspected that Noor was listening to her conversations with Sajida, she would certainly have believed just this when she came across Noor's painting. At first, Nanijaan's attention was absorbed by Ali's handwriting, a neat, exaggerated slant distinct from anyone else's in the family. She was intent on memorizing the spelling of the river so that she might look it up in an atlas to discover where in Bengal a river like that might be. But when she studied the image, the river divided by a rough pencil mark, pink and gray on either side, and the black, wet banks of the river, she heard Sajida's description, *hands tied together*, as though Sajida were standing right next to her.

In the drawing room, supervising the servant to retrieve the old atlas from one of the highest shelves of the bookcase, Nanijaan couldn't remember the last time she'd used the book. Peering through her reading glasses, using a magnifying glass to help decipher the tiny print, she found the river. It was nothing but a thin scribble in the pale green of the map.

It was strange, after so many years, to come across a detail of Ali's war. For a long time after Ali came home, the only reminder of the war was in Lahore, which Nanijaan visited once or twice. There, she recalled, she saw a large red and white banner hung taut across

Mall Road. In bold white print, the banner read BRING OUR POWS HOME. The first time she saw the banner, she told her friend sitting next to her in a taxi that had Ali been a POW, she would have died. When two and a half years passed before the POWs came home, Nanijaan thought she'd been right. Parents were not meant to endure certain things, among them a child dying or languishing in prison a thousand miles away.

As if she were putting many years behind her, Nanijaan closed the heavy atlas in her hands with a thud. It came to her. Indeed, she had questions. They could not be answered by books, intricate maps, or anything else she might read. Something entirely different was demanded. She would have to stand in front of her youngest son, her favorite of all, and find the words. What did Ali *do* in East Pakistan? What did he *see*? What did this boy *find* so far away?

Sitalakhya. She'd seen a river like that once. On the drive to Peshawar, stopping at the astonishing juncture where the Indus and Kabul rivers meet, observing the unlikely blue of one river combine with the silty gray of the other, two distinct streams converged. For all the clarity, it was impossible to pinpoint exactly where the two streams became one murky river.

Later that night, neither able to sleep, Nanijaan and Ali stumbled into each other in the storeroom, in their independent search for sugar to replenish the kitchen supply. Recalling his once sturdy frame and observing the one made more fragile with time and the dim light in the pantry, Nanijaan met Ali's gaze. At that moment, with Sajida's details still ringing in her ears, she was overwhelmed with urgency. She took a step closer to Ali and it tumbled out.

"You killed someone?"

She said it directly. She didn't falter. It came out right the first time, without pauses or stammers or anything that might have cushioned it. Ali liked it that way. Big and whole, in the open, so he could very nearly touch it. And it wasn't, as Ali had feared all along, Sajida who asked the question.

"What did you think I was doing?" he asked, his hands in the air waving the empty sugar bowl.

"Who?"

"Who?" Ali answered incredulously. "Is that what you think war is? Excuse me, before I shoot you, what's your name? So I can tell my mother when she asks?"

"You killed someone and don't know who."

"No. I didn't kill some *one*."

"More than one?"

"You need a number? More than one and less than a hundred? What did you bloody think I was going to do when I told you I was going there? Did you think it would be a party?" Ali hadn't known he could speak to his mother this way. But her questions emboldened him and he fell into the unfamiliar tone as if he were accustomed to this sort of disrespect.

"You knew what you would do?"

"I didn't. But *you* did. You said war was an animal gone mad."

"That's what I said? I was right?"

"You're the one who let me go. Maybe you're the one who should stand trial."

"No one is on trial here, Ali. I just want to know."

"But, why? You've never wanted to know anything else. About Sajida, for example."

"That's not true! I asked you where she came from—"

"You asked me once."

"Listen," Nanijaan said, mustering up her strength, speaking deliberately and emphatically. "Your deeds are yours. I did my part. I taught you the best I could. What you have done is yours to bear. When you stand in front of God—"

"God does not divine what I have seen."

"And what have you seen? Yourself killing? Beating? What else, Ali?"

"War is war, after all," he said.

"Why did you do it?"

"We're not so different. I was running for my life. Just like you."

"What?"

"You killed Papa. What did you say to him that day when he fell over and died?"

The question shocked Nanijaan. Her hands trembled and her legs felt as if they would give from under her. She took a few steps outside the storeroom into the kitchen and sat on a lone chair.

"But, I didn't say anything to him," she answered quietly. "He spoke to me!"

"What did he say?"

"He wished I were dead."

"And then he died? This was his exclamation point? You expect me to believe that? And you were glad—"

"I was glad that he couldn't beat me anymore," Nanijaan said, touching her face where Ali's father had once punched her before slamming her against the display cabinet, knocking knickknacks from their places.

"I didn't do anything to them that they didn't do to us first," Ali offered.

"They didn't *kill* you," Nanijaan said, raising her voice. "You're standing right here."

"That was luck. They meant to."

"There is no such thing as luck in war."

"That's *all* there is!"

"By God's grace, you survived."

"God was nowhere to be found, Mama." When Ali said this, he remembered with certainty that he'd called his mother Mama before Nanijaan became her name.

"Don't pretend to be so high and mighty. You are common, like the rest of us. God sees you as He does everyone else,"

"We were fighting for our lives. Not for you. Or this country.

For ourselves. We were out there in the fucking swamps, fighting stingers, Indians and Bengalis alike; it was just that we couldn't see them . . ."

Nanijaan stood. She walked through the swinging door into the dining room and Ali followed her. Stopping, she turned to him and asked, "How could it be that you could kill someone and not see them?"

Ali thought of saying, *That's why we could, you see?* But he knew better than to give his mother any answer at all, much less to lie. Some he hadn't seen, others he had.

"I didn't mean to," he said, instead, nodding. And this was the closest Ali came to offering his mother an explanation for what he'd done.

"To see or to kill?" Nanijaan angrily retorted before she reached for a tasbee, one of the sandalwood prayer beads strung in a necklace and stored in a deep bowl on the fake fireplace mantel, and left the room.

She'd asked to set the record straight. In her own mind. He was her son, she had a right to know. It had taken years, *how many had it been?*, to realize she'd lacked the courage to ask earlier. All these years, she'd spent being grateful for Ali's life. She was still grateful. But when she and Sajida spoke, sharing what they thought they knew, an urgency set in. Until then, she hadn't wanted to know, and still didn't want to know, because she'd been afraid of the answer. It was as simple as that. But in a strange way, she reasoned, she deserved credit for this. At least she had known enough to be afraid. She hadn't asked earlier, she suddenly thought, because it would have been like asking him when he'd been a child, *Who finished the last cookie in the cookie tin?*, knowing full well it was he. What was the point? Nanijaan caught herself. She wasn't as big a person as she'd hoped.

How many years did she have left, anyway? Life was running out, as it always did once you passed a certain age, and she was long past it. She felt a new responsibility to have answers, and when she was ready, to take them with her when she went. So she'd be equipped in case she was asked, so she could pray for him if it was required, so she could be his closure, if that's what he needed. She could no longer tie his shoe for him, but this she could surely do for him.

Out of all her boys, Ali was the one who'd stayed home. Or, rather, had come back home. Lived his life, with his child, with her. After their conversation, though, Nanijaan would think of him differently: out of reach. He was no longer her youngest son, he was Ali. She looked at him when they sat at the table together, when she poured him his tea, and when she instructed the dhobi to stop starching Ali's shirt collars so sloppily, and thought: *This is Ali, he fought in a war, and he killed someone.* It was in moments like those, rather than in the conversation they'd had or the long months he'd been in East Pakistan, that Ali was separated from her. Her other sons, oceans, land, great distances between them, it was understandable. But this boy, in one night, with words—she hadn't seen it herself—flung himself further from her than any airplane could take her.

Her head spun with questions, but she would not ask any of them. *What does it feel like, to kill someone? Where do you put that knowledge during the day? At night? Ah, sometimes, when it rains, you still can't sleep for remembering! What does it feel like, to know you are the reason for someone else's grief? You've thought of that, right? The mother? The father? The child—one, two, three, perhaps—left behind?*

The next day, entering the bedroom with freshly ironed clothes as Noor, emerged from the bathroom partly undressed, her bra strap falling from her shoulder, her black hair as yet uncombed covering her growing breasts, Nanijaan was almost delirious with fear. *Killing is what you did, right?* she imagined saying to him. *Nothing else?*

Nanijaan tormented herself with these questions and more. The noise overtook her head like a train rushing through a village. The rumbling became the backdrop of her days. She loved and laughed and played despite it, but it was only when she slept that the rumblings did too. Quietly, in a momentary pause, she rested and rested some more.

ഉ

It took hearing the question, feeling it in the space between his hands, for Ali to realize he'd waited his whole life to hear it. But it took answering the question to understand how insufficient it was. Killing wasn't nearly the worst of it. War teaches this. He couldn't remember when he'd learned this for sure.

That night, the order was no different. It was my job on night duty to collect the girls and bring them to the officers. I went to the farthest corner of the barracks, fetched the only girl waiting, and brought her to the officer's rooms. I didn't wave my rifle.

Her eyes were clouded, like I'd seen somewhere else, in the row of Bengalis before they'd been shot by the same bullet. Her eyes were wide open, though, like all Bengali women. We joked that in the face of men, the women could neither keep their eyes nor their legs closed. The man posted near me that morning had repeated this, envying the superiors who found constant use for this weakness. They've never seen anyone like us, he said, hitching up his pants, as if he knew this firsthand, which he did.

It wasn't her first time. She'd been prepared already. I could smell the soap on her, a perfumed fragrance, something Nanijaan might have worn, and I knew it wasn't army-issue. She didn't wear a sari blouse, a preference of the officer in charge. I could see the mus-

cles in her strong back, and I remembered wondering if my cousin bride would have had a back like that. No, she wouldn't have.

We walked the narrow corridor together. I tried not to touch her. I couldn't stop looking at the bruise on her shoulder, deep and swollen. The rest of what I'd seen, the limbs and rotting flesh, birds pecking at a child's arm, had become a landscape so common I hardly saw it anymore. But the bruise, softly risen like a hill, on a body . . . still clothed. Opening the officer's door, I put my hand on her bruise and guided her in. I tightened my grip to show the officer I was, indeed, in charge. The girl didn't flinch.

She stood in the corner of the room and did as she was told. On his command, she let her sari pallu fall to her side, revealing her breasts. I stood behind her. I should have left the room then.

The officer called me forward, told me to look at her bare breasts.

"Right," the officer said. "Take a good look. Haven't seen this before, have you?" He flicked his fingers on her nipples.

Her nipples rose in reflex, the rest of her body so absolutely still it was hardly possible that she was breathing. Her ribs were visible, perfectly aligned, parts hidden behind her breasts, neither big nor small, hanging low. The skin on her belly was patterned with lines, in clusters.

The officer brought his face close to her belly. He untucked her sari with his mouth and the cloth fell to the ground. Underneath, she was naked. The officer pushed his face into her belly. To keep her balance, she took a step backwards. When he took his face from her skin, he left behind two rows of teeth marks. She didn't make a sound.

White dribbled from her breast onto her stomach. Milk is white, cloudy, from the breast. That's when it occurred to me. The milk, the marks on her belly: The woman was a young mother.

I was told to leave the room.

I stood guard by the door. The noises were quieter than usual, but still I heard furniture being shoved to one side, chairs over-turned, the crash of breaking glass, perhaps not a window, but a glass. The officer spoke a few times, but the only fragment I under-stood was Jivai Pakistan. *Long live Pakistan.* Eventually, there were hints of rushed grunts, no sound whatever from the woman.

The officer summoned me.

"Your turn," he said.

"Sorry, sir?" I said.

"Right," the officer said. "Do you have a prick on you or not? It's your turn."

I couldn't take my eyes off the girl. She lay on the desk, na-ked and limp. One knee bent, the roundness of it shocking against the sharp angles in which her body lay. Head to one side, hips to another, chin upward, elbows pointed outward, hands folded on her chest, knuckles sharp and quivering in peaks of their own. Milk flowed from her breasts. There were teeth marks in between.

My pants didn't tighten. I felt sick to my stomach. My first time, offered a woman like that. "Oh, no, sir. She's yours," I said.

"I'll be happy to clean her up for you, sir," I said, trying again.

"No, thank you. Looks like you were too much for her," I said, a bit too frank for a superior officer. He was washing his hands in the corner sink, patting down his hair with oil.

"Behen chod," the officer cursed. "You have a prick or not?"

"Yes, sir," I mumbled.

"Show me."

"In my pants, sir."

"Show me," the officer repeated.

I set down my rifle and unzipped my pants. I could hardly see my penis, shriveled and hidden.

"You're not a soldier," the officer said, calmly. "You only fuck your mother."

The door slammed behind the officer and the comb he'd been using fell from the sink to the floor.

I was alone with the girl, my pants still down. I took a few steps toward her. She was ripped and pried open, the implements used to do this, the scissors, pens, a metal ruler, speckled with blood, lying to her side. The nib of the fountain pen was missing. She was shaved between her legs. I could see her opening in the blood.

I straddled her. She was warm and wet. My penis, soft and small, did nothing and, thankfully, I couldn't enter her. I pulled up my pants and covered the woman with the sari from the floor. I resumed guard duty outside the door.

Later, the sweeper came to fetch the woman. I accompanied them to their quarters. She walked silently, her face still, without expression. Perhaps she'd been spared after all, I remember thinking. She'd taken leave of her life: her body, her husband, her young child. Her soul was already dead, safely warm and wrapped in a peaceful place. I envied her that place. Shameless, right? I knew what I'd done. I could never change that.

ও

The next afternoon, Ali arrived home late from work. Nanijaan sat at the table with him while he ate alone. The cook, undeterred by Ali's years of vegetarianism, refilled a platter with freshly fried kebabs, sprinkling green onions and chilies on the crisp, dark brown surface. Ali turned his face from the rising steam and pushed away the platter. Nanijaan broke off a piece of a kebab and nibbled on it. Ali reached across the table for the plate of mangoes.

The mangoes, out of season, had been frozen in July. They held their shape and most of their color even after many months in the deep freezer. Nanijaan began a tradition of freezing mangoes when Ali's eldest brother left home. She saved her stockpile so that she would be able to serve him mangoes when he returned home, regardless of the season. Time passed, and since he returned home so rarely, she allowed the rest of her family to indulge in the frozen mangoes until eating mangoes off season in Ali's Sector became customary.

Watching Ali suck on the soft green-yellow skin, Nanijaan said, "Beta, why not mangoes?"

"What do you mean?"

"In return for coming back, you gave up meat . . . " Her sentence wandered off without finishing. Ali understood what his mother was saying and picked up her thought.

"You must know," Ali said firmly, still angry with his mother, "I didn't make deals, with God or anyone. I don't eat meat. That's just the way it is."

God and meat, Ali thought. Both were off limits, in the same category, since coming home. God because nothing Ali had seen—or done—could have been divined by God. And meat because he'd smelled flesh in every possible manifestation. Freshly dead, not-so-freshly dead, rotted, singed, burned, baked, and every variety in between, and he never wanted to set eyes on it, much less his tongue on it, again.

Eventually, the cook began to clear the table. Nanijaan remained sitting among half-empty platters, dirty utensils, napkins soiled with pale orange mango juice, and dessert plates piled high with green and yellow mango skins.

Ali was standing, wiping mango juice from his chin with the back of his hand, a toothpick between his fingers to dislodge mango strings from his teeth. He picked at his teeth. Then, with Nanijaan watching, he dropped the toothpick on the table and left the dining room.

ten

It began, Sajida was convinced, when Nanijaan threw out her days in favor of nights. Over the next few months, she took to her bed as if she was suddenly made for it, as if nothing else was possible, as if the years of her life had suddenly added up to a number so great she had to lie down to fathom it.

During that time, Nanijaan was fond of saying that the century was running out. Sajida, on the other hand, had no interest in exaggerated, bigger-than-life events like the closing of the millennium. When the year began, Sajida's only concern lay with Nanijaan. She was the closest Sajida had to a mother or, as she once qualified to herself, at least for the part of her life with which she was most familiar.

As always, Nanijaan took a walk every day, only now she did so with her tasbee in hand, lips moving in prayer as she fingered the beads. She rose in the morning for her breakfast, returned to her bed for a one or two hour nap, rose again to take her forty-five minute walk, and followed it up with a three hour nap, all before lunch. Watching Nanijaan amble down the road, Sajida noticed that with each passing week Nanijaan seemed to walk more and more slowly, until Sajida questioned how much distance Nanijaan was actually covering in her daily constitutional.

One morning, Sajida left a block of distance between them and followed Nanijaan to see for herself. Nanijaan's steps were slow and labored and although she did not stop to take a breath, she might as well have, because she inched along the road as if she were short of air. Sajida hid behind a neighbor's gate when Nanijaan turned around and began her walk home. When Nanijaan passed her, she called out to Sajida.

"Don't be silly, rani jani. I can see your dupatta. What's wrong? Don't you trust an old lady like me?"

"You're walking very slowly. Why so slowly?" Sajida worked to keep the same pace as Nanijaan.

"I've reached the ripe old age, my child, when I'm no longer in a rush. What difference does it make if it takes me one hour or five hours to cover the same distance? No, I don't live like that anymore. I'm not in a hurry."

Even that morning, Sajida would have said it differently. Nanijaan was in a hurry to slow down until there was no more slowing down to do. Sajida sensed it then, but suspected it more strongly during Nanijaan's endlessly long afternoons of somnolence when this woman who had never thought of skipping her afternoon tea decided it did not merit rising from her bed.

The children could not accept Nanijaan's need for sleep. They would storm into her room at all times of day with questions and demands. Adel entered the room one morning before school with his Walkman set so loud that Nanijaan could make out the lyrics without putting the earphones to her ears. Noor passed through Nanijaan's doorway far more than she ever had, bringing with her piles of drawings and displaying them on Nanijaan's bed for compliments.

If Nanijaan had been ill, if she had needed food or water brought to her, the children might have found it less perplexing.

Like the children, Sajida, too, did not want Nanijaan to sleep. Against Nanijaan's protests, she took her to the best doctor in town, who examined her and ordered a multitude of tests, all to find nothing amiss. After the test results came in and after she had seen for herself that Nanijaan was not ill, she found her own excuses to disturb Nanijaan. She requested recipes to give the cook. She searched for imaginary fabric or thread tucked in Nanijaan's closet. She asked Nanijaan's advice on solving fights between the boys. She shared information from the newspaper, anything at all to prompt Nanijaan to converse with her.

Every so often, during these interludes, Nanijaan surprised Sajida. One time Sajida sat on Nanijaan's bed prepared to speak of recipes, but she had other things on her mind.

"If Adel wanted to join the army, you'd forbid him?"

"Absolutely."

"Especially if he wanted to go to war, right?"

"I'd tell him he'd lost his mind."

After a moment, Nanijaan spoke again, as if Sajida had asked a question. "I tried to tell your father. I really did. But he was young. He thought of it as adventure. He was like a little boy, the day he left, waiting to board the airplane. Maybe if his father had been alive . . . ." Nanijaan stopped short of saying that had her husband lived, he would have prevented Ali from joining the army. She had no way of knowing this. In fact, it was likely her husband would not have minded Ali boarding the flight to war that day. But it might have been otherwise, and since Nanijaan had begun her backward glance at life's possibilities, at how things might have been different, she imagined her husband loving his family and worrying about his son embarking on a military venture a thousand miles from home.

"What does Aba say?" Sajida asked, assuming that Nanijaan had spoken to her son about his war of thirty years before.

"Not much. *War is war*, he said. Everyone knows that. It does terrible things to you."

"No," Sajida said, again answering Nanijaan's earlier question. "I wouldn't let the boys go."

"But the thing is, by then they do what they want. They know better. Nothing you can say will change their minds once they're already made up."

"You did your best," Sajida said, squeezing Nanijaan's foot.

"I should have done more, meri jaan. So stubborn, he was. And when he came back, he gave up God. As if he hadn't any use for Him anymore."

"What do you mean?" Sajida asked astonished, unaware her father had ever had a relationship with God. She'd never seen her father pray or hear him utter commonplace, daily phrases like "inshallah," the minute reverences to God that peppered everyone else's speech in Pakistan.

"That was all years ago," Nanijaan said. "Long before you."

Then she turned around in her bed, and went back to sleep.

ൟ

There would never be an explanation. On her walk one morning, Nanijaan stumbled a few yards from Ali's Sector. She lay on the road, grasping her side until Hussein passed in his car some minutes later. He bumped his head trying to get out of the car quickly. Because he forgot to pull the handbrake, the car slowly rolled toward the house as he picked up Nanijaan and ran behind it. At the bottom of the driveway, he hollered for Sajida. She ran from the house and pulled the parking brake.

Noor watched from the driveway as Hussein put Nanijaan in the back seat of the car. Sajida, momentarily frozen, stood by the open car door with a look of horror on her face. Frightened, Noor ran toward the house and into the courtyard. She bumped into a cage of parrots, spilling their water dishes, before falling onto her marble, noticeably dull after many years of summer sun.

Before Hussein had finished making a narrow U-turn on the road, Noor was already at work. She labored with an urgency even more intense than what was her habit. She bit her full lips and furiously worked her colored pencils. She wore a pale blue shalwar kameez, ironed and starched only that morning. A chiffon dupatta hung over her shoulders and against her neck. Except where it was stretched around her knees as she kneeled, her kurta hung loosely on her. As she hunched over her marble slab, the shirt fell away from her chest in a soft balloon of fabric. Noor did not lift her head from her work until she was done, ignoring the carefully carved balls of pink melon the cook put next to her for lunch and, again, for dinner.

The drawing she made was full of color-pencil flowers, every kind Noor had ever seen. They included the make-believe orange and red ones Nanijaan and Sajida had sewn on a razai years earlier, the yellow tuberoses that grew in a pot by the door, the soft pink blossoms on sweet peas that climbed the wall near the driveway, and the white flowers of Islamabad's lovely jasmine bushes bursting with sweet perfume. In the midst of the flowers was a simple charpai, loosely strung and bedecked in a shawl like the one Hussein had given Sajida before Noor was born.

At the hospital, Hussein and Sajida waited in the emergency room until they were seen. By then, Nanijaan's desperate grasping had traveled from her side to her head, and her breathing, at first regular, became intermittent and shallow.

By the time the doctor saw her, Nanijaan could not speak. Sajida answered as best as she could for Nanijaan, given the cold chill that was swallowing her. A nurse put a needle in Nanijaan's back. An hour later, she was lying in the intensive care ward with tubes in her mouth, in her nose, in her stomach, and in her hands. When Sajida squeezed her fingers, Nanijaan, ever so lightly, squeezed back.

"Goddammit," Hussein shouted when the doctor finally arrived at the hospital. "She should have been seen right away."

A few hours later, when Nanijaan stopped squeezing Sajida's hands and Sajida was able to discern and predict the rhythm of all the machines in Nanijaan's room, she leaned her head to Nanijaan's ear and whispered, "We'll take you home."

When Ali arrived, the doctor insisted that she could not travel home. She needed the machines, the one that monitored her, the one that fed her, the one that helped her breathe.

"We'll take them all," Sajida said, speaking up.

"You can't," the doctor said, adding that there was a difference between a hospital and a bazaar.

Somehow, they got permission. Calls were made. A friend of a friend's relative was the eldest son of a cousin of a general whose officer ran the hospital. Money was exchanged, as Sajida later discovered. Ali sold several houses without commission and some staff at the hospital received lifetime supplies of Hussein's bottled water. Two days later, they had all the machines Nanijaan needed in their house, and two nurses, one on night duty and one on day duty, who studied the blinking on the machines and kept notes on hospital forms for the doctor who came to read them every day.

The first night, when Sajida came home from the hospital to shower and change her clothes, Noor would not come near her. Traumatized by the smell of hospitals, the antiseptic solution used to clean the floors, Noor held her dupatta over her nose and mouth while she spoke.

"You smell," Noor said.

"I'm sorry," Sajida answered.

"Your clothes."

"I'll just take a bath."

"Wash your hair. Hospitals stink."

"Nanijaan is coming home," Sajida said, her kurta drawn over her head already, her shalwar wrinkled and dirty, hanging, after the long day, just barely on her hips.

"Nanijaan needs her sleep," Noor declared, nodding her head, her new, dangling earrings swinging with the movement.

"Yes, meri jaan. She needs her sleep."

The drawing was in the bathroom on the toilet seat. For the first time, Sajida felt no anticipation upon seeing Noor's drawing. She knew what it was before she saw the charpai, a shawl flung across it. She picked up the drawing by the corner, where Noor, in big block letters, had hesitantly written her first two words. Bunched together as one, the letters were uneven and crooked: o-v-e-r-t-h-e-r-e. With a heaviness Sajida recognized, she brought the drawing to her face. Silently, she prayed that the place which awaited Nanijaan was filled with color, like her daughter's mind, along with the perfumes of nargis and make-believe flowers alike.

A short while later, Ali saw the drawing. It hung between the *n*'s for Nanijaan, and the *o*'s for Noor's mishmash of two words. He could make out his mother, lying on the charpai. Scrambling for something to say as he stood by her side, Ali explained to Noor that *over there*, although spelled correctly, was two words and not one. Noor raised her voice and pulled her ears. She cried that her grandmother was in one place, not two. Ali folded her into his arms, accepting that the clarity of his granddaughter's grasp on life—and death—surpassed his own. Remembering Nanijaan's trespass (*after all*, he'd wondered, *who was she to have asked questions?*), he relaxed in the embrace of his granddaughter. Ali took Noor's word for it and accepted that his mother had already arrived somewhere else.

❦

It was Sajida's habit, late at night when the house was still, to sit on the bed next to Nanijaan and gently massage special oils into her paper-thin skin. She'd made inquiries of every homeopathic doctor within the area and had settled on a combination of oils that made sense to her: almond oil for strength, ghee for softness, rosewater for fragrance. With this, she mixed drops of holy water brought back from Mecca by a relative. When the holy water was almost gone, she turned to goats to court God's favor. Sajida and her family had more goats slaughtered in the three weeks of Nanijaan's illness than anyone they'd known. Hussein, in charge of sending drivers to arrange the sacrifices, supervising cooks as they cleaned and parceled the meat, and distributing the blood-fresh meat to the needy, had his own opinions. Sacrificing bakras did nothing to win God's mercy. Life was written. Although he prostrated on a prayer carpet, it had been years since he'd felt close to God. Nothing had changed: when it was time, you went, regardless of goats or prayers or (and this he would keep to himself) medicines and machines.

In a rare moment during those weeks when he and Sajida were both in Nanijaan's room at the same time, and the nurse was on her dinner break, he made his point.

"You know, Saji. Nanijaan wouldn't approve. She'd say, *For God's sake leave the goats out of it. Spare them. Don't wipe out the country's goat population on account of me.*" Hussein altered his voice to suggest Nanijaan's: soft instead of raspy, high rather than deep.

"You think?" Sajida answered.

"*All this fuss,* she would have said. *For an old lady with white hair! Stop the nonsense. Khuda ke liye.*"

Hussein looked up to the ceiling at "in the name of God," clasped his palms together, and fell to his knees, mimicking a hero's final plea to the ether in a Hindi film. The two giggled, Nanijaan still and quiet, the machines behind her bed doing her breathing with beeps and lights.

"Khuda ke liye," Sajida mocked, getting up from the bed, laughing for a moment as she reached for her husband.

The next day, when Sajida went to check on Nanijaan, a parrot flapped near the ceiling in the room they had promised the doctor no one would enter without washing. The bird was neon blue with bright yellow painted on its chest. It was Noor's favorite combination, a preference from when Ali had put one just like it in the newly arrived wrought-iron birdcages.

When the household heard Sajida's shrieks, they feared the worst and came running. The cook, first to reach the room, struggled with the door. Hussein threw it open and stumbled in, unwashed, only just home from the office.

"*Tota,* in the room," Sajida said, the clipped sentence the best she could do. She pulled Nanijaan's sheet over her face and the tubes which ran into her nose. The night before, the visiting doctor had told Sajida and Hussein that Nanijaan's new puffiness suggested her condition was deteriorating. Sajida had contradicted him, telling him the extra weight on Nanijaan's face might, instead of an infection, be due to the early stages of a recovery. Sajida smoothed the sheet over Nanijaan as if, so far along, a simple cotton sheet would protect her beloved Nanijaan from a parrot's germs.

The cook entered the room without permission, holding out hands stained with onions and turmeric, calling for the bird. He clucked his tongue and cooed until the bird flew onto his stretched arm and perched near his elbow.

"What was the bird doing in Nanijaan's room?" Sajida demanded, following the cook into the courtyard.

After the latch of Ali's wrought-iron cage in the courtyard was opened and then closed again, fastened with the smooth, whittled branch that was the lock, the cook coughed twice before he answered. He'd put the parrot there out of an idiosyncratic superstition Sajida had never heard of and thought too stupid to contradict.

When Sajida returned to Nanijaan's room, Hussein had washed his hands and face, taken the sheet from Nanijaan's face, and replaced it with a clean one that rested below her chin on her slowly swelling shoulders.

"What was that?" Hussein asked. "The cook put the parrot in here?"

"We should get rid of him," Sajida replied.

"But who would cook?" Hussein said, immediately sorry that in the midst of a crisis he should be concerned with how the cook's potential departure would affect his meals.

"You'd call your mother," Sajida said knowingly. "She'd send food."

She sat on Nanijaan's bed and took a wrinkled, still pliant, hand into her own.

"Did you know?" Sajida spoke to Nanijaan. "We have a real idiot living in the house?"

While Sajida and Hussein hovered over Nanijaan, Ali devoted himself to the children. He set up wickets and took out the cricket bats, produced an unending supply of balls, all in a space that was too small for a real game now that the boys were so much older. Ali retrieved a plastic tape recorder with a microphone, an old toy from a forgotten chest in a storeroom. He replaced the leaking batteries and, microphone in hand, provided running commentary for the modified cricket matches that unfolded.

The rhythms of the house were changing again, and when Sajida ended her shifts with Nanijaan because Hussein insisted she rest, she didn't notice the children playing with bats in the courtyard. Hussein, however, would leave Nanijaan's room and confront the mess outside. Without wasting a word, he'd set to work picking up bats and wickets as if Nanijaan would despair of the mess if she saw it.

In the weeks of Nanijaan's illness, Noor did not enter Nanijaan's room even once and no one sought to change her mind. Noor had always disliked hospitals and when the hospital, in the form of beeping machines and silent nurses, came to her house, she was doubly convinced of her fear. Ali, who found himself shying away from Nanijaan and her machines, spent most of his time with Noor, sitting with her as she did her early morning sketches (before cricket matches began) on her slab of marble, her broken orange bucket beside her, in sight of the parrots. In the beginning, he would still field office telephone calls on his mobile, but later, he stopped these interruptions, along with any others as well.

"Stupid parrots," Noor would complain, her grandfather's attention rapt. "They never speak."

"They're not really meant to, meri jaan. Parrots in these parts don't really speak. Sing is what they do. And they do it rather well, don't you think? *Chee-chee, tooi? tooi?*" Ali mimicked.

"Stupid, still," Noor would say, but in the presence of Ali she was calmed and didn't throw her crayons and crumpled papers at the parrot cage.

"Your Nanijaan," Ali said. "She loves you very much. Do you know that when you were born, she made the mithai herself? I'd never tasted such gulab jamuns. Nanijaan is very sick. One day, meri jaan, she'll be gone."

"I'll go with her."

Noor, her eyes brimming with tears, held on to her grandfather's arm.

"You're special," Ali said.

"Adel is special—he's fastest bowler. Farooq is special—he's got braces. I'm special—my ears are very small, my fingertips are very long and I draw very nicely. You like parrots?" Noor asked.

"I love you," Ali answered.

"Nana, I can draw you a flower?"

"Please."

"Nanijaan will never comb my hair again."

"Your mother will."

꠱

At dinner one rare evening when everyone planned to eat together, Ali was seated at the table, Noor to one side of him, Hussein on the other. The boys were playing with their walkie-talkies, shouting into them as if they were at two ends of the house.

"Talk softly," Ali said. "Otherwise the enemy will hear you."

"He is my enemy," Adel said pointing to his brother.

"Why are you talking to him if he's the enemy?" Ali inquired.

"I'm not," Adel insisted. "He's talking to me."

"Then turn it off," Ali said. "Save it for another time."

"Did you use walkie-talkies in the war?"

"Sometimes. We had a radio in our jeep. Mostly, we used that."

"What did you do there?"

"Oh, lots of things. We tried to keep the enemy behind our lines."

"Lines?"

"The area we occupied, I mean."

"How can you occupy your own country?" Adel asked. "What were you doing there, anyway?"

"Serving our country."

"But they didn't want your help."

"Right," Ali said quietly.

"Then why did you stay?"

"I didn't."

"Ammi brought you home," Noor interrupted. She was the only one among the children eating. She was eating cucumbers again, neat triangles, with rice in her own white-china bowl, which seemed from a distance to be already empty.

"Children," Sajida said, arriving at the table. "Start eating your food before it grows so cold the crows will eat it."

Ali stopped eating.

Black, ugly birds. They smelled death, followed it with a vengeance, as if it were life itself. The numbers were astounding. Where did they come from? Swirling groups, circling above, lower, and then landing, like a blanket on corpses. They'd beat death, sometimes, present for the last cough. It was worse when there were many. The crows came and like the dogs they were always there before the burying was done. Dogs were bold, they didn't always leave when the precious rocks were thrown, but the birds—rocks, sticks—they couldn't care less. They hovered, circled, like hawks ready to pounce on prey. The bathtub of mud. The sky was dark with clouds and rain and birds. Corpses smelled a putrid rotten immediately after death, and the crows, in that place, in those days, lived for the stench. Shit, semen, blood. Right. It was all the same then. All of it.

"So cold the crows will eat it?" Ali asked Sajida when the children left the dinner table.

"Where did you hear that?"

"I don't know. Nanijaan. Someone," Sajida said, finding that the longer Nanijaan lay in a coma, the more clipped her own conversation became.

"I've never heard that expression," Hussein said.

"Well, the children sit there and wait. Until the food is cold. Before they even start!" Sajida said.

"Crows don't wait, you know, until food gets cold," said Ali to Sajida.

"They don't? Always hungry, then?"

"Greedy. Do you know they smell?"

"Of what?"

"When they come, they come in swarms. Did you know that?"

ঌ

Late at night, Sajida would collapse next to Hussein for a few hours of sleep. When she closed her eyes, she tried not to picture Nanijaan slowly being consumed by an untreatable infection, swelling by the day, connected to tubes and wires. Instead, she imagined Nanijaan passing from this life into the next life magically depicted in Noor's drawing.

She shared this with Hussein one night, when he was running his fingers through her hair and letting them trail along the newly set lines of her face.

"No matter how much we love her, Noor does not know everything," Hussein said.

"She knew Nanijaan was going to die before we did."

"Rubbish. First of all, anyone might have made that guess had they seen us put Nanijaan in the car that morning, what with Nanijaan's age and all . . ."

"Noor saw?" Sajida asked.

"She was in the driveway. You didn't notice? Second of all, we don't know that Nanijaan is going to die. Besides, I think it's all good and well that Noor draws. She draws beautifully, in fact. Such details." Hussein recalled the Italian shoe she'd duplicated perfectly.

156

"But nothing but drawing and painting can't be good for her. Maybe we ought to have had a tutor for her. Did we ever talk about that? It's not too late. We could hire someone to give her singing lessons . . ."

"Haven't you heard her sing?" Sajida asked. It was not lost on her that Hussein, who'd once chosen to absent himself from his daughter for years, felt no shame at offering an assessment.

"Jani, I'm just saying," Hussein insisted. "Let's find something else for Noor to do." Although Hussein had reconciled himself to Noor's artwork and was no longer bothered by her galleries on the walls of the house, there was something about her talent that remained unsettling to him. Perhaps if she could be persuaded to sing, he thought, and then his reasoning was interrupted.

"Nanijaan is dying, Hussein," Sajida said steadily. "Can't you feel it?"

Because Sajida was convinced, she made lists of all the things to say to Nanijaan before she died. *Thank you for being my mother. Thank you for dyeing your hair black. Thank you for not killing Hussein that night.* Already, with Nanijaan firmly established in her bow before death, Sajida recognized that there were pieces, so many, of stories and lives that would forever after remain incomplete. *Who was the uncle buried next to the cousin at the back of the family plot? What did the aunt say when she discovered her husband deceived her? Was it "you dog" or "you donkey"? When did Ali start to play field hockey, really play field hockey, become so good? Can you remember the song you sang when we were sewing the razai? Were you born in Kasur or Lahore? What did it feel like when you buried your husband and knew you'd never be beaten again? Why do you think Aba brought me home?*

Nanijaan was Sajida's anchor in this world. Her illness nudged Sajida's bearings, set them aloft. Where there had been peaceful waters, there were currents now, left to right, right to left, swirling. And now Nanijaan was going, taking the anchor with her, leaving Sajida with nothing besides her own two feet to stand on. How, she asked Nanijaan in her dreams, how could she possibly manage?

The answer came shortly after Nanijaan died and Sajida fell into a sleep so deep that Noor's wailing could not wake her. *You must concentrate on the good*, Nanijaan answered in a dream filled with oranges and yellows and neon blues, colors of the parrots drained and mixed in buckets.

The good? As if there was any in a life without Nanijaan.

When Nanijaan died, Ali smelled a bouquet of perfume rising from her body. He stood at the foot of her bed and let the familiar cloud absorb him. He knew it immediately. It was the peppermint-tangerine-almond oil of his childhood, the oil massaged into Nanijaan's bruised skin after his father's beatings.

৯

It took Sajida a while to find assurance of good in her life after Nanijaan died. Her husband, loving as he'd again become, had never been and would never be her anchor. Her children, two of this world and one of another, had found their own bearings, grown their own roots. Even Noor. So grown, so sure, so true. And then there was Ali. The man who'd saved her from the road, wide open like a river. The good in that? There was an answer. She should have asked Nanijaan. Dear sweet Nanijaan. Who hadn't deserved to die swollen like a whale, puss dribbling from her eyes. At thirty-six, God's will was terrifying. It knocked you from your feet and left you speechless. The same as when she was fiveandsix.

In the dream that set it right, Nanijaan came to her. Her embrace immense and all-surrounding. Sajida was lying down and Nanijaan's arms, no longer swollen, wrapped around her, cradling her like a baby. Nanijaan rocked her, as Sajida had done for her children, one after the other, over and over again, night after night, when they were smaller than her arms and later, when they were so much bigger. And when the dream passed, when Sajida awoke reclining in an easy chair, her legs stretched out on an ottoman, she closed her eyes and longed, with all her might, to be rocked again, as in her dream.

When Hussein, shattered and broken himself by Nanijaan's death, said, "Just tell me what I can do for you, Saji," Sajida said nothing. No longer an ache, but still real, the fact that he had left her once had forever sealed a part of her from him. How could she possibly tell her husband? That what she most wanted, no, what she needed, was for him to put his arms around her, hold her like she was, in fact, the meaning of life, and rock her. Slowly. Back and forth. And back and forth. For a minute. That's what it would take. How could she possibly, ever, say this, only this, to him?

Sorayya Khan

eleven

In the months that followed, Sajida succumbed to her grief.
When the boys left for school in the morning, she returned to her bed and hid underneath a pile of Nanijaan's razais, indifferent to the stifling summer heat. Ali, who had yet to return to work, brought her meals on a tray. Hussein curtailed his visits to his bottling factory to spend more time at home and fulfill the obligations Sajida surrendered. He drove the boys to school in the morning and to extra tutorials in the afternoon as they prepared for exams. He gave the cook permission to decide on his own menu in the afternoon. He paid the house staff their monthly salaries by asking them what they were owed, and gave the driver extra money to do the grocery shopping.

One afternoon, the cook drove his bicycle into the ditch while on a quick run to the neighborhood bazaar for Noor's special chips. Hussein took him to the doctor for X-rays and helped wrap his arm in a sling to keep the swelling down. Then, believing Noor would be ravenous because of the delay, he went to the bazaar to fetch the chips. On the way home, he stopped at a mithai shop and although the barfi was not the best in town, he bought the silver-flecked rectangles packed in the gleaming boxes Noor and Sajida loved.

Noor took the chips and sweets behind the curtain which separated her parents' alcove and narrow bed from the room beyond. She sat on the edge of the bed where Sajida lay, breaking the barfi in her fingers, putting crumbs between her mother's lips while she slept. When Sajida felt her daughter's fingers near her mouth and the taste of sugar inside it, she awoke from her slumber. The sweets tantalized her taste buds and as she sat up in bed and devoured the barfi, piece after piece, she suddenly longed not only for sweets, but for an elaborate meal: hot chicken curry and dal garnished with fresh chilies and brilliant coriander, steaming chawal, side dishes of okra and spinach, and her favorite tamarind chutney.

A few hours later, wide awake, Sajida sat at the lunch table laden with all Noor had suggested to the cook and more. Immersed in the aroma of garlic, onions and ginger rising from the food, Sajida made an admission to herself. There was strength to be found, she'd suddenly recognized, in not crumpling up and dying when Nanijaan did. She dipped an expert wrap of phulka and okra between her fingers into the tamarind chutney. The fact that she lived, when she supposed she might not, gave her the strength to embrace her life again.

"I'm so glad you're feeling better," Ali said with a wide grin as Sajida ate.

"Why aren't you at work?" Sajida asked him, only just noticing.

"Because of me," Noor answered for him.

Sajida looked at Noor, who continued to take tiny bites from the slowly shrinking piece of barfi in her hands. "Of course, meri jaan," Sajida said, understanding that Ali had stayed home to care for Noor. "Because of you."

و

Sajida would later swear that Noor drew with closed eyes that morning. It was an autumn day and Sajida pulled a lawn chair into the courtyard to be close to Noor. Time seemed to have taken on a different, unhurried quality for Sajida since Nanijaan's death. She wanted, even more than before, to savor everything about her children—the way they laughed and teased her, how they gazed into the distance when they were deep in their own thoughts, what they looked like when they slept. All the while, Sajida studied them for traces of Nanijaan in the hope that in a gesture or a word, a part of her remained alive.

The sweeper used a watering can to fill the parrots' water dishes through the bars of the wrought-iron cages. He brought Noor water jars for her paintbrushes, and after an hour, as was his habit, replaced them with fresh ones. But Noor's water stayed clean, her brushes hidden at the bottom of her orange bucket.

While Sajida watched, Noor took several pieces of blank paper and folded them into tiny squares. She cut her squares carefully with heavy sewing scissors. Lying on the marble, propped on her elbows with her stiff leg extending behind her, she worked with colored pens and sketched pictures Sajida could not see into the squares.

The sun rose higher and higher into the Islamabad sky until Noor was bathed in a sharp glare that made it impossible for Sajida to continue watching. Instead, she settled more deeply into the lawn chair and listened while her daughter's hand rubbed against the little squares, and above, parrots flapped their wings in the swaying cages and a few single, lost feathers floated to the ground. Sajida tried to imagine what her daughter might be detailing in squares, little and precise, but could not think of what it might be.

When Noor finished, she put the squares, one by one, in a careful stack. Using a thick needle recovered from Nanijaan's sewing box and a piece of old yarn, she sewed together one end of the stack to make a binding. Sajida almost took the needle away from her, but reminded herself that Noor was no longer a child and, more importantly, that even if she did prick her finger, Noor would feel no pain. Sajida offered to help Noor as she struggled to push the needle through the papers, but Noor, immersed in the task at hand, didn't acknowledge her until the booklet, neat and trim, was tightly bound. Just as Noor was about to hand the booklet to Sajida, they were interrupted by the boys. Reluctantly, Sajida left to tend to them.

Ali was still showing houses when Noor rose from the marble slab. She pulled a ribbon from her hair and tied the booklet with it. Standing by the front door, almost underneath one of her earliest paintings, Noor sucked her fingers and waited for her grandfather to return home. When at last Ali arrived, she thrust her booklet into his hand.

"What's this?" Ali asked as he examined the package.

"*Tasveeren,*" Noor said, *pictures.*

"So small?" he asked.

Ali made a show of untying the ribbon, his lips pursed to say what he always did, whether Noor's drawing was a flower, a bird, a mango, a boat, or anything else. Ali opened the booklet one page at a time. Noor snatched it from his hands, bent it back, and let it flip open, page by page scraping underneath her manicured fingernails. A camouflaged jeep bounced on a road before veering off, and tumbling over, the driver lying in his blood in the middle of the road. His passenger, in fatigues, a rifle to his side, bent down to tend to him. The shock of what he saw caused Ali's ears to ring.

The words *wonderful work*, Ali's standard compliment for Noor's work, almost fell from his mouth. Ali stopped himself before the driver was thrown from the jeep. Instead, he mustered a smile and a *thank you* for Noor. In his room, he took off his socks and put on sandals. He washed his hands in his bathroom and recalled Nanijaan's dismay that the room, like so many others in the house, faced the Margalla Hills but hardly offered a view. He slapped water on his face. With a towel around his neck, sitting on his bed where Noor already sat, he found the courage to work the flipbook the way Noor had showed him.

"You know," he said very seriously. "You're an *artiste*."

"I'm big," she answered.

"How did you learn to do this?" Ali asked, waving the booklet.

Noor shrugged.

"Where did you *see* this picture?" Ali urgently inquired, as if Noor had drawn a picture rather than a scene. He was fully aware that Noor could not possibly have witnessed such a thing in the confines of her life in Islamabad.

"In Adel's book or Farooq's?" he asked, continuing with a string of questions.

"Or in a magazine?" he asked, unable to come up with more possibilities.

"It's from one of your brother's videos?"

Noor stood, shaking her head, no, at each question, giggling.

"From the road," she finally said, bouncing up and down. "High like a hill."

It was her description that stopped Ali cold. Ali stared at his granddaughter. The girl, now twelve, was less round than she had been when she was younger. Her dupatta, which had been her idea to make a standard part of her clothes, expertly hung across her shoulders. She had an adult gaze that only seemed to grow in strength every year. Ali looked into her beautiful eyes, trying to imagine the thoughts and feelings lost in the bigness of them.

There was no other way to describe it: the roads *were* high like hills. East Pakistan was the only place where he'd seen roads raised from the ground in long strings of narrow hills. He'd been twenty-three when he'd seen the roads and only a few days older before he was scrambling up and down them in fear of his life.

The roads were raised. They were the only elevations in the fucking flat land. Living here, at the foothill of these great mountains, you can't imagine if you try. The only elevations. If you were to fall in the countryside, you would be surrounded, 360 degrees, by flat fields. The only rises are the roads, built above the fields to protect the corridors from the rain and floods. We built those roads, you know. More money was spent after Partition building their roads than ours. People riding on the land could be picked out in daylight from a mile away. There was no cover anywhere. We were target practice for them. Dead, we rolled—like their pineapples—down the slopes. Our blood and guts fertilized their fields. The land was already so rich, I wonder what it looks like now. We paraded the country like naked idiots. Do you know what that's like?

Noor, sweet little Noor, who hardly ever set foot outside the house, had drawn a perfect picture of an army vehicle and claimed it came from roads which existed a thousand miles away in a place she'd never seen. Noor was still jumping up and down like a young child on his bed, her dupatta falling from her shoulders and her glass bangles jingling on her wrists. Trying to escape the sinking feeling fast overcoming him, he jumped on the bed and joined her. By the time Noor tired of her game, the feeling translated into a short, disturbing question for Ali. What else did Noor know?

౨

As much as Ali missed Nanijaan, without her, at fifty-two, he finally felt grown. Not that war hadn't aged him enough. But without Nanijaan to remind him that he was a son, Ali imagined himself truly his own person. No longer oscillating between his roles of father and son, he was free to devote himself with renewed energy to being a father—and the sweetest progression thereof—a grandfather.

Ali understood it was the children who gave him peace. The boys, growing wide shoulders and big hands, absorbed in their studies and friends, suddenly appeared older than their sixteen and fourteen years. Looking at them, Ali dared to wonder what kind of fathers they would be. Kind, he imagined, and smiled when he envisioned that they might have many children between them. *You only have to look at them*, he thought, *to know their futures were courting them.*

Noor, simpler, was more special yet. When Ali sat with her, the pictures and memories inside his head came to a standstill. He'd loved how, when he was young, strenuous exercising made his world slow down until, in slow and intricate frames, it was comprehensible. Sitting in Noor's presence was much like that now. One morning, when her broken orange bucket lay to her side, Ali had the presence of mind to include her in his healing.

"Do you know what war is?" Ali asked, her flipbook in his pocket.

"Angry," Noor replied.

"Did you know I was in one?"

"You were angry?"

"I suppose," Ali said, unable to remember what he'd felt then besides fear.

"At Bingos?" Noor asked.

"Bingos?"

"Bengalis. Like Ammi, right?"

"I told you that?" Ali said, forgetting that he had explained the term two years earlier.

"The driver had a name?" Noor asked suddenly, as if she could see her work in Ali's pocket.

"Khalid," Ali answered.

"He wasn't a Bingo?" Noor asked.

"No."

"But what did you do in the war?" Noor persisted, playing with the cracked plastic of her bucket.

"Fight people."

"Why?"

Ali couldn't remember. He wasn't certain that, in the beginning, he'd needed or even had a reason to go to war. He'd rushed into it, an adventure of a lifetime. Now, he wasn't certain any of the things he'd been told—except the facts about the Indians—had ever rung true to him. That Bengalis, dark and stupid, not *really* Muslims, didn't deserve their own country, their own leaders. What he did remember had an order to it, like fact books on formations. After he landed in East Pakistan at the Dhaka airport, it took one day before he asked himself, *this is my country?*, another day to know he wasn't fighting the war *for* his country, another day yet to realize he wasn't fighting for Nanijaan or, for that matter, any family. On the fourth day he felt like a mercenary.

What he could remember was that almost immediately after his feet touched the lush ground in East Pakistan and he heard the language, soft, jumbled and unfamiliar, he longed for home. The safety, the certainty, the love. In the end, he'd fought and killed for an unremarkable reason: to save himself.

"Why can't you remember, Nana?" Noor asked impatiently. "You were there!"

"Yes," Ali said without answering her question. "I was there."

Ali took Noor's flipbook and put it on his desk. He spent the night sitting in front of it, running his fingers over the lines his granddaughter had sketched with a pen, where she'd filled in the patterns on the jeep with shades of green and brown. The jeep's tracks were unevenly covered with mud. It had been like that in April's rainy season, and it made Ali's job almost impossible. He could neither recall where he'd been then nor remember the date, and he consoled himself that such technicalities were not meaningful. Although Noor's drawings were tacked to the walls of the house (and pasted on the outside walls in summer before the rains came), Ali cleared space for Noor's flipbook in the first drawer of his desk. It sat there, gently curling along the edges her pens hadn't reached.

A few days later, Ali stumbled into the courtyard later than usual, having fallen asleep just as the day was breaking. The boys were already in school and Noor was planted in front of the parrots' cages. Each year, when the parrots molted, Noor was transfixed by the birds shedding their plumes and the bottom of their cages rising with feathers of all colors and lengths. Ali had often explained to Noor that the shedding and renewal process was not haphazard. The same feathers on each wing molted together so that the birds could maintain balance. *Otherwise*, Ali had said many times, *the birds couldn't fly.* The explanations never made sense to Noor, but every molting season, she empathized with the birds who, she worried, were shedding necessary parts of themselves. Ali watched her convey her sympathy to the birds by trying to sing them songs which had once been sung to her. She sang them as a medley, unable to keep verses of various songs separate. The resulting blend was a mad mix of off-key tunes and tempos that appeared, Ali thought thankfully, not to trouble the parrots.

"Nana," Noor called. "Another drawing?"

"No, meri jaan," Ali said. "You take a break."

"Flowers? Lilies, like my bed?"

"You work too hard," Ali insisted.

"A car, again?"

"No," Ali said quickly. "Flower, please."

"Pink? Yellow?"

"Both," Ali replied, and set off to get his cup of morning tea. Nearing the kitchen, Ali ran into Sajida who'd just dropped the boys at school.

"Good morning, Aba," Sajida said, accepting that day, as she had every day since he'd found her, her father's embrace.

After two cups of tea and toast with malai, Ali decided not to go to the office. He called his office and asked that his appointments be cancelled for the day. Ali showered and shaved, choosing a loose kurta pajama to wear instead of the usual shirt and trousers that were his office suit.

A few hours later, Ali knocked on Sajida's bedroom door. Inside, he sat on the marriage bed he'd paid for, as far away as possible from the piles of clothes sprouting on the bed cover.

"Why don't you get someone to do that for you?" Ali asked, watching Sajida fold laundry, mostly white underwear and boys' socks.

"It's easier for me to do it. I know where it all goes," Sajida replied reaching into one of the laundry baskets.

After a few minutes, Ali cleared his throat and addressed Sajida again. He spoke in a tone reserved for serious chats, although he couldn't recall when they'd last shared a conversation worthy of that tone.

Unexpectedly and for the first time, Ali asked Sajida, simply, what she remembered.

"The day I picked you up from the street," Ali said slowly and carefully. "What do you remember?"

"Sorry?" Sajida said, not making sense of her father's question. She was examining two socks that appeared a match, keeping a trained eye on the open door beyond where Noor ran in dangerously tight circles around the parrot cages in the courtyard.

"Before you came here," he said. "Do you remember when I picked you up from the street?"

"You mean before coming to Islamabad? From Dhaka?" Sajida asked. Then she recited, word for word, almost a poem, what Ali had told her when she was a child. "You saw me. You found me. You took me. Right?" Satisfied that the socks were a match, she put them next to Adel's pile of undershirts.

"Do you remember the color of the truck, what was in it?"

Sajida needed a moment. There *was* a truck in her memory. Near the pyramid of thirty-six oil drums, on the curb of a road wide like a river, there was a truck. It sped so close to her that it ran over the end of her dupatta. The truck kicked up dust and gravel and she'd wiped her face, still holding the heavy iron rod in her hand.

"Pipes," she said, recalling what Ali had once told her. "And the truck was blue," she said, making a guess.

"It was green, Saji, green. Do you remember the jeeps? Army ones?"

"I rode in one once," she recalled. "It was white. A blue flag hung from it. There were others, army ones, but I don't remember them very well. Camouflage paint?"

"The bumpers, of the jeep we rode in, do you remember them? The jeep had doors? What did the license plate look like? Was there a step on the driver's side? Treads on the tires. The noise they made?"

Ali threw out the questions one by one, as if he didn't know the answers. The events of that day so many years ago when he took Sajida from the side of the road were so clear to him they might have happened yesterday. But he wanted Sajida to share what she knew, suspecting that if she put it into words, something important might be laid to rest.

While Sajida thought about what he'd asked, Ali remembered.

The person who had driven the jeep that day was Ali's senior by a few months. They pulled to the side of the road to stop for cigarettes.

He paid for them. Ali watched him put money on the counter. But he'd also flashed his pistol in daylight and Ali remembered his own worry: he might still be killed before getting to the airport.

The child was a few yards ahead of where Ali sat in his jeep. Her kurta, far too big, hung off her shoulders, revealing one of her shoulder blades. Her hair, black and blue at the same time, swirled down her back in a thick plait. She held a rod in her hand and moved it back and forth as her plait danced to the rhythm across her back. The girl sat hunched, half on the curb and half not, her back rounded, and from that angle, with heat rising in waves from the road, it was impossible to know how old she might have been.

Without knowing why, Ali opened his door, walked a few steps and picked her up. She was dry. In the suffocating heat of summer, the child's clothes were not damp with perspiration. In his weakened state, still recovering from typhoid, reaching for the child and lifting her, his hands virtually on her bottom, made Ali dizzy. He set her in the back of the car, putting her down roughly, wanting to take his hands from her quickly. He closed the door after he checked that her kurta was not hanging outside.

As they began to drive, the officer opened his window for a moment. The hot outside air mixed with his cigarette smoke. The child's kurta slipped down her front: collar bones poked out as did the tiniest buds of nipples Ali had ever seen. The girl continued to look at him, as unaware as any child of her nakedness.

"Where are your parents?" Ali asked in the broken Bengali he'd learned.

They drove through the city, circling one roundabout after another in which, one day, remnants of the war they were living would be memorialized.

The child said she'd lost her family in the cyclone, and Ali's companion interrupted.

"That's what's wrong with Bingos," he said. "Always trying to make us feel sorry for them. So they have floods, cyclones. Lazy bastards. Can't do a thing by themselves. So they blame us."

She looked directly at Ali, without seeing, he thought, but the quality in her eyes, the unwavering directness, gave him pause. *Why wasn't she afraid?*

Ali made his decision. He would take her home.

The same day, hours later, they boarded the cargo flight together, a C-130 packed with people as if they were cattle. He asked her name while she cried, engines roaring in their ears. He heard her say, "Sajida."

At the time, he'd believed his intention was to help the child. But as the years passed and he'd had more and more time to consider his actions, he knew he'd done it, not for her, but for himself. In the shape of the child crouched over a curb in downtown Dhaka, Ali imagined making amends, atoning. Taking the child home, making her his daughter, Ali worried that in pretending to save her, he remained what he wanted, so badly, no longer to be. Ali preferred not to focus on this. He pushed these thoughts farther and farther away, trying to concentrate on the daughter he'd raised and the beautiful children she'd made, rather than scrutinizing his intentions that hot day on the side of the road.

Sajida was still considering the barrage of Ali's questions. The bumper, doors, license plate, steps, treads. She didn't have any answers for him, but she didn't tell him that.

"Tell me why, Aba," she finally said, putting down the next pair of socks and turning to him. Standing, she was taller than her father. "You don't remember? You've forgotten? How long were you there, anyway?"

And, with those words, Sajida began a conversation which Ali had not imagined having with his daughter.

"Eight months. I rode in jeeps," Ali spoke slowly. "Who told Noor?" He took Noor's flipbook from inside his kurta and flipped it in his hands.

Sajida took a step closer and examined Noor's booklet in Ali's hand. She saw a jeep on a bumpy road and was almost relieved at the simplicity of Noor's new drawings. Suddenly, and quite unexpectedly, she heard her mother's voice, the *Bismillah* from so long ago, the one that had met and then been swallowed by the wall of water.

"You mean your jeeps looked like *that?*" Sajida said, stretching her hand to stop the flipping pages. To her, Noor's jeeps looked like exaggerated versions of her son's Matchbox cars. Outside, Noor ran the handle of some paintbrushes against the parrots' cages, but neither Ali nor Sajida noticed the racket.

"Just a minute," Sajida said. "You drove them?"

"I had drivers."

"More than one?"

"Yes."

"Why?"

"They'd die," he added. "See?" he said, opening the last page of Noor's flipbook. Then he left the room with it.

Khalid, the first, died from one bullet. It was the most merciful killing I saw although I didn't know that then. The bullet went in and out of his chest and the windshield cracked. The car ran off the road. There wasn't time to tend to him. The gunfire was too close. I pushed him to the passenger side and took the wheel myself. There didn't seem to be a lot of blood, but when we got to base the seat had turned brown. The batsman couldn't get rid of the stains. After that, I sat on the stains. He died the first day he drove for me. He had four children, all small. Their names rhymed, someone said. All girls. Samina. Safiya. Sakina. Names like that, maybe. His body went home. When his widow saw him, she said it wasn't him. In death, he had a look on his face that wasn't recognizable. Fear. But nothing in the world could scare him, she insisted, not meeting the enemy or meeting his Creator. Some asshole had shaved his beard and that must have confused her as well. His family never did claim him. He was buried by a sergeant who took pity on him. In Pindi. I don't know where. I'd visit his grave if I knew.

৯

Sajida lay down between the piles of folded laundry on the bed and rested her head against the wooden lilies of the headboard. She closed her eyes and tried to clear her head. For the first time, she had a need to string together, like laundry on a clothesline, the snippets of what she'd known, long ago, of her father's war. Not what she knew now (*hands tied together*, among other things), but what she'd known then. She didn't so much as pause. She was certain that as a child she'd known of the war.

She recalled that when she'd been in Nanijaan's house for a few months, someone pulled an atlas from a shelf and let her absorb the shape of the country. *Wings*, she thought to herself, *it's a set of wings!* The only fact that disturbed her image of a bird in flight was that Nanijaan kept pointing to the body, an upside down triangle in between, and giving it its own name: India. Nanijaan identified other countries in the area as well, many of which Sajida had never heard before. Each country corresponded with one shape on the map and it confused Sajida enough to ask why Pakistan, in its east and west wings, was two. Ali was not in the room at the time. Nanijaan, who'd never seen the borders of her country with her own eyes, merely replied that as far as she knew, long before Sajida was born, the borders had been drawn quickly and carelessly like lines in a child's drawing.

"Not yours, though," she'd said, patting Sajida on her head where her hair was carefully parted before being pulled into the long, black plaits that ran down her back.

Some days later, Ali studied the atlas and gave the east wing, where she'd once lived on an imperceptible edge at the mercy of the ocean, another name. *Bangladesh* was comprehensible. Sajida had not been gone so long that she couldn't comprehend that Bangladesh, simply translated, meant home for Bengalis. Sajida recognized that the bird she'd first believed she'd seen in the jagged map hadn't been that at all. It hadn't even had a body or the good sense to hold on to what belonged to it. As time passed, she recognized those moments with the atlas as her first geography lessons.

That December, when the war was lost, Sajida knew that Ali had fought in it, but not because he ever said so. She knew, instead, because of the black and white television and the metal antennae that sat on top of it. She loved the television when she arrived at her new home and she would watch it for entire evenings sitting on the sofa between Ali and Nanijaan. Generally, Ali watched the nightly television news without comment. But she remembered the one time he rose from his armchair. He stood in front of the television, almost touching the screen, when a photograph of a bombing run at Dhaka airport was being shown. At Sajida's prodding, Nanijaan repeated the newscaster's description of what they were seeing. An airman, perched next to an aircraft, interrupted in his preparations, had lain on top of the pilot to protect him. In the bombing run, the airman died, not the pilot. Ali ran his fingers alongside the man's shoulders. Sajida remembered Ali's hand lingering in the static of the television screen, as if he were touching someone he'd known.

"He's Aba's friend?" Sajida had asked Nanijaan, but Nanijaan shook her head, no, explaining that Ali had also fought in that war but he'd returned home early.

The formal war, those few, official days in December, was not completely lost on the city of Islamabad. Roadside trenches were dug in scattered places. Drapes and blinds were drawn tightly at night and chics, the cotton and bamboo exterior shades meant to protect houses against the summer sun, were unrolled at night to prevent

any scrap of light from being seen by Indian aircraft which, every so
often, hovered above the mountains in Pakistani airspace. Sleeping
next to Nanijaan, Sajida heard the airplanes. But after escaping the
cyclone, a threat as distant to her as airplanes flying miles high in the
sky was hardly worth considering. She dug her head into her pillow
and, on the instructions her mother announced to her in dreams, she
thanked God for sparing her life in the cyclone. But giving thanks
like that made her feel guilty. Her family had not been as lucky as
she, and thanking God in her prayers made her dwell on the lopsid-
edness of what had happened.

Sajida remembered, then, that at fiveandsix she'd been saddened
to consider that God behaved in random ways.

Sajida's conversation with Ali stayed with her. She wasn't immediately bothered by the jeeps Ali had ridden in or the drivers who had died
or the flipbook Noor had made depicting all this. But speaking with
her father about that morning long ago had sharpened her memories. The open road, the truck, the holes in her dupatta. *You saw me.
You found me. You took me.* After their conversation, her memories
had a different feel to them which Sajida tried to comprehend.

At breakfast the next morning, before they were joined by the
children, Sajida spoke to Hussein.

"I'm from somewhere else, really," Sajida said to Hussein, stating
the obvious.

"What do you mean?" he replied.

"You know, I'm not from here." Sajida, sitting next to Hussein,
marked where she meant with her stockinged foot on the floor of the
dining room.

"Don't be silly, Saji, I know that."

"I'm from somewhere else," she said again, and Hussein looked
up from the newspaper.

"Do you know the name of the place?" he asked.

"Village." Sajida shrugged. "I can't remember."

"Perhaps we could find out. You'd like to visit? I can arrange it. We can go together."

"Don't be silly, I'm not going anywhere. It was by the water. We used to walk on the beach. My father was a fisherman. I told you this?"

It was strange for Sajida to say these things. The images she'd had in her head for so many years suddenly became real. The sand, water, boats. The hut, *or was it a house?*, she suddenly wondered. Over the years, her impression of where she'd come from had faded to almost nothing. In Pakistan, as far as she could tell, the only evidence of Bangladesh, what had been East Pakistan, lay in her children's geography books and in the unfinished house at the end of a nearby street that had, by now, all but gone to rot.

"What kind of fish do they have there?" Hussein asked.

"On a lucky day, the nets were full."

"You'd keep some?"

"That's how we ate."

"He cleaned the fish?"

"I did."

"We never eat fish here," Hussein said looking around. "We could get some. I can put in an order at the new market. They'd get it for us. Fish curry—I've had that in Karachi. It's very good."

"I don't like fish," Sajida said.

"To try, I mean."

"No. Thank you," Sajida replied. She began buttering the toast in the basket for the boys who were just arriving at the table.

That night, Sajida shook Hussein awake.

"What do you think," Sajida asked forcefully, "what do you think Aba did in the war?"

"He helped with the inventory of bridges. He told me that a long time ago," Hussein said, rolling over to face her in the dark.

"What does that mean?"

"He went where bridges had been destroyed, inventoried what was left over, and shifted the parts to storage locations. In case anything could be used again."

"What else did he do?"

"Whatever else they did," Hussein said, tugging at the sheet.

"You think, maybe, he killed someone?"

"I don't know," Hussein responded, shaking his head. "What does it matter? The war's been over for years. Forget about it."

"Maybe I should ask Aba." Sajida said after a moment.

"Don't," Hussein said quickly. "It isn't respectful."

"Why not?"

"You don't have the right. It's not your business. For God's sake, Saji, he's your father!"

"Not really, you know," Sajida answered in a small, hushed voice.

twelve

Noor worked alone. Her drawing, almost a photograph, was in pencil on heavy paper. A cluster of troops stood in messy rows. Hands at their sides, their attention was directed ahead to the unseen presence addressing them. Afternoon shadows fell on their khakis, making for pants in varying shades of drabness. Berets sat on the tops of heads, slanted as they were meant, to the side. One officer was drawn in more detail than the others. He stood in the front row. He was tall, his shoulders broad, his feet slightly farther apart, his uniform wrinkled in uneven creases. The expression on his face was firm with anticipation. One hand at his side was a fist, the other open and flexed in preparation for a salute.

Noor put the drawing in a silver frame from Nanijaan's room. She leaned it against a vase on the dining room table, not far from where the gallery of her paintings had begun.

Hussein saw it first. He picked up the frame, cold to the touch. The drawing was different and, in a flash of clarity, Hussein saw why he'd never been especially keen on Noor's drawings. He understood

Noor's previous drawings to be mere suggestions, but he'd always feared, he realized, that she might one day take to recording facts. Her latest drawing was exactly that. It was evidence of what Ali had been: a soldier in uniform. Although this fact was not a secret, Hussein suspected that Noor, *so different*, might have access to secrets yet to be revealed. He was certain that there were truths, buried or forgotten, that were best left untouched in Ali's past. But Hussein hadn't known how to say this without alarming Sajida when he spoke to her about Ali and his war.

Hussein was determined not to focus on his own past, the harsh facts of how he'd once abandoned his wife and daughter. It was best that way. Hussein knew Sajida's kindness and generosity afforded him such a luxury, and for this, among other things, he would always be indebted to her. He'd accepted his destiny in Noor—even if it had taken him years—and he'd resolved to live his life looking forward rather than backward. The frame slipped from Hussein's hands, and when he picked it up again, the glass was slightly cracked and the frame was dented. Hussein took the damaged frame into the lounge and placed it in Ali's lap.

Without looking at the picture, Ali spoke to Hussein. "Bad habit of yours, breaking frames," he said. They both knew Ali was alluding to the day, years earlier, when Hussein had intentionally stumbled on empty picture frames Ali had stacked for Noor.

"It's you?" Hussein asked, pointing to an officer in the front row.

"I suppose," Ali said, studying it. Treating it as if it were a photograph from a holiday trip, rather than one of Noor's still lifes, he added, "Now, where would I have been?"

Interrupted by calls for lunch, the men didn't have a chance to finish their conversation.

Sajida came across the drawing next. It lay on the side table next to the chair where Ali had left it. So accustomed to labeling her daughter's drawings, the first thing she thought was, *t* for troops.

Where? she suddenly wondered. Although the pencil drawing was black and white with the shadings of a pencil tip in between, Sajida saw the men standing against a background of blue. The clear sky fell into a foaming sea behind the troops, a sea so immense it could raise itself at any moment and erase land and light the same. She could hear the sound of the ocean, gentle at first, and then loud and unforgiving as she had heard it last. One man's face stood out. He was young and confident, steady with his gaze. *I know him,* she thought, suddenly frightened at seeing him how he'd once been. *Aba.*

The part of the drawing that now held Sajida's attention had gone unnoticed by Hussein. Ali wore knee-high boots. Along with the others, he stood in ankle-deep mud, a shifting plane of mire dried to a thick slush. Somehow, Sajida knew that Ali had, at least once, stood in mud that seeped into his socks and clothes and the hidden crevices of his then young body. Holding the frame to her face, Sajida could almost taste it: mud in Bengal was a nauseous mixture of dung, salt, and clay. As if she could smell it, she set it down, away from where she stood. She propped the frame against the lamp on the side table near Ali's easy chair and walked away. There it remained until the following day when Sajida and Ali were in the room alone.

Ali looked at the drawing again. The light from the lamp bounced off the glass in the frame, mimicking daylight in East Pakistan. There, the light was always sharp, even when overcast, and rather than illuminate targets it obscured them. Ali saw the mud this time, and as he sat on his chair, his feet resting on a stool, he could still feel the difficult surface beneath his boots. Thirty years later, instinctively, he cursed how willingly it gave.

Attempting to keep his memories at bay, Ali began to wonder where he might hang Noor's drawing. Would it be *b* for Bengal or *m* for its mud or what, in the end, was demanded from them: *s* for surrender?

I was with Nanijaan during the surrender, five months after I re-
turned home. In the last days—the official war—the Indians fought
alongside the Bengalis. We all heard when Pakistani soldiers were
rounded up in East Pakistan. Some were stripped, locked in cages.
But they would have seen their enemy, their black faces, their short
bodies and the Indians, uniformed and bold, standing tall. There
you are! I can hear them saying. They were directed to walk on
mines they'd planted themselves. I can see it. Limbs flying through
the air, different-sized torsos torn open, showering blood and guts.
No, I wasn't there. I know because I saw something like that once
during a bombing run. Had it been the other way round, if we'd
finally won a war against the Indians, we'd have done the same.
Anything goes. I'd bet my life on that. War is war, after all. You
know that, right?

Leaning his head against the chair, Ali accepted that these conversations, if that is what such snippets were, were one-sided. Of course,
Ali thought, he was speaking to himself. He'd been having these conversations inside his head since he'd returned from East Pakistan.
In the beginning, he'd meant to pack it all away. But when whiffs
of stories rose like a stench from the file cabinets inside his head,
he discovered that the only way to force the birds from the sky, return the details to where they had come from, was to put them into
words—to himself—and then return the memories to their drawers.
But the words were always wrong, lacking. They were never quite the
memories, the sounds and smells, sharp and crystal clear. The mother
shaking, begging for the life of her child. The child whimpering. The
smell of a mother's milk: sweet. She: wet, cut open, on the desk. The
river, rushing reds mixing with slower silt, separate streams of color
at first and then not.

With Noor's framed drawing between them, Sajida spoke. Her
voice trembled as it never did.

When she asked, when the question sat in front of Ali, he looked at it: the words, the emphasis, the question mark. *Could it be?* he wondered. Had he been practicing all those years? Rehearsing the stories, making them right?

Sajida asked again, and when she did, he knew he'd been waiting for it.

"What *was* it like? There?" she asked.

After a pause, he opened his arms, parentheses around her question, and answered, "Green."

"In the summer, too?"

"Always."

"What was it like for you, though?"

"Adventure. First time on an airplane."

"You didn't know you were going to war?"

"No," Ali said and laughed, remembering Nanijaan and her predictions. "We were back here for the real war, those few days in December."

"When you went, you didn't know what was happening?"

Ali shook his head. "You know, meri jaan, I was scared of the dark when I was small. I slept with a flashlight underneath my pillow. Nanijaan tried to get me to stop. She told me to use my head, instead. *Imagine the sun*, she'd say. It didn't work for monsters or gunfire."

"Like when?"

"Let's see," Ali said, considering what he should say next. "The first night in Dhaka, I patrolled the dark streets. I heard gunfire and moving bodies. I could hardly breathe, I was so afraid. I was twenty-three, you understand," Ali added, apologizing to his daughter for his fear. "Someone shot at me. He missed. I dove behind a rickshaw."

"That's when you knew? How big the trouble was?"

"Well, I was on the airplane still, the first time it really occurred to me there might be something wrong. A commercial flight. DC-8, I think. I got my rifle and bullets in Karachi and after many hours, after flying around India instead of across, because of the airspace ban, we tried to land in Dhaka but we couldn't. We went to Sri Lanka, where we waited on board for twenty-four hours before taking off again. While we waited, I wondered. What on earth could be happening in Dhaka that we couldn't land? When we finally got there, rubber from the plane's tires marked the tarmac. It stank."

The cook interrupted Ali.

"*Khana laga doon?*" he asked, inquiring whether to put lunch on the table.

"What was happening anyway?" Sajida asked Ali, ignoring the cook.

"War," Ali answered. "But never mind about that. It was a long time ago. You were very small, remember?"

Afterwards, Sajida was reminded of her own secret.

Even if Ali hadn't said anything specific, he'd offered Sajida a different glimpse of himself. She couldn't imagine him afraid. It was a bit like imagining him lost in a crowd. As her father, he'd always seemed strong, fearless. Months earlier, when Hussein had confided that Ali stumbled as Nanijaan's body was lowered into her grave, Sajida was forced to think of the obvious. In addition to being her father, Ali was Nanijaan's son. Likewise, when Ali allowed that he'd been afraid during the war, that he'd been shot at, she was given the space to think of him slightly differently. She wondered how fear manifested itself in her father. Did he cry? Shake? Run?

Imagining her father, she once more considered the secret she'd kept from Hussein. Intermittently, during the thirteen years of Noor's life, Sajida felt remorse at what she sometimes thought of as her deception. She'd consoled herself with the belief that Hussein would never have accepted her version of what had happened the night Noor was conceived. But she sometimes felt as if she ought to have given him a chance. If only for herself, anyway, she thought, she really ought to have spoken. After speaking to Ali, however, she felt she had a responsibility to let Hussein into the one event of their life she'd kept from him.

The night after Ali and Sajida spoke with Noor's drawing lodged between them, Sajida was slow to get ready for bed. She brushed her hair one hundred strokes, leaned forward to let it fall into a long curtain, and then did it again. She filed her toenails and rubbed lotion into the dry skin on her feet. She poured herself a glass of water from the thermos next to the bed and wiped a trace of dust from the books beside it.

Then, Sajida spoke.

"I knew about Noor," she said.

"What?" Hussein said.

"Before she was born. I knew the night she was conceived. I knew she would be special. I knew she would be different."

"You knew?" Hussein asked, confused.

"I dreamed it," Sajida added by way of explanation. She sat next to him on their narrow bed while Noor slept in their marriage bed beyond the curtain. "I think."

Hussein looked at the woman who'd been his wife through three children and almost eighteen years of marriage. He recalled a detail of their surreptitious meetings in the Margalla Hills before they were married. They'd parked their cars pointing down toward the city of Islamabad, which unfolded like a planner's blueprint from where they sat on boulders perched high above. Below, the main sector avenues ran like airport runways and cut the city into now unimaginably precise rectangles. Hussein couldn't remember the last time he'd been in the hills. Sitting close to him, the hennaed streaks in Sajida's hair were easily visible where her strands of gray became orange during her monthly hairdresser appointments.

"Ah," Hussein said and smiled.

"But I knew!" Sajida insisted. "I could have warned you about her. The way she'd look. The things she'd do."

"You knew she would draw?"

"Oh, no. I didn't know that."

"Even if I'd had the dream myself, it wouldn't have mattered," Hussein said.

"You'd have had more time. The same nine months I had to get used to having a different child. Who knows? You might have loved her right away," Sajida said softly, offering a thought she'd had so often in the months after Noor was born and Hussein—she granted him this—had struggled to love the baby.

"No," Hussein said, after a while. "Impossible."

"Many times," Sajida said. "Many times I meant to tell you, before you left, I meant to tell you . . ."

"Forget it," Hussein said, brushing wisps of hair from her face with his fingers. "You sound like you're apologizing. Don't do that. Please," he whispered. He was aware that when it came to apologies, his had been the tardiest—that evening when he filled her bedroom with all the plucked flowers he and his servants could find in Islamabad.

"Good thing, after all those years, you came to your senses," Sajida said, only half mocking.

"Good thing," Hussein repeated and took his wife into his arms.

৯

In the two days before Sajida and Ali were alone, again, Ali remembered. Noor's drawing, most definitely, was of April. They were dressed in boots in anticipation of the first monsoon of the year.

Only a few weeks had passed since the day in March when Dhaka had been overcome by his army and death hung like a cloud in the air. When he heard, Ali was grateful to have been spared. He was on assignment miles away on a shallow river bank looking for salvageable materials among remnants of a narrow bridge. Ali remembered another detail. Noor had drawn a shaded plane of mud on which they stood. It was black and rich with the promise of life. But the ground Ali recalled standing on in knee-high boots was far softer than the flatness Noor's pencil suggested. Something else was wrong with the drawing. The ground, which gave and gave, was not black.

Until then, I hadn't believed that death was the problem. But rotted, piled, and dumped in mud, it suddenly was.

On the return trip to the barracks, my ears rang and I couldn't hear the others. Worse, I didn't care. I sat in the front of a jeep. When it was my turn to stand, I stood watch and saw nothing. We were on the road later than anticipated, and our convoy of jeeps completed the journey without encountering so much as sniper fire. If I'd still believed, I would have said, "By the grace of God."

Back in the presence of my superior officer, after a shower and a change into fresh clothes, my ears stopped ringing. In the makeshift office, I offered estimates for the people buried.

"Forty-three," I said, only accounting for the already decaying corpses intended for the mass grave.

I predicted most had been dead more than a day, maybe as many as three or four.

"How many days? One, three, or four?" the officer asked.

You know, in the camaraderie of war, once in a while, rank falls away? "Planning on death certificates?" I asked, and we both laughed.

Each time he passed Noor's drawing, Ali paused to study it. He searched for details, hints of who he'd once been. He saw himself standing at attention, prepared to follow orders. He was little more than a child, and it shocked Ali to realize he'd been only a bit older than Adel. As he contemplated his first grandson, he grimaced, trying to recall why he'd wanted to go to war. He could no longer remember what he'd felt when his cousin-bride had died and he'd imagined running full-speed into a life that was unscripted and abounding with possibility.

In the middle of the day, Sajida and Ali crossed paths in the courtyard. The boys were in school. Hussein was attending to a breakdown of machinery at the factory. Noor was in the kitchen seeing to it that shortcuts were not taken in Nanijaan's recipes for the lunch vegetable pulao. One of the servants was cleaning the parrots' cages, talking to the birds as he wiped the cages with a wet rag and refilled water bowls.

"Why did you come home?" Sajida asked him, picking up the thread of their conversation as if it had not been interrupted.

Noor's drawing alive in his head, Ali answered immediately.

"A bathtub of mud sent me running," he joked, chuckling to himself, not realizing which drawer inside his head he was about to empty for his daughter to see.

Sajida could not think of bathtubs without thinking of Noor. She recalled the endless days and nights she'd spent with Noor, long ago, alone in her bathroom, when Noor's cries could only be comforted by the steady sound of running water filling the tub.

"What do you mean?" Sajida inquired.

Ali began. He had been given orders to direct a convoy of a dozen soldiers to a remote spot south of where he was stationed. The soldiers were part of a cleanup crew, he was told, and Ali was asked to accompany them because he'd been near that spot a few weeks earlier on another assignment. The roads were less dangerous than others, better traveled, and in the midst of flat, unforested land, they were almost, unbelievably, covered on one side with trees.

"You remember?" Ali asked Sajida. "Not so many trees in East Pakistan?"

"Where?" Sajida spoke, picturing a different landscape, a road lined with trees and a UN jeep rushing over it, a river on one side, rice fields on the other.

Besides, Ali went on without answering her, the enemy was yet to grow as bold as it would soon become, which left the roads quiet, at least on that day.

While they drove, they took turns standing on their seats, surveying for attacks. It was like a mime, Ali explained, watching those of lesser rank than he sit and stand. East Pakistan was becoming something like that: being there and not being there at the same time. More often than not, he felt himself removed, as if he were watching himself do what needed to be done. He imagined this came from not believing in the war, not believing he was fighting it for his mother, his family, his country.

"Nanijaan, you know, was a smart woman. She knew what awaited me before I got there."

The jeeps arrived at the appointed station without incident. The stench was thick and putrid. Soldiers held handkerchiefs over their mouths. A pile of bloated corpses lay at the edge of a shallow, sunken pit. Ali realized that he'd been ordered to assist in the digging of a mass grave for enemies.

"Enemies? Mass grave?" Sajida whispered.

Ali oversaw the unloading of shovels and pickaxes. Others were there already, working ahead. He talked to the drivers of the jeeps. They were allowed a few minutes to offer prayers. Ali didn't pray. Although he was yet to abandon God, he preferred to pray in solitude, except when he was burying someone. Then he stood next to others, if there were others, to offer namaaz-e-janazah, funeral prayers, for it was his duty to respect the soul of the dead. He'd never said so many as in the last months.

"War is war, I'd say to myself, standing graveside, reciting prayers. People die. Study war," Ali said gesturing to Sajida. "History, great battles fought and lost or fought and won, right? In all of them. People die. War is war. You understand?"

Sajida didn't, but she continued to listen.

After prayers, Ali and the young soldiers carrying their tools on their backs made their way up ahead, toward the stench. Ali didn't think much of the assignment. Digging graves was something he'd become good at, although he'd never done something so big before. He didn't mind death too much. It was just another reminder of what he was not. He was not dark or small like the Bengalis ("No disrespect meant, meri jaan," he said to Sajida), and he did not eat fish. He was not dead like the bodies he buried. Which made him alive.

Right there, Ali thought to stop. To end the conversation, stand, leave the room. But his daughter's anticipation was tangible, almost a spell, and after all the years of silence, it was impossible to break free. He cleared his throat. It was too late. When he spoke again, his chin trembled.

The pit was already dug. It was wide. Deeper than what he'd seen. But not empty. Soldiers, the ones who were already there, were knee deep and further in it, still digging. The earth, black, fertile as it was, yielded easily. Ali listened. Shovels hitting the earth. *Aagh.* Men grunting. Scooping up the earth. *Thump.* Falling over their shoulders onto higher ground. Phlegm coughed up and spat out. The army had done that for Ali, sharpened his senses. It was one of the things he would remember most clearly about the war. Forever on the edge of what he might see or hear or smell.

Surveying the work, Ali realized that the pit was not deep enough. Who'd been in charge? They hadn't dug deep enough or measured accurately enough or, as far as he could tell, done this much before. Those who'd already been working for hours were tired, the pit unevenly dug. And where were the stones? Nobody had thought to gather a pile of stones and put them near the pit. Ali had learned that early on. No digging unless the stones were right there.

Otherwise, someone had told him, *your work will go to hell.*

Either that, Ali had thought to himself, *or to the dogs. Same thing.*

Suddenly, it was raining. In a matter of minutes, the earth was soaked. The April rain drowned what it touched, giving life, as he would discover, to mosquitoes in sizes he'd never imagined. Stingers, they'd call them. The bandana around his neck was wet with dirt and sweat from the drive, but then his shirt and pants were soaked as well, and the sky, a low blanket for as far as he could see, poured water as if from taps.

"For the first time," Ali said to Sajida, "I wanted to take my clothes off, too. All of them." Then he added, "Of course children dance in the monsoons! Why wouldn't they?"

Waves of heat, a fog, rose from the baking ground as it drank the rain. The soldiers kept at it. Their movements were cumbersome, the soaked earth too heavy for them to do a good job. The piles of dirt thrown over their shoulders slid back into the pit with the rain. The rain came down harder and harder all the time, and the pit was becoming a filthy pond.

In desperation, some of the soldiers scrambled to complete the assigned work. From the pile, corpses were being moved. *Wait*, two or three of them shouted, their pleas overrun by the rain. One after the other, corpses—some with their hands tied together—were being thrown and pulled into the pit. The soldiers continued to dig. The earth, dripping, was only getting heavier.

It was too late to stop the corpses from being pulled into the pit. Ali jumped into the pit and set to work. The shovel, heavy even without a load, shifting in his grip. He worked as fast as he could.

Before long, he was just another soldier struggling to move his share of dirt. It was mud now, sliding, slipping, from his shovel and everyone else's.

Before Ali or Sajida realized it, Noor was standing beside them. She smiled at her mother and grandfather, her teeth white against lips wet with what Sajida knew was a tinge of lip gloss.

"Remember, Nana! *We* danced in the rain!" she said. She stood on a chair and lightly tapped Sajida's head in the rhythm of imaginary raindrops. She skipped to her marble and threw her head toward the sky the way she and her grandfather had one summer, years earlier, celebrated the arrival of the monsoons in Islamabad late in July.

Startled, Sajida stood up and reached for Ali. "Come," she said. She led him from the courtyard to the driveway where the rusted cement mixer which had twisted Noor's leg still stood.

"Ammi!" Noor called after them. Noor stopped where the driveway dipped into the road at the edge of the imaginary line, the border she'd set for herself. Sajida pulled Ali's arm. They crossed into the road, leaving Noor and Ali's Sector behind.

They walked slowly, and sometimes Sajida had to remind herself to take a step. She remembered Nanijaan, then, the halting nature of her last strolls and Nanijaan's explanation: she wasn't in a hurry anymore. As Ali continued to speak, Sajida knew what she had meant. Ali's words, sometimes little more than a whisper, were difficult to make out at first above the sounds of bicycle bells and car horns, the chants of newspaper and bottle collectors, and the calls of shopkeepers in fruit stalls lining the road. Sajida was in no rush to know. But the longer they walked, the more powerful Sajida's need to hear Ali grew. Finally, the sounds around them fell away, until, in hushed silence, there remained only Sajida, Ali, and the story he was recounting.

The mud pit filled with rain, corpses, and soldiers with shovels. In the distance, hidden by the fog of rising heat, a lone group of Bengalis was making its way toward the pit. They walked along a path swelling with water and mud. They approached the pit from the opposite side from where the jeeps had come. They walked slowly, unable to keep their legs steady, tripping over each other as if they were blinded. The jeeps were parked on one side of the pit, the soldiers inside attempting to keep watch during the downpour. Eventually, the approaching group came into view. A driver honked his horn to alert the command, and a gunman on one of the jeeps fitted with a rifle held his position below a plastic poncho, a slippery finger on the trigger, his eye on a blurred lens.

A tremendous thunderclap exploded above. The group staggered forward through the soaked and shifting ground, clothes plastered against their bodies. Behind them was a child. She ran after them, finding her way on her short legs in the mud without falling. The gunmen on the jeeps swung guns to keep pace with the group and then the child. Everything, it was understood, was a potential danger in this war. Especially children who appeared from nowhere to throw grenades. Some soldiers, on the perimeter of the pit, stood with their hands on their guns and tried to make their way through the drenching rain toward the staggering group. They shouted at the group to stop, but their calls drowned in the roar of the rain.

Inside the pit, along with Ali, soldiers were weighed down in the thick mud. Some struggled to rise, sloth-like, from the pit they'd dug. They held their shovels in one hand and tried to protect their rifles with the other. Ammunition belts hung over their shoulders and were reduced to ripples in the mud.

The group staggered out of the fog at the edge of the pit. Ali and the other soldiers who witnessed its arrival, froze with surprise—what all of them had been most stringently counseled against in their training. Ragged, angry shouts rose between the noises of thunder as the people in the group grew suddenly frantic, moving much more quickly, making their way around the edge of the pit to the diminishing pile of rotting corpses on the side.

As Ali spoke, he remembered that the rain was like beating drums, the mud was shit, the fog a dream.

"How could we have known?" Ali said.

A soldier outside the pit, possibly from one of the jeeps, pulled the trigger on his rifle. Then, Ali recalled, they all seemed to follow suit.

Why? He didn't know. His body took over. There was no explanation.

"Honestly," he whispered to Sajida.

Removed, again, he watched himself. He pulled his trigger. He wasn't the first or the last, but he did it nonetheless. He aimed ahead, into chaos, where some of the Bengalis stood at the rim of the pit.

"Screaming, sobbing," Ali recalled the scene for Sajida. "And, all I knew was I might die," Ali said.

It was impossible to see. Rain pelted in currents to the ground. Almost night. Sounds of rapid gunfire. Ali watched as lightning dissolved the crowd of Bengalis into people. Shot, they fell, one by one, from the edge. They landed in the rising pit, swimming with soldiers and rotting corpses. The fresh bodies sank, but the decaying, stiff corpses, *frozen* is all Ali could think, floated. Ali didn't see the stinking corpses, eyes and tongues pecked clean by crows, really *see* them, their skin stretched beyond compare, until they were pitted against the newly dying and drowning.

Ali noted the slow dance that transpired before his very eyes. Corpses rose, lifted by rising bubbles of mud as bodies landed and sank beside them. Before long, a singular red spread slowly in the pit. The striking color glistened like oil paint in the rain-made twilight. Later, in the open jeep, the wind dried the mud on their own bodies and Ali watched as they shed slivers of pinkish red from their uniforms into the wind.

Even as he spoke to Sajida, thirty years later, unable to convey how gracefully the dance of death was choreographed that war afternoon, the first day of the short monsoons, he needed a moment before he could continue.

"Nothing," Ali said to Sajida, "but a bathtub of death." Remembering what he had seen, he added, "No place for a child."

There was a child in the pit, tugging on the dead as if they were alive. She pulled a corpse by its foot, long and thin amidst the swells of death, and it moved. Ali hadn't thought it possible to move a body, fixed, folded into the earth.

"How old could she have been?" Ali asked Sajida and waved his hand low to the ground, marking an imaginary height.

Her head was barely higher than the mud in which she stood. She turned, with ferocity, to another body which almost fell on top of her. Managing to make a path for herself and the body, she whipped her fists in the mud with a frenzy that would have shamed the soldiers with their shovels, had they taken note of her accomplishment. Just as the girl arrived at the side of the pit, but before the head of the body emerged, she abandoned her efforts. The corpse sank further into the mud. The little girl shouted a name.

"Mukhtiar," Ali said, remembering it for its familiarity and ugliness. "Who would name anyone such a . . . throatache of a name?"

The child disappeared.

Eventually, the rain ended. Streaks of yellow light shone through a break in the clouds. After sunset, but before the darkness of true night, in that solitary hour, the soldiers rediscovered a rhythm. They helped each other out of the pit using shovels and, finally, standing above the pit, they threw the last of the corpses into it. Exhausted, they shoveled mud into the pit. In the jumbled nature of the war they fought, when night fell, they left the job unfinished, climbed into their jeeps and returned to their base.

"That's how I came home," Ali said to Sajida. They were sitting on a bench in an open space behind the neighborhood bazaar. The bench was all there was in what had once been intended to be a sector park. Aware he'd spoken too much and concerned by what he'd revealed, he finished abruptly. "I got typhoid from that stinking hole and they sent me home." Then he crossed his arms over his waist and waited.

The two of them, the faint sounds of the city growing audible again, a soft breeze carrying the aromas of frying chilies and cumin from the bazaar into the air, sat in silence for a few moments. Sajida bit the insides of her cheeks. Listening to Ali's story was like being on the airplane that day as a child, transported, lurching in the air, her stomach never quite in sync with the rest of her. When Ali had described the child in the pit of corpses, Sajida felt as if she couldn't breathe.

"There *were* trees there," Sajida finally said. "In East Pakistan."

Inexplicably, she heard her mother, a garbled voice, still from the bottom of an ocean. *Bismillah.*

"You're certain . . ." Sajida asked, finding courage, "of that name?"

"Tell me, beti, how can one bloody forget a name like that?" Ali responded. He looked at his daughter, the blue in her hair, her delicate collarbones making knobs against her thin kurta. He picked up her hand and studied her palm, running a thumb over her lines. Her hands, neither soft nor rough, reminded him of Nanijaan's.

"Goddamned war," Ali mumbled.

There was a cavity inside him. He'd climbed out of the mud and taken the pit home with him. It was as deep as the boots he'd worn when he stood thigh-deep in the mass grave. It was a sinking hole forever filling with muck, the stink of it, the frozen stiffness of bloated, rotting corpses, the soft sound of bullets hitting live flesh in stinging rain. He'd done his level best to fill it with the ready-made family he'd had the fortune to make. Because of them, he hadn't drowned in the rising, bubbling mud. But exposing it to Sajida made it perfectly clear: what he had done, what he had seen, what had, in

196

fact, been the war, would go on happening inside of him for as long as he lived.

"The girl . . ." Sajida said, taking her hand from her father. She spoke quietly. Ali leaned his ear toward her face to hear her words. "That name. Mukhtiar. He was her baby brother."

"Pardon me?" Ali asked and hiccupped.

"I," Sajida said, the realization coming to her in the pause between her words, "was there."

৯

The remainder of Sajida's day passed in a haze. She checked on lunch and dinner preparations in the kitchen, she made out a grocery list for the cook and driver, she greeted Hussein when he returned for lunch, and after the boys were home she remembered to set out with afternoon tea a gift of sweets Hussein's business associate had brought from Europe. She watched in wonder as her sons complained that the Belgian chocolate already had a white film on it, although it hadn't been refrigerated for more than a few days. The boys gave their share to Noor, who wrapped the chocolates in a tissue with a hair ribbon and tried to give them to Sajida.

Hussein did not come home that night. He was at the factory dealing with another machinery breakdown on the eve of when a special order of bottles was due. After the gate and outside doors were bolted, Sajida took her evening bath and retired, wrapped in a shawl, to the only place in Ali's Sector where she thought she might find air. She climbed the stairs to Nanijaan's ledge, a place that hadn't been used for years. She settled on the chair which hadn't been cleaned in as long, without noticing the dirt or the slight puddles of rain.

Bathtub of mud, she heard her father say. As his story had unfolded, the pictures in her mind became so vivid she could see the pit he was describing, including details he didn't share, the mud smoothly sliding from the ledge down the sides to the bottom. The pit was twice a school bus, deeper than the inflatable swimming pool she'd bought for the children years ago in which Hussein had waded through the lukewarm water. There was, Sajida knew, a distinct feel to the earth and monsoons over there, an uncommon tinge to the mud. In this land where she was now, where the ground shifted only when tremors ran far, far below, she'd almost forgotten. How, she thought incredulously, could this be?

If she tried, she knew, she could conjure a trace of the dead.

Sajida was squeezed between two old men. The one in front of her was hit first by a bullet from behind and he fell over the side. The second one, to whom she clung, stood behind her. He was also hit from behind and when he fell he took her with him. She plunged into the filling mud pit, smothered by the weight of the old man and pulled down further by the suction of shifting mud below. When she thought her lungs would explode, she broke through the surface to gulp at the thick, putrid air. The mud was inside her cheeks, high in her nostrils, deep in her ears, her eyes, her mouth, her throat, between her teeth, her legs, her toes. She choked on the mud and, simultaneously, she vomited.

The rain fell in sheets, mud sprayed as corpses and bodies fell around her. She almost expected her father, lost in ocean water, to miraculously rise from the sea of mud. She tugged at one corpse and then another and pulled it a short length. She looked up. A body, open-mouthed, fell on top of her. Teeth struck her head, and she was sucked deep into the swirling mud. Before she was swallowed, she shouted her baby brother's name, *Mukhtiar*. Slapping at the mud, she imagined that she had become him. She was in a cyclone. She was being swept from the arms of an older sister into the loud and blinding sea.

The next thing she remembered was the Land Rover taking her away from the camps, a foreign relief worker putting a tin of sugar biscuits into her hands, and the city, Dhaka, miles away, whitewashed buildings and wide streets. In a language she couldn't comprehend, bolstered by wild gesturing, she learned from relief workers that only she had been pulled from the mud to safety. A few weeks later, a man picked her up from the roadside: Ali made her his.

After absorbing Ali's account, Sajida speculated that she'd sunk, unconscious, in the mud. Miraculously, she'd been spared. By being almost dead, by the cover of the thick mud in which she'd almost drowned, by the rain that blinded everything, and afterwards, by careless, hurried soldiers.

She tried to imagine her father holding a gun. She couldn't. *What would it have been? A rifle? How big, how heavy?* She didn't recall seeing the shots fired. She heard them, soft, as they hit. *Oh, but the mud.* Falling into it, sinking further and further into the suffocating thickness. *That*, she would always remember.

Little did he know, Sajida thought. Even if Ali hadn't stopped on the Dhaka road, wide like a river, that hot, dry, early morning on the way to the airport, the two of them would have been forever joined by a pit of mud at the beginning of the monsoons in a land more than a thousand miles removed from the shadows of the Margalla Hills, where the two of them—and Nanijaan—became family.

Sajida concentrated on the facts. Once, her father had been a soldier. In those nine months, he'd killed. He hadn't wanted to, she insisted to herself. *War is war*, he'd said.

Sajida considered the story of her beginning. She recognized it was different now from the one she'd carried with her since she was the girl of fiveandsix. First came the cyclone, she repeated to herself, and then, a few months later, the swirling pit of war.

"Right," she muttered to herself, pulling her shawl more tightly around her head and shoulders. *That was how it had been.*

With that thought, she carefully raised herself from Nanijaan's chair. She heard the parrots below and the voices of her sons carrying from inside the house. Standing, she arched her back and searched the night for the outline of the quiet Margallas. Descending Nani-jaan's spiraling stairs, her grip firm on the railing, she prepared to set aside the facts as they might have been. Ali, her father, might once have lifted his rifle and blindly aimed in a torrent of rain and rising waves of heated fog—and shot her dead.

thirteen

Inside the room that Sajida, Hussein, and Noor shared, Noor sat on a low wooden stool in front of the corner full-length mirror, observing the particulars of her face. She ran her graceful fingers along her hairline, her ears, her eyelashes, and the light fuzz of hair on the farthest edges of her cheeks. The drawers of the dressing table stood open, their emptied contents lying in a heap to one side of her. There were lipsticks and nail polish, eye shadow and eye pencils, and an array of cosmetic brushes, some still wrapped in plastic sleeves, which Sajida had collected over the years. In its own pile were hair wax strips, eyelash curlers, tweezers, overnight creams in smoky bottles, foundation and powder blush. In front of Noor sat a new paint box of primary colors and a mug of water filled with paintbrushes of different sizes.

Noor started to mix colors on the new palette Hussein had bought her. She mixed and remixed combinations of blue, red, yellow, and brown, washing the palette in the bathroom sink each time she decided to begin again. When she found the right balance of color, she thickened the mixture by adding some of Sajida's powders, a bit of red blush and blue eye shadow, scratching the round cosmetic plates with her fingernail until powder fell onto her palette. Finally, she opened a tube of glitter Sajida reserved for special occasions to dab on her cheekbones and the edges of her eyelids.

With her eyes half closed, in front of a mirror that captured her reflection and more, Noor painted herself. She dipped her paint-brushes, one in each hand, each of different thickness, into the mixture on her palette. She ran them over her jet black hair, knowing exactly where to begin on her hairline and where to end at the full tips of her thick hair. She worked methodically, beginning on one side and working her way to the other. When she finished with her hair, she dug into Sajida's pile of cosmetics and applied lip liner, lipsticks, blush, kohl, eye shadow, and lastly, the special glitter.

When Noor sat down to paint herself, she hadn't had a plan. But when she saw herself in the mirror, she noted, with pleasure, what had become true: she'd transformed herself into a doll. The purple sheen in her hair, the reds, blacks, and browns on her face, the glitter on the slant of her eyes, all of it suggested she had been plucked from a shelf in a toy store. Noor observed herself from every angle, tipping her chin this way and that, rotating her head from side to side. She gathered her thick hair into a loose knot near her neck.

She settled on the low wooden chair, and when she was ready, her head began to gently sway, as if to an invisible pulse of music. Gradually, in slow waves, her body began to move, from her shoul-ders to her arms, her chin to her neck, the heel of her foot to the toe, her good leg to her other one, and then, finally, into her hips, until she stood, in utter submission to her own private dance.

Some time later, when Sajida opened the door, she faced Noor's back. In the mirror's reflection, she watched as an adolescent girl of thirteen with curves of her own hovered above a wooden chair in the corner of the room. The girl seemed to float in her movements, her hand rising ever so slowly in the air until the arc stopped on her painted lips. She moved close to the floor as if some tremendous emotion did not permit her to stand or sit. Her long hair, an electric combination of oranges and pinks, was thick like a rope and the knot waved gently over one shoulder and then the other. The girl's color was dark like Sajida's, she had a flat nose bridged by oddly slanted eyes, and her perfectly sculpted miniature ears appeared as if they were meant for a far younger child. The girl's white teeth seemed too big for her mouth, yet the crowded rectangles fit one after another in an impeccable row of white. Her wrists ended in pudgy bracelets, like those of a healthy baby.

The scene was vaguely familiar to Sajida, as if she'd seen the barest of its outlines once before, as if it were an apparition transformed into life.

Suddenly, the suspended girl focused her attention on Sajida. Noor picked up the mug of water no longer filled with paintbrushes. The velvet texture of her big black eyes poured into the plea that followed. Noor threw the mug into the mirror with all her force and called out in the high-pitched voice of a young child registering an urgent, all-consuming need for her mother, "Ammi!"

The sound of the word, the fact of it, made Sajida's sight blur. As it had in her vision the night Noor was conceived, it appeared to be the utterance itself that caused Noor and the small stool to dissolve like pieces of a scattered puzzle into sheer darkness. The shards of glass finished falling and the mirror lay broken in thousands of pieces. Sajida stumbled across the room, tripping over the wooden stool, caught by her daughter who, underneath her paints, was still soft and round.

Hussein and Ali found them that way: Noor and Sajida covered in paint and glitter, lipstick, nail polish, and more, standing amidst the remains of the full-length mirror. Mother and daughter watched astonishment spread across Hussein's face. When a sudden snort escaped his lips, his fright returned Noor and Sajida to the moment. Clutching each other, first by their hands and then their shoulders and arms, they shrieked with laughter, gasping for air, until they ached so much they collapsed on the floor and fell on top of each other. His hand still on the door knob, Hussein saw what had always been: Sajida holding on *for dear life!* to the child who was hers.

Outside, the wrought-iron cages swayed in the courtyard. Almost dusk, the parrots began their calls, *keeak-keeak, tooi? tooi?, chee-chee-chee.* Ali entered the bedroom. Gently, he pushed Hussein aside. He moved to where his child and grandchild lay tangled in a giddy embrace. Upon reaching them, he stood perfectly still. Then, as if he'd never stopped believing, as if he'd never known otherwise, he dropped to his knees the way Noor surrendered to her marble slab and paints every morning.

Prostrating before his ready-made family, his forearms touching the sides of his folded legs, he rested his left cheek on the floor. He took in the sight of his child and granddaughter. His eyes roamed, then settled, above.

The moan, deep and immense, rose gradually. It began in Ali's belly. It rode through his strained vocal chords and gaping throat. It hurled out of his mouth stretched wide like the dead buffalo's. The groan filled Ali's Sector like no other sound ever had. Noor pulled free of her mother. She covered her perfectly sculpted, miniature ears with the heels of her beautiful hands. Still on the floor, Sajida leaned towards her father. Stretching, she locked her arms with his.

૭ ૭ ૭

Acknowledgments

Douglas Unger, first and foremost.
All the people (I regret I cannot name) whom I
interviewed in Pakistan and Bangladesh during my research.
Lisa Loomis and Laura McNeal Rhoton.
Dawn Douglas Coker, Pat Dutt, Rebecca Thompson.
Omar Khan, Kamini Ramani, Ayesha Khan, and Ahsan Jamil.
Thera Khan and Munir Khan.
Kamal Naeem and Shahid Naeem.
Always, Naeem Inayatullah.

Glossary

aba	father, dad
Alhamdulillah	praise be to God
Allah	God
Allahu-akbar	God is Great
aloo ki bhujia	potato dish
ammi	mother, mom
bakra	goat
barfi	fudge-like sweet
bazaar	market
behen chod	a vulgar curse
beta or beti	son or daughter, an endearment
bevakuf	stupid
bharis	type of hut
bharta	smoked eggplant dish
biryani	rice dish
Bismillah	in the name of God
bister	bed
chaddar	shawl
chapattis	type of unleavened bread
charpai	cot
chaukidar	watchman
chawal	rice
dadi	grandmother
dal	lentil dish
dhobi	washerman or woman
dhuri	woven cotton rug

dupatta	scarf
Eid ul-Fitr	Islamic holiday that marks the end of Ramadan
ghazal	semi-classical song, lyrics in verse, in the North Indian tradition
ghee	clarified butter
gulab jamuns	confection
goonda	rogue
halwa	sweet
inshallah	God willing
jani	life, an endearment
kameez	long shirt
kalima	testament of Islam
kebab	burger
khana lagadoon	put food out
khuda ke liye	for God's sake
khussas	type of shoe
kurta	shirt
kurta pajama	shirt and pants
kutti	female dog
kya	what, question
laddus	sweet
larka	boy
lassi	yogurt drink
loadshedding	the practice of cutting power to certain lines when the demand surpasses the supply
malai	cream
meri jaan	my love, an endearment
mithai	sweet
namaaz-e-janazah	funeral prayers
nana	maternal grandfather
nanijaan	maternal grandmother, an endearment

nargis	narcissus
oloo ki pati	mild curse, literally child of an owl
pulao	rice dish
pallu	part of sari draped over shoulder
parathas	type of fried unleavened bread
phulka	another word for chappati
rani jaani	queen life, endearment
rasgulla	sweet
razai	quilt
rickshaw	three-wheeled vehicle
sari	traditional dress worn by women in many parts of South Asia
shalwar	pants
shalwar kameez	pants and shirt
tasbee	prayer beads
tasveeren	pictures
tota	parrot
vark	silver decorative paper for sweets
yaar	my friend, colloquial

An Interview with the Author

Cara Cilano

Sorayya Khan and I began this conversation in March of 2005, and it continued for months via e-mail. The extended nature of our exchange allowed both of us to consider each other's points at great length and even to revise our own questions and comments. Additionally, this conversation draws from presentations Khan gave to various audiences during her visit to the University of North Carolina Wilmington in March 2005.

Cilano: I'm curious if you agree with the assertion that, in the aftermath of war, fiction can help bring about a just remembrance and thus encourage a national healing. Why you would think that is possible or impossible?

Khan: I suppose it would be possible, particularly if you were putting together an anthology around Partition. That's what the framework could be. But it strikes me that fiction is not the only place where that could happen. And not necessarily the best place where it could happen, because look at what they did in South Africa with the Truth and Reconciliation Commission. That had nothing to do with fiction. People were asked to confess whatever it was that they had participated in and were granted immunity because of that. The idea is, with that sort of confession, that sort of testimony, the victims get to hear it also. The articulation of what's happened and the listening to it by the people who have been adversely affected—there's healing in that process. It's really direct. I'm not sure about fiction. I haven't thought about fiction in terms of contributing toward a process of healing. I think of it as a manifestation of testimony of pointing out where the silence is as opposed to doing the healing. But I suppose that pointing out the silences and acknowledging them is the first step.

CC: Do you think healing hinges upon the directness the immediacy of articulating one's deeds in front of the person who has been wronged, who has suffered? Is there something to be said about the moment when that happens?

SK: Well, the premise of that process is that if there is recognition on both sides of the crime that has been committed it's possible to move on. That's not the premise of fiction. With fiction, the premise is that the writer is inviting someone into her fictional world. Or, it's the reader who is inviting herself into a fictional world; I'm not even sure that it's the author who is doing the inviting. That's different.

CC: I view the narrative mode you've employed in your novel as realism. At the same time, Noor herself defies "reality." Were you seeing Noor as introducing a magical-realistic element?

SK: Someone asked Gabriel Garcia Marquez about his use of magical realism, and he responded that his work is absolutely and completely grounded in truth. There's not one thing in his books that comes from a fantastical source. People have said to me that there is a magical realism element in the novel *Noor*. But, I don't think about it like that because the realm of war is so beyond our imagination that, unless you've gone there, there's no way to understand how mad it is, how insane it is, how horrifying it is. The use of Noor is the introduction of a character whose head is different from our heads in that she is able to understand or able to see the horror and insanity of something that you and I might not be able to see. So, her mind can stretch and open in ways that ours can't. Due to that elasticity, she can see something that we can't in this realm, that we don't know what it is. I don't think of her as being magical. She just has access to something that we don't have access to. She's real in that way.

CC: She's not just an instrument through which Sajida, Ali, Nani-jaan, and Hussein grapple with their demons.

SK: Although, of course, she is a vehicle that makes all of this possible. Because she is a vehicle, the book is dependent upon her and her ability to do this. But, I don't think of her as a magical-realist element.

CC: That brings to mind questions about what's representable and what isn't representable. Noor's uniqueness manifests itself in her paintings and drawings. Aside from the last one, in which she draws her grandfather Ali, they are abstract paintings. While you write in a realist mode, the paintings do not adopt a realist mode. That's suggestive that there's part of the story that you wanted to convey in a transparent way so that we would trust what's going on. But then you give us these paintings that are refusing mimesis; we don't really know what their subject matter is.

SK: And it takes the character's interaction with the paintings to figure out what the representation is.

CC: Did that seem a way to address war atrocities—that there was no other way to contend with them?

SK: I don't think so. Maybe subconsciously I was thinking something like that. The book was written in many drafts. It was not originally the intention for each chapter to be based on a painting, which is the way, structurally, it ended up being. There was always a progression from paintings that were very abstract that she painted when she was one or two—the blues. They eventually progress in detail to where she's drawing her grandfather in military uniform, that last photograph-like picture. The purpose of the paintings and the reason why we're not told what they are when they're being described is because I wanted different characters to get different meanings from the paintings. I wanted that to be open so that Sajida could look at a painting and think one thing. Nanijaan could look at it and see something else. Hussein could look at it and see something else. The idea being that the secrets that they have inside their heads affect how they're seeing the world.

CC: Their interpretation is dependent upon what they're carrying around with them, independent of what they're interpreting?

SK: Exactly. Hussein recognizes his Italian shoe from that date, but we don't see that painting. It's entirely possible that if you and I looked at it, it would be something entirely different. Right? I wanted that possibility to be open. Although most likely that painting was of a shoe, if someone had looked at it, they might have seen something different. Somehow the paintings operate independently but in conjunction with the other ones. Noor's gallery is alphabetized. So, there's this order to them. Each painting fits in some place to produce a continuum of experience of life, of love, of death, of something.

CC: What's interesting is that this continuum is far from linear. The book is linear—you do have the italicized flashbacks and the filling of story here and there—but it is a very linear plot line. But Noor's paintings fill in here and there.

SK: That's a reflection of how children learn language. They don't learn language linearly at all. Their initial first words could be anything. But also, that's reflective of how memory works. When I settled upon the device of the paintings to structure the novel, I wanted the idea of memory as being nonlinear to come through even though the paintings have a progression. When Ali starts remembering what he's remembering, it's not in a linear fashion. It's moments he's remembering.

CC: Then he tries to piece together, to try to explain to himself and eventually to Sajida, what it meant.

SK: Also for Sajida, too. When she sees that painting with the buffalo, that's just one moment. It's not the first moment.

CC: How important is it, in terms of the potential ending of the book—it's not entirely clear if there's forgiveness and reconciliation—for Sajida to see that all of this has been constructed by Ali—how he found her, who he is to her, all of these things? She's experiencing a bit of an earthquake in her own identity. You've said you wanted to think about war "in the theater of the family." If there are tremors going through this family, how is that supposed to be instructive as we step back from the personal story of the family and try to think of how this is suggestive of the overlapping between the personal and political?

SK: The conclusion is supposed to be open-ended. All I know is that, probably, Noor wouldn't draw anymore. That's what I think had I written further. Because her work as an artist is done. Done in the sense that Sajida has the memory of the mud pit, and she recalls something that really defines her existence that was hidden from her. Now the choice is what to do. There are multiple possibilities. In terms of Sajida and the earthquake she's feeling, it is suggestive of the overlap between the personal and the political in the sense that the politics of what her father has done has finally come home to roost. Eventually, whatever it is you've done comes home to you in some fashion. That was the point of it. Now we don't know what she's going to do. Chances are that they're still in that house. What is she going to do anyway? It's not as though she has another home to go back to. Though maybe someday they'll take that trip to Bangladesh that Hussein suggests earlier in the book. There's interaction between the personal and the political all the time; we just don't know about it. Even if we think that our lives are not affected by the political realm, that in itself is an effect of the political realm. Here she's gone through her whole life not really understanding, not making the connection with what her father did in Bangladesh. Why is she where she is? There's suddenly this moment where she has to recognize that her personal life is tied to issues that are much larger than she is. Issues of nationhood.

CC: Say more about that.

SK: In a concrete way, her birth as a East Pakistani, as a Bengali, forces her to have to recognize that now that she is in [West] Pakistan. That moment is true, more real to her than ever before. Probably even more than when she came to West Pakistan, because at that age she probably had no conception.

CC: In *Noor*, there are no Western characters, and I appreciate some of this is due to historical circumstances. It's an interesting way of thinking about the dynamics of the subcontinent's colonial past.

SK: Actually, the first book I wrote was so large with so many things in it that I felt one of its problems was its scale. When I started to write *Noor*, it was an experiment. I wanted to see if I could write about one family in one geographic space. To see if I could define plot in a very small box, in Ali's Sector. The other stuff is not like that at all. There was no possibility of having foreigners come in; the life in *Noor* is completely different than life in anything else that I've written. I needed it to have a very clear perimeter.

CC: Is place-based-ness a move toward looking into the domestic? Is it a way to explore the personal and political things you've been talking about?

SK: It must be. I hadn't thought of that. Location is important to me. That's how I see, that's my lens. When I'm thinking about narrative, it springs from location. I'm not sure if the choice of location has to do with the desire to explore domesticity or the personal aspect of life in a confined way. Or to examine how the politics affect the personal in a confined situation. I'm not sure that that's how the scheme happened. Without location I couldn't write. I need that ground. It's a way of reclaiming my memory, a certain way of remembering what I saw. Ali's Sector—this is how Islamabad was built. It was very scripted. Initially. It didn't turn out that way because growth is uncontrollable; it's sprawl. Initially, the older sectors of Islamabad are built in exactly this sort of fashion, where a grid almost virtually put down on the land. You could go to a certain place in the Margalla Hills called Viewpoint. You can drive your car up to Viewpoint and you can look down. When we first moved to Islamabad, we would drive up to Viewpoint. You could look down at the two Seventh Avenues, which at that point, were the largest roads in the city, and they looked like airport runways going out of the city. That's what our life was circumscribed by. Now it's not like that at all. Now if you go up there the Seventh Avenues blend in with everything else. You have a hard time picking them out. It was all blocks and roads and numbers and sectors. The city itself is divided into sectors. You move from a point from where the Margalla Hills begin to where they just stretch out. Sectors are just lined against the hills.

CC: So you can really only return to the place in your mind because it's changed so much.

SK: Exactly, because it doesn't exist anymore. In those days, when we were kids, there was no traffic. It was uncongested. There were two or three sectors. The drive to school was forty-five minutes through barren land. Now there are sectors that go from "F" to "H" and "I" and "J" and "K." The school was in "I." Now it's built up the whole way.

CC: How did your interviews and conversations with both Pakistanis and Bangladeshis help you come up with your own narratives?

SK: The interviews I conducted were paramount in helping me come up with my narrative. But let me say that very little of the minutiae, the details of what I learned in those interviews, actually made it into my book. I approached the interviews in this way. I had a writing teacher, Douglas Unger (without whom I might never have taken the prospect of my writing fiction seriously), who stressed that the purpose of gathering information for a piece of fiction was about determining possibility. That is, it doesn't matter whether something is true or not in fiction, it only matters if it is possible. When I set about trying to figure out how to approach my research, I kept hearing his words. My goal was simple. If I could only get one soldier to tell me his story, talk to me about his fears and motivations, reveal to me who he was, then I'd know what was possible and could write a novel around this (which is very different than writing a novel *about* this). As it turned out, I found several people who were willing to share their stories with me. I "used" those narratives by thinking of them as trajectories around which my own character's possibilities might derive. So, the conversations I had with interviewees were essential to my writing. Without them, I would not and could not have written *Noor*.

CC: I'm interested in this distinction that you draw between "around" and "about."

SK: The information that I received in interviews provided me with a concrete understanding of events/incidents that had actually happened. I think of this chronicle as a collection of signposts or markers. For example, I was told of incidents where soldiers sometimes shot out of fear rather than because they were ordered to. I was provided with the understanding that this sort of behavior was possible, even likely. Subsequently, the scene where Ali is randomly shooting into the mud pit is made possible by the reality that soldiers shot out of fear. I wrote the scene "around" the information (the signposts or markers) relayed to me. I didn't write expressly "about" any of the incidents that were relayed to me, but the fact that the incidents had happened, made it possible for me to come up with a scene like that. This is what I mean when I say writing "around" the possibility.

CC: How does writing "around" anyone's experiences, particularly as it opens up countless and unexpected possibilities, offer space to the soldiers with whom you spoke, for instance, to self-invent or to fictionalize their own stories because they're relying on their memories?

SK: Writing "around" someone's experiences does open up countless and unexpected possibilities. When you ask how this offers space to the soldiers to self-invent or to fictionalize their own stories because they are relying on their memories, I'm not sure what you mean. I'm not sure if we're equating here the writing "around" and talking "about"? I suppose talking "about" is really talking "around." No one jumped up during my interviews to say they had raped—it was always in the context of others engaging in such activities (hence, talking "around").

During interviews, the subjects talk around their experiences because what they say is filtered not only by their memories, but also by what they feel comfortable revealing to me and to themselves. But for the purposes of my research, I had to take what they said at face value. Of course, they could have been making up stories, but I believed that if someone took the time to participate in an interview, it was because he wanted to give a voice to what had been happening inside of him all these years since the war rather than use the opportunity to make something up. Also, my most effective and useful interviews were group interviews where soldiers corrected each other in details and specifics, helping each other along if they could—and perhaps this was a way of checking themselves.

But perhaps you mean offering space to soldiers a bit differently. In regards to my work, the space they filled is the provision of markers, signposts, laying out of information I took to be true. In regards to the soldiers, my interviewing them offered them space to present their stories any way they wanted (assuming they wanted to—there were plenty whom I spoke to who declined to be interviewed). Specifically, with regard to the novel *Noor,* it is their presentation of stories that provided the possibilities around which I could write the story.

CC: You've expressed an interest in attempting to represent the unrepresentable or, to paraphrase your words more closely, to dispel with language the silences that are created by the stories that are told.

SK: Here I think I'd say I write "about" the silences. I mean this in a general sense—there being a distinction between the abstract notions of writing and the doing of it. My overall and abstract purpose/interest in writing *Noor* was to address the silence, to pinpoint it as something that is out there, that defines the history of '71 in Pakistan, the way we think about who we are, as a way of not taking responsibility for what's been done. It's in the doing of the writing (the mechanics—the details, the plot development, the structure, the story)—the writing "around" the soldiers' stories—that I'm writing "about" the silence.

CC: This interest seems to be another way to approach the idea of writing "around" rather than "about" insofar as it asks us to think about how the stories that the soldiers shared with you gave voice to certain aspects of their experiences that they were willing to make explicit (both to themselves and to you). Does writing "around" let you write in the gaps of what they said?

SK: I'd say it differently. I'd say that writing "around" allows me to guess at the gaps of what they said or, at a minimum, to explore them.

CC: How would you characterize the growing tradition of contemporary Pakistani writing?

SK: It's actually odd to think that I might fit into a tradition, although I don't have any problem being included as such. I think that quite clearly if I didn't have the heritage that I do have, I wouldn't be writing about Pakistan. Pakistan is a place where the personal and political are intricately woven together. People are interested in politics, even though they don't always have a say. My father belonged to a generation of people who fought for the right of independence, who rallied against the British. And most everyone in Pakistan of my age has a parent who was involved in the struggle in one way or another. Also, the act of Partition left millions dead, and there are countless stories about this reality as well; the shadow of those days hangs over us still. So there's a historical memory and political reality that binds us together. But I'm not sure that's what you're really asking. I don't know how to characterize this tradition. Except that it comprises a lot of people who've found their voices and want to vocalize their stories in a public way—and they all come from the same country, which means they've shared in some form or another something of what that means.

CC: I'm interested in hearing more, particularly with respect to the various languages in which Pakistani literature is written and to where the literature is written and/or published.

SK: I do think balance is important. In fact, it is wrong to characterize Pakistani writing as comprising only Pakistani-American or Pakistani-British writing because this ignores a whole crucial [element] of writing in local languages. I fear that Pakistani writing done in English is used to represent Pakistani writing to the West, and this is not honest. Those of us who employ the language of the West can engage in dialogue with the West, but this limits considerably the conversation by excluding a host of other representations of Pakistani writing.

And I guess this is my discomfort with being labeled a "Pakistani" writer, because I am perfectly aware that I have led an utterly privileged existence in Pakistan, the type of education I had (in the international school system) is not at all the norm, my heritage is both Pakistani (father) and Dutch (mother), my Urdu is not fluent, and I could go on and on. In principle, I don't have a problem with being incorporated into some sort of category that includes both Pakistani writing by outsiders and more indigenous Pakistani writing by "insiders" because what does provide some connection is that both subsets of writers have their experience of Pakistan at the core of what they write.

CC: I'd also be interested in hearing you speak about the publishing industry here in the U.S. and in Pakistan. For instance, how does publishing in English in Pakistan predetermine an audience? What sort of reader have you envisioned for your work?

SK: Following right from the discussion above, publishing in English in Pakistan predetermines my audience in terms of class and the elite. The audience is very, very small, even if it is an extremely engaged, hungry audience.

The next question is tricky. I don't know if I've envisioned the kind of reader for my work. Just anybody who will read it, either here or in Pakistan or Bangladesh or anywhere the book is available. I wish for my work to reach the widest audience possible in that I think of the text as organic and coming to life through interactions with multiple types of people. I know, of course, that the type of writing I do limits my audience.

Which leads me to the issues of publishing in this country [the United States]. Without being specific, and keeping in mind that there are a few exceptions, the audience in this country isn't widely interested in "knowing" about the rest of the world in an active way that recognizes complicity. Is it? While there is an awful lot of great fiction out there, my feeling is that often the fiction from the third world (specifically, the Muslim world) that is grabbed on to in the West is work that reflects Western sentiment (bias) with regard to the societies under discussion. In a perverse way, this makes sense. Why would people want to read novels that leave them uncomfortable, with the suggestion that they are complicit in the troubles of other people? This is not the role of literature, at least best-selling literature, in the West.

CC: English-language fictional treatments of 1971 are limited in number. In addition to Noor, Kamila Shamsie's 2003 *Kartography* and Mohsin Hamid's 2000 *Moth Smoke* both feature that time as an important element in their stories. Yet yours is the only novel that features so prominently a Bengali perspective. In my estimation, then, *Noor* succeeds at calling into question Pakistan's sense of itself as a nation through, to borrow your words, the "theatre of the family." Do you think that it's important that Noor begins to point toward (West) Pakistan's imperialistic treatment of East Pakistan?

SK: Hmmm. Perhaps it is significant that *Noor* begins to point to West Pakistan's imperialistic treatment of East Pakistan, but whether it is important is another matter. I don't really believe that my book will make a difference in the overall milieux of discussion. I felt the need to write something that would point to the silence in Pakistani society—which is different than believing that this would make a difference. Maybe I should say, rather, that I was interested in exploring the silence—as I think I said in my talk, my hope was that history and memory would meet, and in this dance a moment of silence and forgetting might be explored.

I think that the need to write about the silence differentiates my book from Shamsie's and Hamid's. In Shamsie's novel, the 1971 crisis is a backdrop in a literal way, but I think in mine it serves a different function. The trauma of '71 isn't only individualized, it's also presented as a collective, national trauma. What is curious, I think, is that in Pakistani Urdu literature, where the '71 crisis has been dealt with more frankly than in Pakistani-English literature, there isn't much depiction of the '71 violence. But I suppose some of the reason why there isn't more literature on '71 is due to the state of publishing in Pakistan. I almost feel that there must be other manuscripts out there that tackle the issue directly and that these manuscripts have yet to come to light.

CC: How do you see your novel in particular fitting into this tradition of Partition literature? Is your novel also forging a new path, given the dearth of literature (in English) that deals with the Partition of East and West Pakistan?

SK: I guess the novel does, by nature of its subject matter, fit into a tradition of Partition literature. I hadn't ever really thought of it as such until you pointed this out. The difference, I guess, is that partition literature which deals directly with 1971 isn't very vast. That goes right along with the idea that the war itself isn't something that is happily discussed, even now. Pakistanis can afford this because the war—for the most part—happened "over there" and the scars of it (evidence of people killed and raped, and the disruption of landscape also) is safely ensconced in the part of the country that became its own entity. I don't think I'm really forging a new path. If I hadn't begun to think about this subject matter in an explicit way, someone else would have. It's partly a question of timing. Enough time has passed, perhaps, for some exploration to begin.

This book was composed in the Adobe Garamond Pro and
Minion Italics typefaces, with heads in Papyrus. It was composed
in Adobe InDesign CS on the Macintosh computer in
The Publishing Laboratory in December 2005.

≫

Printed in the United States
58952LVS00005B/185

9 780971 930872